INTO THE GAUNTLET

INTO THE GAUNTLET

THE 39 CLUES

MARGARET PETERSON HADDIX

SCHOLASTIC INC.

NEW YORK TORONTO LONDON AUCKLAND
SYDNEY MEXICO CITY NEW DELHI HONG KONG

ISBN 978-0-545-34130-1

12 11 10 9 8 7 6 5 4 3   11 12 13 14 15 16/0

Printed in the U.S.A.   40

This edition first printing, May 2011

Book design and illustration by SJI Associates, Inc.

For Todd and Will and all
the other Clue hunters
— M.P.H.

CHAPTER 1

Amy and Dan Cahill forgot to look for bugs in London.

They knew the drill. Arriving at a new hotel, they always had to scour their room for any listening devices or other top secret spy gear their enemies might have planted. They always checked for all possible exit routes and anything that could serve as a weapon, as well. Amy and Dan were only fourteen and eleven. But they'd developed the instincts of CIA pros.

Arriving in London, though, Amy stumbled three steps into the hotel room and collapsed onto the bed. Dan wobbled past her to sprawl on the couch. He sat, then slipped backward, weighed down by his backpack. He looked like he'd been flattened.

He has, Amy thought. *We both have. Now that we know the truth. Now that we know how many lies we've been told all along, how many secrets were being kept from us, how much is expected of us . . .*

Only the kids' wild-haired au pair, Nellie Gomez, seemed to have enough energy left to keep standing.

She even had enough energy to sway slightly to whatever crazy music she was listening to on her iPod as she tugged their duffel bag and cat carrier into the room. Dimly, Amy thought that she or Dan should have offered to help. But even carrying a duffel bag seemed beyond Amy right now.

Nellie turned to shut the door. Then she, too, seemed to collapse.

Did she faint? Amy wondered.

Before Amy had time to do anything, Nellie was standing again. She hadn't fainted. She'd just dipped down to the floor to pick up something Amy and Dan must have walked right over: a plain manila envelope.

Nellie held the envelope in the air like a prize.

"What do you think, kiddos?" she asked. "Wanna bet this is your next lead?"

They'd been warned to expect one — coded, of course, in case any of their enemies intercepted it. Normally, the two siblings would have dashed to grab the envelope, raced to open it, scrambled to break the latest code. At the very least, they would have told Nellie that at their ages — and with the fate of the world depending upon them — they were way too old to be called "kiddos."

Now Amy just shrugged.

Dan tilted his head back and stared at the ceiling.

"Kiddos?" Nellie said in a puzzled voice. She popped out her iPod earbuds. "Didn't you hear me?"

Nellie flipped the envelope over.

"Yep, addressed to Amy and Dan Cahill," she said. "*And* Nellie Gomez. Wow. Now I really feel official. This must have been slipped under the door, waiting for us." She held out the envelope toward the two siblings. "Who wants to do the honors?"

Neither kid moved.

Nellie shook the envelope at Amy and Dan.

"Come on, guys," she said. "It's a *lead*." She acted like they were as simple as Saladin the cat, always easily distracted with his favorite red snapper. "Don't you want to see what this says? Somebody's trying to help us!"

"If *somebody* wanted to help us," Amy retorted, "they would have just given us all the answers back in Jamaica."

She knew why they hadn't, but it was too much to think about right now.

"Or way back at the beginning," Dan added. "At the funeral."

Just over a month ago, Amy and Dan had gotten a huge surprise after the death of their beloved grandmother Grace. They'd been among a select group of relatives given an odd offer in Grace's will: They could have a million dollars apiece or a single Clue.

Amy and Dan had picked the Clue.

Since then, they'd been traipsing around the globe, scrambling to outsmart or outrun or simply avoid some of their least-charming relatives in the race to the final prize. They'd lost count of how many times someone had tried to kill them.

When Amy wasn't completely terrified, there had also been moments she'd absolutely loved. Learning that she was brave enough to jump off that roof in Vienna. Being the only team to figure out the Clue in Cairo. Flying to the top of Mount Everest.

But only the day before, in Jamaica, Amy and Dan and Nellie had learned what the Clue hunt was really all about. Then the cruelty of it had sunk in on their long flight over the Atlantic. Before yesterday, they'd thought they were no different from the other teams—if you didn't count being younger, poorer, orphaned, and less informed. They'd thought their *goal,* at least, was the same: Win. Beat everyone else to the final prize.

But no, Amy thought bitterly. *We're younger, poorer, and more ignorant—and it's not enough for us just to beat everyone else to the prize. For us to win, we also have to make everyone else forgive and forget five hundred years of backstabbing, infighting, double-crossing and . . . murder.*

How could anyone forgive or forget that?

"It's impossible," Amy muttered.

"The lead?" Nellie said, a baffled look spreading across her face. "You haven't even heard it yet."

"The whole clue hunt," Dan corrected. "It's useless. We can't win. Not the way we're supposed to. Why'd we even bother coming here?" He gestured toward the window. Since they were on the twelfth floor, all they could see was a patch of gray sky. "I hate London. Doesn't it ever stop raining?"

Amy had a flash of remembering Dan's wild enthusiasm checking into another hotel, weeks ago, back in Egypt. He'd run around the room, delightedly calling out the names of every new object he discovered — "Stationery!" "Umbrella!" "Bible!" Amy felt guilty thinking about what the Clue hunt had done to that enthusiastic kid. It was like he'd turned into a grumpy old man about seventy years early.

"Well . . ." Nellie frowned uncertainly. For a moment, Amy thought she would say, *You're right, kiddos. It never stops raining in London, and this clue hunt is insane. I'm only twenty years old, and you aren't even my real family. I'm going home. Now.* Then she shook her head, her black-and-blond-dyed hair flaring out. "Look, kiddos. I promised your grandmother —"

"She's dead," Dan said in the same old-before-his-time voice. "She's dead, Lester's dead, Irina's dead. . . ."

Mom and Dad are dead, Amy finished in her head. Back in Jamaica, they'd counted all those deaths as reasons to complete the Clue hunt. Lester had been an innocent bystander, drawn into things only because he'd been willing to help. Irina was a former enemy who'd given her life to save Amy and Dan. And the children's parents had gone to their deaths trying to save a single Clue from falling into the wrong hands.

What did any of those deaths mean if Amy and Dan didn't keep trying?

But how could Amy and Dan keep trying when everything was impossible?

Nellie looked from Amy to Dan as if she could read their minds.

"Let's take this one step at a time, okay?" she said quietly. "Just listen."

She tore open the envelope and began reading aloud:

"'Lest our hopes vanish into thin air at the crack of doom, you must follow the longing of your heart of hearts. Can't you see in your mind's eye how everything can come full circle?'" She looked up. "Does that make any sense to you? Some of the words are underlined—that might mean something."

She held out the note first to Amy, then to Dan:

Lest our hopes vanish into thin air
at the crack of doom, you must follow
the longing of your heart of hearts.
Can't you see in your mind's eye
how everything can come full circle?

Something tickled Amy's mind, but she ignored it. *Doesn't matter,* she thought. *We can't win.*

"It doesn't mean anything to me," Dan said bitterly.

Mrrp, complained Saladin from his cat carrier. He sounded just as cranky as Dan. Nellie bent down to push the lever that set him free.

"At least I can make the cat happy," Nellie mumbled.

But Saladin didn't rub against her leg in thanks. He stiffened and growled low in his throat. And then he sprang straight toward the window.

"Saladin!" Amy shouted.

She glanced quickly to see if the window was open — it was, but there was a screen. Saladin, mid-leap, hissed at it. No, he was hissing at something beyond the screen, perched on the window ledge outside.

It was a monkey.

Amy blinked. And then, in spite of everything, she grinned. The monkey reminded her of one of her favorite books set in London: *The Little Princess,* where a monkey homesick for India climbed across the rooftops to visit a lonely girl who was also homesick for India. And then the monkey led to her finding a new family, even though her parents were dead. . . .

Amy's grin faded.

Fiction, she told herself. *Something else that isn't true.*

Anyhow, this monkey wasn't carrying treats. He was baring his teeth at Saladin, slamming his hand against the screen. He must have had something sharp in his hand — just his claws? Or a *knife?* — because the screen split. The monkey sprang over Saladin, dropping to the floor. And then in three quick bounds, he was at Nellie's side. He leaped up and snatched the paper from her hand.

"No! That's *ours*!" Nellie yelled.

She dived for the monkey, trying to snatch the paper back. But the monkey darted away.

"I'll get him!" Dan called.

He jumped up from the couch. He must have forgotten he still had his backpack on because he just fell forward, missing the monkey by a mile. The monkey skittered sideways toward Amy.

"I'll try!" Amy hollered.

She scrambled up and darted to the right. The monkey darted to the left.

Saladin jumped down from the windowsill, as if he thought he and Amy could corner the monkey together. The monkey easily sprang past them.

He turned around once he reached the windowsill again. He grinned and nodded up and down, making a *kee-kee-kee* sound.

"Is that monkey *laughing* at us?" Nellie demanded, outraged. She rushed toward the windowsill.

The monkey only laughed harder. Then, just as Nellie reached for him, he tossed a coinlike object into the room and plunged out the window.

He was gone.

With their only lead.

CHAPTER 2

Dan picked up the coin. It was some sort of thick metal, stamped with a fancy script "K" on each side.

A "K." Of course.

"The Kabras," Dan said darkly.

The Kabras had become Dan and Amy's worst enemies in the Clue hunt. They were filthy rich — and pure evil.

"Of course they even have their own trained monkey to do their bidding," Amy said bleakly.

"They probably have their own private zoo," Dan muttered.

He rushed to the window, getting there just a few steps ahead of Amy. The monkey was several stories below them now. He had the paper rolled up in his teeth and was climbing down a rope suspended from the roof. While Dan, Amy, and Nellie watched, the monkey reached the ground and scrambled across the sidewalk. Then a pair of hands reached out of a waiting limo and scooped up the monkey. The door shut; the black limo sped away.

"Those were Isabel Kabra's hands," Amy said. She pronounced the name carefully, as if every syllable hurt.

It does, Dan thought.

He didn't ask how Amy thought she could recognize Isabel's hands from twelve stories up. Isabel had murdered Amy and Dan's parents. She'd tried to murder Amy and Dan themselves back in Indonesia, and threatened them with death in Australia and South Africa. Then there were all those times she'd sent her nasty children, Ian and Natalie, to attack them. Back in Korea, the Kabra kids had tried to leave Amy and Dan to die in a collapsed cave.

When someone has been so incredibly cruel and awful to you so many times, you develop a sixth sense about them. You know when they're around.

Dan was just as certain as Amy that those had been Isabel's hands.

Dan turned away from his sister because he couldn't stand seeing the agony on her face. He wished he could run after Isabel, beat her up, throw her in jail, take back everything she'd taken from them. But he was an eleven-year-old kid. He didn't have much to work with. The best he could do was to hock up a huge glob of phlegm and spit it out the window. He aimed precisely toward the speeding limo.

"Dan!" Nellie exclaimed.

"What?" Dan said innocently. "She's *evil*. Getting spit on her limo—that's the least she deserves."

Dan could tell Nellie was trying not to laugh. The advantage of having an au pair who was only twenty was that sometimes she thought and acted like a kid herself. But then she put on a stern face.

"I just don't think your aim is that good," Nellie said. "Not at this distance."

"Oh, yeah?" Dan said. He was glad of the distraction. He thrust the "K" coin into Nellie's hand. "Throw that out the window, anywhere you want. I promise, I'll hit it on the first try."

Before Dan had a chance to really prove his spitting ability, he felt a tugging behind him. Now what? Was someone trying to steal his backpack? Right off his back?

Dan whirled around. It was only Amy.

"What are you doing?" he said.

"We need to check the Internet," she said. "Immediately."

Dan's eyes met his sister's. Sometimes he wondered how they could be related. She was shy; he was a chatterbox. She liked books and quiet libraries; he liked noisy video games and any sort of joke that involved burping or farting. Still, there had been times—

INTO THE GAUNTLET

11

especially during this Clue hunt—when Dan felt like he and Amy were practically the same person, thinking the same thought at the exact same time.

Now was one of those times.

"Right," Dan said. He lowered the backpack so Amy could get the laptop out faster. She handed him the cord. He plugged it into the wall while she plugged the other end into the computer. While they waited for the laptop to fire up, she gave him a pen and a piece of hotel stationery from the desk.

"What are you two doing?" Nellie asked as Dan began writing on the paper.

"We're figuring out the lead," Amy said. "I have a hunch, but I want to check it out online."

"I thought you were giving up," Nellie said. "I thought you said you couldn't win."

Dan looked at Amy and went back to writing. He'd let her explain.

"I still don't think we can win," Amy said. "Not the way the Madrigals want."

Once she would have said that word—*Madrigals*—with the same kind of fear and disgust she reserved for Isabel Kabra. But in Jamaica, Dan and Amy had found out that the Madrigals were really the good guys.

The way-too-good guys, Dan thought. *The ones who think we can end this all holding hands and singing "Kumbaya" around a campfire someplace. They're nuts!*

"You agreed with everything the Madrigals wanted in Jamaica," Nellie said. "So did I."

"Yeah," Amy said. She sounded distracted. The computer had booted up now, and she was logging on to the Internet. "It just doesn't seem possible. But if we can't win the Madrigal way, the least we can do is make sure the Kabras don't win instead."

Dan looked up from his paper. "Can you imagine letting Isabel Kabra take over the world?" he asked.

The words hung in the quiet hotel room. This, finally, was something Dan could hold on to. Everything the Madrigals wanted was too big and slippery: peace, love, forgiveness. . . . Dan hadn't even been able to keep those goals in his mind during a single uneventful plane ride. He would *never* be able to look Isabel Kabra right in the eye and say, "I forgive you." But keeping her from winning the Clue hunt, stopping her from gaining ultimate power, preventing her from being able to cause even more unforgivable deaths . . . that would be close enough, wouldn't it?

It would have to be. That was the best that Dan could hope for.

The rain kept falling outside, harder now. The room stayed gray. Nellie was shaking her head, her expression grim.

Then Nellie, irreverent as ever, grinned. She lifted the "K" coin Dan had given her toward her mouth.

"And now we have yet *another* game-changing turnover," she said, as if she were some sort of sports announcer and the "K" coin was her microphone. "For those of you scoring at home, the evil Kabras may think they just surged ahead, but their little monkey business has backfired. They seem to have *completely* reenergized the scrappy Cahill kids, who are just seconds away from figuring out their latest lead, thanks to Dan's photographic memory and Amy's *amazing* research skills."

Dan finished writing the exact replica of the note the monkey had stolen. (Exact, that is, except for Dan's sloppier printing.) He did indeed have a photographic memory, which had already saved them many times during the Clue hunt. He was sure he'd gotten everything right, even the underlining. He handed the paper to Amy and turned to Nellie.

"Nellie," he said, almost scolding her, "this isn't a game."

Nellie watched Dan and Amy bent over the computer together. She had no doubt that in a few moments they'd turn around with some brilliant deduction. And then they'd announce that they needed to depart immediately for some dramatic location.

Personally, Nellie was hoping for Stonehenge. She'd always wanted to see that. But maybe not on this trip—Nellie wouldn't want to have to explain to some proper British authority why her two charges were rappelling down such a major landmark. That's how these Clue hunt adventures often turned out.

It had been amazing—and a little scary—to watch

the transformation in Amy and Dan over the course of the past month. Nellie tried to remember what she herself had been like at eleven or fourteen. Eleven was the summer she'd done nothing but hang out at the local swimming pool, right? And fourteen was the year she'd gotten her nose pierced.

And . . . that was the year Dan and Amy's grandmother had entered Nellie's life. Not directly — Nellie didn't meet Grace until later. But opportunities had begun falling into Nellie's lap the year she started high school. For a kung fu "scholarship." For flying lessons. For more advanced classes than she'd signed up for at school, with demanding new teachers who seemed to care way too much about a certain girl with a pierced nose and multicolored hair sitting at the back of the room.

It had taken Nellie a long time to figure out where all those opportunities came from. But now Nellie saw that Grace had changed her life completely.

And Grace was one of the good Cahills, Nellie thought. *What could someone like Isabel Kabra do to people like me if she's in charge?*

Nellie fingered the "K" coin Dan had handed her. It had seemed just like a coin toss — random luck — that Grace had chosen Nellie to be Amy and Dan's au pair. But in Jamaica, Nellie had found out that her family had been linked to the Cahills for generations. In her own way, Nellie had been as fated to take part in the Clue hunt as Amy and Dan.

And, in Jamaica, Nellie had accepted that fate.

Nellie kept fingering the "K" coin. And then she wasn't thinking about families or fate. She was thinking about the coin, which didn't exactly seem like a coin anymore. It had a thin line that went all the way around the edge. A crack maybe?

Nellie forced her thumbnail into the crack. Under pressure, the "coin" popped open, revealing a miniature electronic network inside.

Just then Amy whirled around in her chair.

"I've got it!" she said. "The answer is—"

Nellie dived toward Amy. She clapped her hand over Amy's mouth.

"Don't say it!" Nellie commanded. "We've been"— with the hand that wasn't on Amy's mouth, she flicked miniature wires out of the faux coin—"bugged!"

In the limo a block away, Isabel Kabra leaned forward, intent on the headset piping an uncultured girl's words into her ears: "We've been—"

Static. Nothing but static. The audio link was gone.

So they discovered the listening device. So what? It had been overkill anyhow. Isabel had the Cahill children's lead, and she had vastly more resources than they did for figuring it out. She had vastly more of everything that mattered than they ever would.

This was just . . . annoying.

Isabel almost frowned—*no, don't do that. Remember?*

Frown lines? There's only so much that Botox can do. Those brats aren't worth getting wrinkles.

They really weren't worth noticing, but just in case, she mentally sorted through everything she'd heard, checking for any significance at all in those pathetic children's pathetic conversation.

"You agreed with everything the Madrigals wanted in Jamaica" . . . *"If we can't win the Madrigal way . . ."* This meant they'd joined forces with the Madrigals, the shadowy ne'er-do-wells who had been the bane of Isabel's family's existence for centuries. Ah, well. In Isabel's experience, loyalties were nothing more than opportunities for betrayal.

Isabel mentally fast-forwarded to something the boy had said: *"Can you imagine letting Isabel Kabra take over the world?"*

Isabel let herself smile, even though smiles were nearly as likely to cause wrinkles as frowns.

Yes. She could imagine that. She could imagine it perfectly: the power, the glory, the *rightness* of it. Isabel Kabra was superior to everyone else in the world. When she won the Clue hunt, everybody would finally see that. She would rule, and everyone on the planet would obey.

They would obey—or they would die. Exactly as they deserved.

Amy and Dan Cahill certainly deserved to die.

Isabel's smile widened. She was almost grateful to those brats for managing to stay alive so long. This way, she could think of even crueler ways to kill them.

"Mummy?" Isabel's eleven-year-old daughter, Natalie, half whined from the opposing seat in the limo. "You look a little scary right now."

Isabel realized she was still holding the disgusting monkey.

"Here," Isabel said, thrusting the nasty creature into her daughter's lap. "You and Ian take the paper out of his mouth and figure out what it means. Justify your superior abilities and education for once in your life."

Isabel had trained her children well—the girl cringed away from the monkey, instinctively knowing that monkey hair would look horrible on her haute couture black dress. And fourteen-year-old Ian looked nauseated at the thought of potentially exposing himself to monkey spittle. These instincts would serve Ian and Natalie well someday, if they ever became the heads of the Kabra empire—after long decades of Isabel's astute rule, of course. But right now, Isabel's children were mere underlings, and she couldn't have them failing to obey a direct order.

"Whatever happened to, 'Yes, Mum. Whatever you say, Mum'?" Isabel demanded. "When did you stop obeying instantly?"

Ian mumbled something Isabel couldn't quite catch.

"What's that you say?" Isabel asked. "Speak up!"

"W-we—" Was Ian *stammering*? Ian, whom she'd

trained to be smooth and suave, who'd known how to wear a tuxedo properly since he was three? He cleared his throat and managed to get the words out: "We haven't stopped obeying. We just think first now."

Isabel slapped the boy.

CHAPTER 3

Amy lined up listening devices on the desk. After Nellie had destroyed the Kabra bug, the Cahill kids had belatedly searched the entire hotel room, as they should have from the very beginning. They'd found three more bugs: an ingeniously tiny one inside a lamp; an elegant one on a picture frame that Amy had originally thought was part of the artwork; and, under the bed, a rather crude one that looked like it might have been built by a football player with thick fingers.

"Ekat," Amy said, pointing at the ingenious one.

"Janus," Dan said, pointing at the artistic one.

"Tomas," Nellie said, pointing at the crude one and rolling her eyes.

"And the Kabra one was Lucian, so that's everybody," Amy said.

They were naming off branches of the Cahill family—the other branches searching for the Clues. Each branch was descended from one of the four feuding children of Gideon and Olivia Cahill: Katherine, Jane, Thomas, and Luke. Only the Madrigals—Amy and Dan's branch—knew that there'd also been a fifth sibling born after the family fell apart: Madeleine.

My ancestor, Amy thought.

It was nice to know where she fit. She'd been longing for that knowledge ever since the Clue hunt began.

But do I really fit if I don't try to do what the Madrigals want? she wondered.

Dan shoved the three bugs a little closer together on the desk. He raised his fist above them, ready to smash them all in one blow.

"Three, two, one . . ." he counted down dramatically.

At the very last minute before his hand hit the bugs, Amy grabbed his wrist.

"What are you doing?" he asked, trying to jerk away from her. "Are you nuts?"

"I have to talk to you," Amy said. She gestured toward the bathroom and pulled on his wrist. Dan frowned but followed along. Nellie pointed to herself and raised her eyebrows as if to ask, "Me, too?"

Amy nodded.

In the bathroom, Amy turned on the faucets in the sink and the bathtub full blast. Together, they made a sound like a waterfall. Nellie and Dan had to lean in close to hear what Amy was saying. There was no danger her words would be picked up by any bug.

"If we're just trying to make sure the Kabras don't win, should we throw some help to the other teams? Let them know our lead?" she asked. "And . . . doesn't that fit with what the Madrigals want us to do?"

"Are you kidding?" Dan said. "You want to just give away our hard work?"

"What if you share your answers and then, I don't know, the horrible Holts end up ruling the world?" Nellie asked.

The Holts were the Tomas representatives: Eisenhower and Mary-Todd Holt and their three kids — Hamilton, Reagan, and Madison.

"Hamilton's not so bad," Dan said.

"Okay, but *Eisenhower*?" Nellie said.

Eisenhower Holt was a muscle-bound, knuckle-headed buffoon.

And he was there when Mom and Dad died, Amy thought. She clenched her fists, as if that could smash the Holts' clumsily made bug.

"Uncle Alistair can be okay," Dan offered. "He hasn't betrayed us . . . recently."

Alistair Oh, an Ekat, had teamed up with them more than anyone else. But he'd also double-crossed them again and again. Then, during a horrifying fire on an Indonesian island, he'd made sure that they got to safety before him. He'd even seemed willing to sacrifice his life for theirs. Was that enough to redeem him?

He lied to us in China after that, Amy thought. *And he was also there when Mom and Dad died. He didn't start the fire that killed them, but . . . he didn't save them, either.*

"How do you know the Ekat bug is Alistair's, not Bae Oh's?" Nellie asked, making a face.

Bae Oh was Alistair's uncle and a completely unpleasant old man. He would have let Amy and Dan die in Egypt if Nellie hadn't rescued them.

Amy's fists clenched tighter. The Ekat bug would have to be destroyed, too.

"So that leaves the Janus," Nellie said. "You want to tip off Jonah Wizard? Want to let him add 'king of the world' to all his other titles?"

Jonah Wizard was already an international hip-hop star, bestselling pop-up book author, and Pez dispenser model. The only thing bigger than his fame was his ego.

Amy waited for Dan to defend Jonah so she could squash his arguments flat. Dan had kind of bonded with Jonah in China. But Dan just got a stunned look on his face.

"Whoa," he said. "Are you sure Jonah's still on the hunt? When was the last time we saw him looking for a clue?"

"He wasn't in Tibet. Or the Bahamas. Or Jamaica," Nellie mused. "Could the great Jonah Wizard actually have given up?"

"There's a bug out there that has 'Janus' written all over it," Amy pointed out.

"Maybe Cora Wizard is doing her own dirty work now," Nellie said.

Cora Wizard. Jonah's mother. Amy could barely remember ever meeting the woman. No, wait. She could.

That night, Amy thought. *I saw her there the night our parents died, too.*

Amy had to grip the counter. She felt the blood drain from her face.

"We can't let Cora Wizard win," she whispered.

Nellie and Dan looked at her. Both of them seemed to understand instantly.

"So that's it. You can't trust any of the other teams," Nellie said. "Not really. Not all together."

"Duh," Dan said. "We knew that a month ago."

Amy blinked back something that might have been tears. She hoped Nellie and Dan would just think it was steam from the sink and bathtub faucets running full blast.

"Then how do the Madrigals possibly think we can—" she began.

"Power," Dan said. "We have to win. And then—then maybe we'll have enough power to knock everyone else into shape."

For a moment he looked like a miniature Napoleon, plotting world domination. Then he was Dan again, gleefully darting out of the bathroom.

"We'll stomp on the bugs," he called back over his shoulder. "Come on—we'll each do one. I call first dibs!"

Amy and Nellie looked at each other and shrugged. Then they raced after him. Together, all three of them swept the bugs from the desk and began jumping up and down, crunching the electronic devices beneath their feet.

Two men sat in a darkened room. One had a beaked nose and a dour expression. The other was dressed all in gray and had headphones over his ears. The first man, William McIntyre, kept looking expectantly at the other and asking, "Can you hear them now? Now?"

Finally the man in gray, Fiske Cahill, pushed the headphones back.

"They are figuring out the lead," he said. "They are proceeding with the hunt. But . . . they have destroyed all the bugs."

Mr. McIntyre was silent for a moment.

"Except ours," he finally said.

"We had the advantage of having ours built into the wall," Fiske said. "They are staying in a Madrigal room. One we arranged for them." He winced.

"You don't feel right about eavesdropping on them," Mr. McIntyre said, interpreting the other man's wince.

"There is much that I don't feel right about in this clue hunt," Fiske said. "We are gambling on children. We are gambling with their lives."

"Doesn't every generation gamble on the next?" Mr. McIntyre asked.

Fiske made a barking sound that was much too bitter

to be a laugh. "Says a man who chose never to have children," he said. "But . . . I made the same choice." He stared bleakly at the wall. "Something else to regret," he murmured.

Mr. McIntyre started to lift his hand, as if he might pat Fiske's shoulder. But William McIntyre wasn't the type to give comforting pats. He lowered his hand.

"I thought you'd become more optimistic," Mr. McIntyre said. "You're wearing gray now instead of all black."

"It's dark gray," Fiske said. "Allowing only a little hope . . ." He tapped his fingers on the table. "I wish we could know what they're thinking. Why they decided to destroy the bugs but continue the hunt. They must have been discussing it somehow." He pictured scribbled notes being passed back and forth, or a whispered conversation in a closet while the water ran in the bathroom, masking the sounds for the bugs. Knowing Amy and Dan and Nellie, he suspected they'd made it fun. Fiske himself hadn't had much familiarity with fun.

"They know the fate of the world depends on reuniting the entire Cahill family," Mr. McIntyre said.

"Is that enough?" Fiske asked. "Should we have given them exact details, spelled out precise consequences — told them *everything*?"

Mr. McIntyre pushed back from the table. "How much of a burden can two children take?" he asked.

He sat in gloomy silence for a moment, then added, "You could just *ask* them what they're thinking. After all, they've told us their clues. We've told them ours. They know we're on their side."

"Yes, but . . . don't you see how this clue hunt has taught them to lie?" Fiske asked. "Taught them to be suspicious of everyone?"

Mr. McIntyre frowned.

"They know we're in this together," he said.

"And that's why we're sitting in a safe, dark room, while they're about to head out into danger?" Fiske asked. "Danger that *we're* going to make worse?"

"And the solution is"—Amy paused dramatically—"William Shakespeare."

Dan blinked.

"Okay, Amy, I know you've read, like, every book ever written. And you know a lot more about words and writers than I do," he said. "But how do you get from 'thin air' and 'crack of doom' and 'heart of hearts' and all that other stuff to *William Shakespeare*?"

"Because he's the one who made up those expressions," Amy said. "Look." She brushed aside the debris of the destroyed bugs and pulled out the chair to sit down at the computer. She touched a key, and the screensaver disappeared, replaced by the site Amy had been looking at before they'd discovered the first bug. "This is a list of all the words and expressions Shakespeare coined. 'Into thin air,' 'crack of doom,' 'heart of hearts,' 'mind's eye,' 'come full circle' — all the underlined phrases are on this list."

Dan watched as Amy scrolled through the words and phrases. There were hundreds of them.

"Sheesh, did the English language even exist before Shakespeare?" Nellie asked. "'Bated breath,' 'gossip,' 'leapfrog,' 'mimic' . . ."

"Aw, come on. Nobody ever uses a lot of these," Dan said. "Have you ever in your life said something 'beggars all description'?"

"Some of these sound a little weird now," Amy admitted. "But here's a word you use all the time, Dan."

She let the cursor rest on a single glowing word: *puke.*

"Shakespeare made up the word *puke*?" Dan asked.

"Yep," Amy said.

"Well, then . . . I guess he kind of knew what he was doing," Dan said.

Dan wasn't about to admit it to Amy, but he'd always regarded *puke* as pretty much the perfect word. It sounded exactly like what it was.

"And how about . . ." Amy was scouring the list for other good words.

Dan wasn't in the mood for a language lesson. He liked it better when the Clue hunt pointed to swordsmen and kung fu experts.

"Okay, okay, I'll take your word for it." He wanted

to say, "Whatever," but he was afraid Shakespeare might have made up that word, too. "Now that we know our next clue has something to do with William Shakespeare, what are we going to do about it?" he asked.

Just then the hotel phone rang.

All three of them jumped, then Nellie reached over and answered it. She listened for a moment, then put her hand over the receiver.

"It's the hotel's concierge service," she said. "They want to know if we'd like them to get tickets for us to any attractions. Or" — she raised her eyebrows significantly — "theatrical productions."

Amy beamed.

"Oh, no," Dan moaned. "No!"

"What's playing at the Globe?" Amy asked eagerly.

"I am not going to a Shakespeare play!" Dan protested.

Nellie ignored him.

"Yes, I'd like three tickets . . ." she said into the phone. She finished making the arrangements and hung up, a dreamy look in her eye.

"It's *Romeo and Juliet*," she told Amy. "*Romeo and Juliet*, in London, where Shakespeare wrote it, performed at the Globe, just like it was originally done. . . ."

Amy's expression turned just as awestruck and dreamy as Nellie's.

"Amazing," she whispered.

"Torture," Dan muttered. "Cruel and unusual punishment. Worse than those poisonous snakes and spiders in Australia. Worse than almost being chopped up into lollipops in China. This has got to be the worst thing we've had to do yet!"

But nobody was listening.

As far as he knew.

CHAPTER 4

Ian Kabra tiptoed across the cold marble floor. He was related to just about every notable spy in the last five hundred years. He himself had been trained in subterfuge practically since birth. But this was the one place he'd never suspected he'd have to employ his stealth skills: his own home.

Somewhere high overhead — on the third floor of the Kabra mansion, or possibly the fourth — a beam creaked. Ian froze.

It's an old house, he told himself. *It makes sounds like that all the time. Doesn't it?*

Normally, Ian wouldn't have even paid attention. But normally, he wasn't breaking into the one wing of the house that had always been off-limits to him and Natalie. The wing where all the Kabra family secrets were stored.

Ian's eyes darted about, looking for the first glimmer of telltale light coming toward him. He rehearsed excuses in his head: *Why, no, Mum, Dad, how could you ever think that I would be out of bed tonight doing something wrong? Or sneaky and underhanded? I'm just . . . getting a drink of water. Yes, that's it. I was thirsty, and I thought the water would taste better down here than near my bedroom. Haven't you always taught me I deserve the very best of everything? How could you think that I would be here because . . . because I don't trust you anymore?*

No light flashed at him. No accusing parent — or suspicious servant — leered out at him. He took a deep, silent breath and began inching forward again. No matter how carefully he stepped, he could hear a soft *tssk-tssk* with every brush of his socked feet across the floor.

What will happen if they catch me? Is this worth the risk?

"I just want to know the truth," Ian whispered, so desperate that his lips actually formed the words, his vocal cords actually pushed out small bursts of sound. He froze again, but nothing happened.

Truth . . .

Ian had always been taught that truth was a very flexible thing. His mother could smile brightly at another woman and say so charmingly, "Oh, that dress is just perfect for you. Wherever did you get it?" And then behind the woman's back she'd go on for hours about how such a hideous, shapeless old hag could not possibly have picked an outfit any more repulsive than that one. Or — Ian had heard both of his parents, at different times on the phone, talking to business associates and assuring them, "Why, yes, of course, we have your best interests at heart . . ." — and then hanging up, telling a subordinate, "Close down that factory. It's worthless." Or, "Sell that stock. Every last share."

But that's just how they treat losers. Outsiders. People who aren't Lucians like us.

He remembered how his mother had treated Irina Spasky, who'd been loyal until almost the very end of her life.

She wasn't a Kabra. Mum and Dad have a code of conduct — the Kabras are the only ones that matter. It's just their way. Yes, they can be ruthless with everyone else, but really, they're doing it for their family. For Natalie and me.

Was that why his mother had slapped him earlier that day? Why she seemed not to care anymore if Ian or Natalie lived or died, as long as she won the Clue hunt? Why she'd had Natalie on the verge of tears for, oh, weeks, now? Ian had always found his little sister a bit annoying, but lately he'd actually felt sorry for her, watching her try so hard to please their mother, who'd become completely impossible to please.

What changed? Ian wondered. *What happened? Is it really just that we're . . . losing?*

Ian was reaching for a doorknob now. Willing his hands to stay steady, he slipped an old-fashioned skeleton key from the pocket of his silk pajamas and slid it into the lock. His parents had ordered that he be trained to pick locks so he could steal information, if necessary, from business rivals, family enemies, international spies. He'd never expected to become so confused about who his enemies really were.

It's time to find out, Ian told himself coldly.

Just then the lock clicked. One twist of his wrist, and the door sprang open.

With a glance over his shoulder, Ian stepped into the secret wing and pulled the door shut behind him.

Jonah Wizard gave a final wave to the fans crowding around his limo and slid into his seat. His driver shut the car door firmly behind him and pushed dozens of girls out of his way getting back around to the front of the car.

"You're so hot, Jonah!" one of the girls yelled, kissing the window as the car pulled away. She left a smear of lipstick across the glass.

Jonah stared at the lipstick. He'd asked his father to schedule this concert in London at the last minute. He'd sung and danced his heart out for the past three hours. He'd even added a surprise encore at the end. The crowd and the screams and the excitement were his reward, exactly what he needed right now: proof that his fans loved him. Proof that he deserved that love.

So why did he keep thinking that the smear of lipstick looked like blood?

Because of the clue hunt, Jonah told himself. *Because if my fans only knew what I almost did . . . If they knew what my mother expects me to do . . . If I did it . . .*

Jonah had been thinking like this since China: in incomplete sentences. He couldn't form a complete thought because that would mean he had to make an impossible decision. An irreversible decision, one Jonah would have to live with for the rest of his life.

"Good show." Jonah's dad, Broderick, spoke from the opposite corner of the limo seat. He was doing calculations on his ever-present BlackBerry. "Ninety thousand people at seventy-five pounds per head, minus overhead, that's a take of . . ."

Jonah shoved at the BlackBerry, almost knocking it out of his father's hands.

"Oh, money," Jonah said, his voice cracking. He reminded himself to at least try to sound normal. "Yo, don't you care about anything except the Benjamins?"

"Elizabeths, in this case," Broderick said.

Jonah stared at him blankly.

"Queen Elizabeth?" Broderick said. "On the British pound?"

"Oh," Jonah said. "Yeah. But . . ."

And he'd arrived at another incomplete sentence.

What does Dad think I should do? How much does he know, anyhow? Jonah wondered. *What does he want for me? Just more money? Or . . .*

Jonah couldn't even bear to think the question.

Everything had always come so easily for Jonah. The first time he'd picked up a musical instrument—a child-size guitar—he'd been able to play "Twinkle, Twinkle, Little Star" by ear. (He'd written about that in his pop-up book *Twinkle, Twinkle, Li'l Gangsta*.) Even in the early stages of the Clue hunt, things had just fallen his way. He was a Janus; it was no big deal to sing, tour, record, blog, Tweet, promote, and find Clues on the side. He'd had to do a few crazy stunts—stretch a little—but, hey, things worked out. He already ruled the music world. Winning the Clue hunt and conquering the rest of the world just seemed like the next step.

Until China.

In China, Jonah had come face-to-face with evil.

Evil inside himself.

He'd almost let Dan Cahill be sacrificed for the Clue hunt. He'd been so close to letting Dan die. Horrified, Jonah had quit. He remembered how relieved he'd felt in that moment, telling his mother he was done with hunting Clues, done with threatening his relatives, done with lying and keeping secrets. In that moment, he'd pictured the rest of his life as one long, happy concert, one great performance after another—fame and fortune without a single complication.

But his mother had told him no. She'd said he couldn't quit. She'd said—

Broderick's BlackBerry beeped, signaling an incoming text. He read it, then held out the BlackBerry for Jonah to see.

"This is what your mother wants you to do tomorrow afternoon," Broderick said.

Jonah braced himself against the back of the seat. He narrowed his eyes to such tight slits he could barely read. He'd stayed away from his mom for the past several days. He'd ignored her messages. He'd let her think whatever she wanted. But was this it? The moment when he'd have to choose?

He'd worked so hard to make his mother proud of him. He was Jonah Wizard, international star. Was tomorrow the day she'd also expect him to become Jonah Wizard, murderer?

"Father-son bonding time!" Eisenhower Holt screamed at the top of his lungs. He gave his son, Hamilton, a punch in the gut that would have felled most grown men. But Hamilton had been on an Olympic-style training regimen since he was two. He merely grinned at his dad.

Eisenhower was looking around at the spectacle before them. Down on the field, men in red-and-white uniforms were chasing a swiftly rolling ball. In the stadium around them, thousands of people rose and cheered, moving almost as one.

"Brits!" Eisenhower yelled. "The best soccer fans in the universe!"

"We call it football around here, bozo," a voice growled behind them.

Eisenhower and Hamilton both turned around. Eisenhower Holt was six foot five, and Hamilton was nearly that tall. But the man behind towered over both of them. He was shirtless, revealing muscles that probably would have looked like rock if they hadn't been covered — like his stony face — in red and white paint.

Eisenhower grinned at the man.

"Sure thing!" Eisenhower agreed. He gave the man a chest bump, his muscular chest hitting the other man's like giant boulders crashing together. "Go, Manchester United!"

It took a minute — stone moves slowly. But then the man grinned back at him.

That's my dad, Hamilton thought proudly. *He knows how to handle any situation having to do with sports.*

Eisenhower and Hamilton turned around to watch the game again.

"Dad," Hamilton said after a few minutes. "You don't mind too much, do you, that, um, we kind of lost our trail? In the clue hunt, I mean?"

"We'll find it again," Eisenhower said confidently. "We Holts specialize in come-from-behind victories."

Hamilton nodded, as he did any time his father imparted Holt family wisdom. Even when he didn't quite believe it.

That had been happening more and more lately.

"Besides," Eisenhower said. "Your mother needed time to buy new tracksuits for Reagan and Madison. The way those girls are growing — they might even end up taller than me!" He beamed proudly. "And how could I come to England without going to a soccer — er, football — game with my son?"

"You couldn't," Hamilton agreed.

The two of them watched the fancy footwork down on the field in silence for a moment. Before the Clue hunt, Hamilton would have savored one-on-one time like this with his dad. But something was nagging at him tonight.

With the clue hunt . . . Sure, I want to win as much as Dad does. But the way we've been trying to win . . .

Ever since South Africa, any time Hamilton closed his eyes, he pictured the same image: a man in a bowler hat — Alistair Oh — sweating. Sweating because Hamilton's dad was threatening to kill him.

Sometimes when Hamilton saw that, he imagined himself standing up to his father, yelling, "Dad, *no!* You can't kill Alistair!"

Sometimes he imagined Alistair dying.

What had actually happened in South Africa was that Hamilton had intervened secretly, without his father knowing. Hamilton and Dan Cahill, working together, had saved Alistair's life.

I had to! Hamilton thought. *That was my only choice! It doesn't mean I betrayed my family! Reagan and Mom didn't want Alistair to die, either!*

But that wasn't the only time Hamilton had gone rogue. His father didn't exactly know how often Hamilton had teamed up with Dan and Amy, how much Hamilton had tried to help them rather than his fellow Holts.

Am I a traitor? Hamilton wondered. *Or just . . . doing the right thing?*

Before the Clue hunt, right and wrong had seemed so simple to Hamilton. Right was doing what his father wanted him to do. Wrong was everything else. Complexity was for football strategy, not ethical decisions.

But what if . . . when it came to the Clue hunt . . . Hamilton's dad had been wrong from the very beginning?

Hamilton glanced at his dad again.

"Dad," he began, "do you ever think—"

"Nope," Eisenhower said quickly. "I try to do that as little as possible. Gets in the way of muscle development." He laughed at his own joke.

"Seriously . . ." Hamilton tried again.

"Seriously?" Eisenhower lowered his voice. He glanced around, as if to make sure that no one could overhear. "Seriously, I'll tell you something nobody else knows about me. I'm not very good at thinking. Never have been. But I want better things for you and the girls. That's why winning this clue hunt is so important."

Hamilton gulped. Now how could he say what he was going to say?

Eisenhower's cell phone rang just then, cutting off the conversation.

He lifted the phone to his ear. "Yes, sugarcakes?" he said into it.

Several people nearby turned around, snickering. But Hamilton glared down all of them. There was nothing wrong with his parents using sticky-sweet terms of endearment with each other. Nothing.

The other people quickly looked away.

"Really?" Eisenhower said into the phone. Then he cheered, "Yahoo!" He put his hand over the phone and said to Hamilton, "Didn't I tell you? The Holts are back in the game! Your mother and the girls found a lead!"

He did a little victory dance, right on the spot.

Evidently, Hamilton's mother was still talking on the other end.

"Okay, okay, you got a phone call, and . . ." Eisenhower said. Then he almost dropped the phone. "We have to go *where?*"

Ian Kabra sat in the midst of dozens of manila folders. He'd hoped that everything would be computerized in the Kabra secret wing. That way, he'd just have to decode a secret password, download everything to a flash drive, and then browse through the info in the privacy of his own room. He'd forgotten how paranoid his parents were about computer hackers. Having to sort through paper files meant he was completely vulnerable to being discovered.

Ian sighed and resolutely picked up the next folder. Massacres authorized, betrayals approved . . . thousands and thousands of people sent helplessly to their deaths by generation after generation of Ian's family.

Ian supposed that most people reading these files would be horrified. He supposed that whenever Mum and Dad planned to show him these files—when he turned eighteen, maybe?—his parents would expect him to be proud. The files around him recorded dazzling tales of power. Raw, throbbing power, wielded brilliantly, century after century.

But Ian felt neither horror nor awe. He simply felt . . . unsurprised. He'd always known that his family was both powerful and ruthless. It truly was the Lucian way. In his turn, Ian would be expected to act just like his ancestors. He'd already demonstrated—on his preschool playground, at those ridiculous Cahill family reunions in New England, in the Clue hunt as his parents' emissary—that he was perfectly capable of living up to his Lucian heritage.

What exactly was he questioning now?

Ian realized that the folder he'd just picked up held a newer label: THE HOPE CAHILL AND ARTHUR TRENT SITUATION.

Ian's heartbeat quickened. He recognized those names. They were Amy and Dan Cahill's parents, people who had died in an accidental fire years ago.

Or maybe not so accidental.

Ian quickly scanned the papers in the file. They were mostly letters. He could see the skill with which his parents had organized the other branches of Cahills—a Janus, Cora Wizard; an Ekat, Alistair Oh; and two Tomas, Eisenhower and Mary-Todd Holt—to confront Hope Cahill and Arthur Trent about Clues they'd gathered, advantages they'd gained. It was brilliant the way Isabel and Vikram Kabra had drawn sworn enemies together for a common goal.

But the confrontation itself had gone badly. Isabel Kabra had struck a match, intending to force Hope and Arthur to play by her rules.

And . . . Hope Cahill and Arthur Trent had died rather than give Isabel Kabra the total power she wanted.

Ian felt the papers slip from his grasp.

My mother caused the deaths of Amy and Dan's parents, he thought, horror finally catching up with him. Another wave of horror hit him with his next thought: *Do Amy and Dan know?*

Ian thought about the way Amy had smiled up at him back in Korea, the way she'd let him flirt with her, the way she'd blushed and stammered over his suave overtures. She couldn't possibly have known the truth then.

And afterward?

Certainly Amy — and Dan — had been a bit cold to him since Korea, but he'd mostly thought that was because he himself had betrayed them, making it look like he was leaving them to die. Not that they were really ever in any danger. (Were they? Would he have cared if they were? Was he any different from his mother?)

Of course they know that's just how things go on the clue hunt. . . .

Unbidden, another memory came back to him, one that had been haunting him for weeks. One from the peak of Mount Everest. Ian had been falling, plunging toward certain death. Even though he'd paid an entire pack of Sherpas to get him safely up and down the mountain, Amy was the only one close enough to reach him. But she'd faced a choice: save the test tube of valuable Janus serum they'd all been searching for or save Ian.

Ian had known, in the split second he'd had to think, that the logical, rational, *likely* thing for Amy to do was to choose the serum. It's what Ian would have done in her place. The serum was priceless, possibly even irreplaceable. And Ian was just someone who'd said fake nice things to her and then betrayed her, more than once.

But Amy had saved Ian and let the serum fall.

Ian still couldn't understand why she'd done that. It was so . . . un-Lucian. Un-Cahill.

Everyone had been so bundled up then, with every inch of skin covered against the brutal Everest cold. So Ian couldn't see the expression on Amy's face at that moment; he couldn't gauge what she was thinking. But he'd looked into her eyes. And her eyes had been . . . knowing.

She knew then that my mother caused her parents' death. And she still *saved me.*

This made everything even more incomprehensible.

Ian picked up the Hope Cahill/Arthur Trent file

again. Maybe he'd missed something. Maybe his mother had tried to make up for Amy and Dan's parents dying.

The file held both documents leading up to the fire and a flurry of letters sent afterward. It wasn't hard for Ian to piece everything together. As soon as the flames grew out of control, the non-Lucians panicked. None of them seemed to have understood that Isabel *wanted* Hope and Arthur to die. Alistair Oh, Cora Wizard, and Mary-Todd Holt had all, eventually, called 911. Eisenhower Holt had grabbed a neighbor's garden hose and aimed it at the blaze.

And Vikram and Isabel Kabra had masterminded a cover-up, trying to hide all evidence of their involvement.

"They felt guilty," Ian whispered to himself. "Otherwise, why would they sound so defensive?"

It was cold comfort, grasping at straws to convince himself his parents weren't really *that* bad.

Ian turned over the second-to-last piece of paper in the file and was surprised to find that the last sheet had nothing to do with the deaths of Hope Cahill and Arthur Trent. Rather, it was a report his mother had written about the death of Irina Spasky.

"She completely betrayed us," his mother wrote. "She disobeyed a direct order from me and went to rescue Alistair Oh and Amy and Dan Cahill when I told her they had to be eliminated. . . ."

Eliminated. Just a few weeks ago, his mother had

tried, in cold blood, to murder Alistair and Amy and Dan. Not by mistake, not as collateral damage, but intentionally. Ian scanned the entire document. The murder attempt wasn't even a bargaining chip, something threatened in exchange for her actual goal. It was carefully planned—a goal in and of itself.

And Irina had died in the others' place.

"When I saw what Irina was doing, I could have gone back and rescued her," Isabel had written. "But why bother?"

So cold. A woman's life dismissed in three words.

It wasn't that Ian had had any great sentimental attachment to Irina Spasky. She'd threatened to use her poison fingernails a few too many times to be close or cuddly with anyone. But there'd been a moment years ago when Ian was little, when she'd said to him quite wistfully, "Do you suppose you could call me Auntie Irina? You're the same age now as another little boy I once knew. . . ."

She'd covered her mouth immediately with her hands, as if she hadn't actually meant to say that. And Ian had certainly never called her Auntie. With his parents' encouragement, he had treated her like a servant, slightly beneath his notice. But she had served his family faithfully for years. Even Irina Spasky didn't deserve to be left to her death with the words *Why bother?*

Furrowing his brow, Ian flipped back and forth between the papers describing the three deaths.

Something *was* different. The faint hint of remorse that came across in the earlier papers was completely missing in connection to Irina Spasky. It was like his mother wasn't even capable of remorse anymore—not remorse or guilt or doubt or loyalty to anyone but herself.

Why not? Ian wondered.

Something rattled across the room, and Ian froze. Quickly, he extinguished the small reading light he'd been using. In the sudden darkness he felt blind. He didn't know if he should leap up and hide or if it was wiser not to move, to stay as silent as possible.

It's just a noise outside in the Kabra family zoo, Ian told himself. *Probably that blasted monkey Mum insisted on using today.*

The rattle sounded again, and Ian could no longer pretend that it wasn't the doorknob to the secret wing. Before he had a chance to move, the door swung open and the beam of a flashlight caught him right in the face.

Someone gasped. It was a gasp Ian recognized.

"Natalie?" Ian said.

"Ian?" his sister whispered. She dropped the flashlight, and the beam of light swung crazily around the room.

Ian scooped up the flashlight and pointed it directly toward the ground, confining the light to a narrow space.

"No—no—don't let it show through the windows," he said frantically.

Now Natalie gulped.

"What are you doing here, Ian?" she asked in a small voice.

Ian thought fast.

"Mum and Dad wanted me to pick up some files for them," he said. "They trust me in here. Because I'm older than you."

"You're lying," Natalie said, almost offhandedly. "If Mum and Dad knew you were in here, why would you be so worried about the light showing?"

Ian had forgotten that Natalie had gone through all the same logic and analysis training classes that he had. He waited for her to say, "I'm telling," so he could say, "I'm telling first." And then he could figure out how to negotiate her silence.

But Natalie said nothing. She just sniffed.

It was funny—just that one sniff made Ian determined that Natalie would never have to find out what he'd just learned about their parents. He never wanted her reading about how Irina Spasky had died.

"Go back to bed," Ian said. "There's nothing to look at here."

"There are secrets here," Natalie said stubbornly. "Explanations."

She looked up at her big brother.

"You don't trust them, either, do you?" she said. "That's why we're both here."

Ian sighed. Sometimes Natalie was too smart for her own good.

"Don't worry about it," he said. "Just think about the next Prada bag Mum will buy you."

"No," Natalie said. "I have to know—what's happened to her? Why is she being so mean? Mean all the time, even to us?"

Ian shrugged helplessly. Keeping the beam of the flashlight low, he backed up slightly so Natalie wouldn't see the mess of files on the floor. He accidentally backed into a desk, knocking himself off-kilter. He reached around and grabbed at the edge of the desk, but his fingers brushed something else. A . . . test tube?

Ian spun around and held it in the light.

It was a test tube Ian had seen before, with oddly spelled words on it. Ian knew that the words themselves didn't actually matter anymore. They were anagrams of instructions that Amy Cahill had followed weeks ago in Paris. She had risked her life to follow those instructions right before Ian had swooped in and stolen the test tube out of her hands.

"So *this* is where Mum and Dad have been keeping the Lucian serum," Natalie said, peering over his shoulder. "Wouldn't you think they'd put it somewhere safer?"

Ian shook the test tube, which was supposed to hold some of the most valuable liquid on the face of the earth. Maybe *the* most valuable liquid, period, since the Janus serum had been lost, and nobody knew what had happened to the Tomas serum, the Ekat serum, or the original master serum created by Gideon Cahill himself more than five hundred years ago. Ian was pretty sure the master serum was going to be the final prize in the Clue hunt; he could remember back in Paris, when he'd been so proud to have at least captured the Lucian serum.

He'd been so ignorant then.

"It doesn't matter what happens to the test tube," he told his sister. He turned it upside down. "See? It's empty."

Natalie looked up at him with troubled eyes.

"Then they drank it," she whispered. "Just Mum, do you think? Or Mum and Dad both?"

"Who cares?" Ian asked harshly. "Either way, no one saved any to share with us."

"That's not fair," Natalie said, a familiar whininess back in her voice. But this time it was whininess on Ian's behalf. "You're the one who found the serum. They should at least have shared it with you."

"We're just servants to them," Ian said. "Minions. Like" — he swallowed hard — "like Irina."

CHAPTER 5

Dan felt cheated.

Nellie and Amy had convinced him that he *had* to come to *Romeo and Juliet* because it would be a good place to look for a Clue.

"It's about feuding families," Nellie had said. "Don't you think that's related?"

Besides, the two had told him, the play would be exciting.

"Back in Shakespeare's day, theater wasn't seen as high class and literary and all that," Amy had said, practically reading the words right from the computer screen. "It was meant to appeal to common people. On the same level as the other big entertainment in Elizabethan London—bear baiting."

"What's bear baiting?" Dan had asked.

Amy had put her hands over Saladin's ears before answering.

"Oh, it was awful," she said. "They'd chain up a bear and then let a bunch of other animals—usually dogs—attack. Everybody would watch to see if the bear killed the dogs or the dogs killed the bear."

"Sounds like *Survivor*," Nellie said. Her face turned grim. "Or this clue hunt."

"Well, anyhow," Amy said quickly. "There are sword fights in *Romeo and Juliet*. Two or three of them. You'll love those."

So now Dan had been sitting in the Globe Theatre for what felt like hours, and he was bored out of his mind. Sure, there'd been a sword fight. One. But Dan had missed most of it because he was leaning over to Amy and asking, "Wait—what are they fighting about? Just because the one guy bit his thumb at the other guy? What's wrong with that?"

"It was a terrible insult in Shakespeare's time," Amy had explained.

"Well, then—can I bite my thumb at Isabel Kabra the next time I see her?"

Just then the sword fight had ended. And ever since, the play had mostly been people saying sappy things about love.

Now the girl, Juliet, was standing on a balcony that jutted out above the stage.

"O Romeo, Romeo," she sighed. "Wherefore art thou Romeo?"

Dan dug his elbow into Amy's side.

"What's her problem—is she blind?" Dan asked. "Can't she see that Romeo dude on the stage right below her?"

"It's supposed to be nighttime," Amy whispered. "It's dark, and he's hiding."

"He's not hiding very well," Dan said.

"Anyhow, 'wherefore' means 'why,' not 'where,'" Amy said.

That was crazy. "Wherefore" sure sounded like it was supposed to mean "where." Dan's opinion of Shakespeare was sinking lower and lower.

"But—" Dan began.

"Shh," Amy hissed. "I want to hear this."

She settled back, a dreamy look on her face. Beside her, Nellie looked every bit as rapt.

Dan glanced around. It seemed like every single other person in the theater was staring up at Juliet with that same goofy expression that Amy and Nellie had. Even the people standing in the middle of the theater where there wasn't a roof, where the rain was pouring right down on their heads.

Amy had said that those people were called groundlings, and they didn't have a roof over their heads because this theater was supposed to be historically accurate, as much like theaters back in Shakespeare's time as possible.

Dan thought that if he'd been standing in the rain watching a stupid play about love, he wouldn't have minded a little historical inaccuracy to keep his head dry.

Dan's attention wandered further. He looked toward the top of the theater, three stories up. He and Amy and Nellie had seats off to the side, near the stage, so he had a good view of the ring of thatched roof that protected everyone who wasn't a groundling. Amy had told him it was the only thatched roof in London — and it was allowed only because they'd used special flame-retardant thatch.

The original Globe Theatre had burned to the ground.

Another fire, Dan thought. *Probably set by feuding Cahills even way back in the 1600s.*

Dan's stomach churned. This had been happening to him ever since Jamaica, ever since he'd watched an innocent man die. Dan had gone into shock right afterward, but since then he'd worked very hard to convince Nellie and Amy he was back to normal.

I am, Dan told himself.

Except when he thought about Lester too much, or when he remembered how dangerous the Clue hunt was. Then his stomach churned and his vision blurred and his mind blanked and he wasn't sure if he was going to throw up or faint or just start screaming and screaming and screaming. . . .

Dan forced himself to focus very intently on the thatch. Maybe there was a Clue hidden up there and he would see it while Nellie and Amy were watching the play.

A hand appeared in the section of thatch Dan was staring at.

Dan jerked back and blinked hard.

Was he hallucinating? Imagining Lester reaching up out of the quicksand all over again?

Dan made himself look again. He wasn't hallucinating. There was a hand holding on to the thatch. While Dan watched, a dark figure appeared behind the hand: Somebody was holding on and peering over the peak of the roof section directly opposite the stage.

Two more dark-clad heads appeared beside the first.

Dan tugged on Amy's arm. He reminded himself not to act like he'd just thought he was hallucinating a dead man's hand.

"You didn't tell me there were going to be ninjas!" he said excitedly.

"What are you talking about? There aren't ninjas in *Romeo and Juliet*!" Amy said.

"Sure there are," Dan said. "Look!" He pointed toward the back section of roof. "How soon until they rappel down onto the stage?"

Amy looked up at the roof, too.

"Oh, no," she moaned.

In the brief moment that Dan had looked away, the three ninja figures had begun pulling other clothes over their dark costumes. They were the same kind of clothes the people on the stage were wearing: old-fashioned dresses for two of them, and breeches and a tunic for the third. Then the ninjas began following the peak of the thatch around, toward the roof section that hung over the stage.

"What are they looking for?" Amy muttered, because every few steps they plunged some sort of testing stick down into the thatch.

The ninjas in Elizabethan clothing passed on to a section of roof that Amy and Dan couldn't see because it was practically right overhead. Amy surprised Dan by diving over the people sitting in front of them.

"Excuse me, excuse me, sorry to get in your way," she said on her way down, as people gasped and grumbled. Only Amy would apologize in the middle of a dive. At the bottom, Amy did something like a flip and landed on her feet in the groundling section.

"They're pushing something down the drainpipe!" she hissed back to Dan.

Dan glanced at Nellie—still, amazingly, staring raptly at Romeo and Juliet onstage. Then he imitated Amy's dive and flipped into the groundlings.

"What drainpipe?" he asked Amy.

She pointed.

A tube ran down along the side of the stage from the roof, painted to blend in with all the frilly stage decorations. Dan thought about telling Amy that it wouldn't really work as a drainpipe because it'd been capped at the top. But the pseudo-ninjas had taken the cap off and were putting some sort of chain down the tube.

"That's a plumber's snake," Dan told Amy. "One of those things you use to clear out clogged—"

A rolled-up paper popped out of the bottom of the tube.

Amy dived for it.

"That's ours!" the breeches-clad ninja yelled down at her.

"Too bad!" Dan yelled back. "It's ours now!"

The people around him turned and glared and made shushing noises, but Dan didn't care. He was sure the paper was another lead. That was all he could think about. He didn't even care which team the ninjas were from. They were still three stories up, on the roof. Dan and Amy had all the time in the world to escape.

Then the breeches-clad ninja pulled out a rope. He staked one end of it in the roof and shinnied down it, straight toward Amy and Dan.

Dan glanced around frantically. Back at their seats, Nellie had stopped watching the play and was watching them. She was white-faced and worried looking, gesturing wildly.

"Go! Run!" she screamed, pointing toward the exit. "I'll meet you outside!"

But the groundlings around Amy and Dan surged toward the ninja on the rope, angrily muttering things like, "That's not supposed to happen in the balcony scene!" Dan was caught between a man's large belly on one side and a woman's dripping raincoat on the other. He couldn't even see Nellie anymore.

Amy grabbed his arm and pulled.

"This way!" she screamed.

There was only one way to escape: up.

Onto the stage.

Jonah had a bad seat at the Globe.

Before the play started, he'd distracted himself from thinking about his mother's plans by sending a text to his dad:

```
Yo Can hardly see stage b/c column
in way Make sure this never happens
2 fans at my shows
```

But his mother must have been intercepting his father's messages because she was the one who texted back:

```
U R not there to enjoy the play
```

Jonah's seat was in the section above Amy and Dan's. They couldn't see him, but he would be able to watch their every move when they left their seats. And then he would be able to . . .

Don't think about it, Jonah told himself.

The play started. The actors sang and laughed; the actors fought. Jonah stopped thinking of them as actors. He could almost believe that what he saw was real. The prince of the city came out and said anyone who started another fight would be put to death.

Jonah started to sweat.

And then he couldn't hear anything else because the prince's words kept echoing in his ears: "If ever you disturb our streets again/Your lives shall pay the forfeit of the peace . . . On pain of death, all men depart."

Your lives shall pay . . . Your lives shall pay . . . On pain of death, depart . . .

Jonah didn't depart. He sat there, numbly, until he saw Amy and Dan scramble down out of their section and grab something from the floor of the theater.

Can't I just tell Mom they were too far below me to attack? he wondered.

His mother didn't like excuses.

A rope dangled off to the side, not far from Jonah's seat. Jonah couldn't have said if it had been there all along or not. But he squeezed his eyes shut and leaped for it. He planned to just climb down — quickly, before anyone saw him — but the rope swung forward. Panicked, he let go.

He landed on the stage.

Before he had time to figure out what to do about *that,* somebody else landed right on top of him — somebody in a tunic and breeches over a ninja costume. Jonah didn't even bother trying to make sense of it. He shoved the person away and stood up.

The confused-looking ninja grabbed the rope again and started running toward the stairs to Juliet's balcony. Jonah turned and saw that Amy and Dan were clambering up onto the stage off to the side. They froze when they saw Jonah.

Mom thought they'd trust me again, but they don't, Jonah thought bitterly. *And now I'm onstage, in full view of everyone....*

Jonah looked out at the audience. He had never known a moment of stage fright in his life: Audiences calmed him. He felt like he needed an audience right now—his fans, his millions and millions of homies. *Romeo and Juliet* aficionados weren't his usual crowd, but in a pinch, they'd do. Only this audience was stirring about angrily and screaming, "Get off the stage!" and "Stop ruining Shakespeare!"

This audience was also so much smaller than anything Jonah was used to. He could pick out individual faces. He could see Alistair Oh advancing toward the stage in the center, knocking people aside with his cane. He could see Isabel, Ian, and Natalie Kabra—the ruthless Lucians Jonah's own mother wanted him to imitate—slicing through the crowd from the left. And the Holts had evidently been in the section past Jonah's but in the highest seats. They were swarming down the wooden frame.

Everybody's here, Jonah thought weakly.

Behind him, Juliet screamed.

Jonah whirled around. He was glad of the distraction, glad he'd have another moment before he had to decide anything. He saw Juliet plunging off her balcony—she'd jumped to get away from the confused-looking ninja.

"Catch me, you fool!" Juliet shrieked to Romeo.

Romeo held out his arms and caught her awkwardly, but then he ad-libbed, "Uh, hark! What *girl* through yonder window breaks?"

The entire audience—except for the advancing Clue hunters—began clapping and cheering.

Jonah wanted that kind of applause. He always wanted applause—from his fans, from his parents, even from his single-minded Clue-hunting relatives. He looked back and forth between Amy and Dan and the audience, all his choices so clear before him.

Why do I have to choose who loves me? he agonized.

And then, just like that, Jonah knew what he had to do.

He took a step forward.

"This is for you, Mom," he whispered.

"Amy! This way!" Dan called.

Amy shook off the paralysis that had hit her the minute she'd seen Jonah land on the stage. She dashed off behind Dan, onto the front part of the stage where the rain had blown in. She skidded on the wet wood.

"Amy! Down here! I'll help you!"

Amy saw that Alistair was out in the crowd, waving at her. Could she trust him?

"Throw me that paper! I'll keep it safe!" Alistair

called. "Then you can hold on to my cane—I'll help you down."

Don't think so, Amy told herself. If Alistair cared so much about her safety, why had he asked for the paper first?

She veered away from the front of the stage, her head whipping back and forth from watching out for Alistair, watching out for Jonah, and watching out for the pseudo-ninjas. Alistair was getting closer and closer to the stage. The ninja had tied the rope to the balcony so the other two costumed figures could climb down behind him. Now all three ninjas were rushing toward Dan and Amy.

Amy put on a burst of speed.

If only we can make it to the other side of the stage . . .

Dan must have had the same thought because he sped up at the same time. He was right in front of her. They were almost there, almost to safety. . . .

Dan skidded to a halt.

"What's wrong?" Amy shrieked.

Dan's face was turning a sickly shade of green. He clutched his stomach. He reeled backward and barely managed to stay upright.

"Is it—?" Amy began. Then she saw what Dan was staring at. *Who* he was staring at.

"Kabras," Dan whispered.

Right at the edge of the stage—right where Dan and Amy had thought they would reach safety—Isabel Kabra was rising out of the crowd. Amy was close enough to see that the woman wasn't really floating in midair. She was climbing over the backs of her own children, Ian and Natalie.

In spike heels.

That's got to hurt, Amy thought.

It was easier to think about shoes than to think about Isabel Kabra and everything she'd done. But Amy couldn't hold back the horror.

The last time we saw Isabel face-to-face, Lester died, Amy thought.

Isabel hadn't held his head underwater. It'd been her hired thugs chasing him. . . .

Amy cast a quick glance over her shoulder, suddenly even more worried about the bizarrely dressed ninjas.

"Give us that paper!" the breeches-clad ninja growled. He was only a few steps away.

On Amy's other side, Isabel stepped from her children's backs onto the stage.

"Oh, no, I believe these are *my* victims," Isabel purred.

So the ninjas weren't working for Isabel. That made Amy feel a little better. She could think more clearly now.

She slipped the paper into Dan's hand and whispered in his ear, "We'll have to divide up and distract them. Run! I'll go the other way, and they'll chase me instead."

But Amy caught a glimpse of Isabel's smug face —

Isabel had seen what Amy did. And now Amy and Dan were both trapped between Isabel and the ninjas, with Alistair climbing up onto the stage to their right.

Maybe if we dart toward the left, if we run back-stage . . .

Just then Jonah stepped up on their left, blocking any chance they'd had of escaping in that direction.

"Yo," Jonah said. Oddly, he seemed to be addressing the entire audience, not just Amy and Dan.

He slipped his arm around Dan's shoulders.

Odd way to try to steal the paper, Amy thought. *Or — he wouldn't try to strangle Dan, would he? Here in front of everyone?*

There was something desperate about the way Jonah was holding on to Dan. Even Isabel was watching Jonah as if she didn't quite understand what he was about to do.

Amy grabbed her brother's arm and pulled him away.

"Yo," Jonah complained, turning toward Amy. "No. It's not like that. I was thinking —"

The breeches-clad ninja shoved at Jonah's chest. Jonah was caught off balance. He flailed about wildly, knocking over a barrel at the edge of the stage. The barrel rolled into Isabel, knocking her off the stage. The barrel rolled after her. It hit the ground and exploded.

The crowd shrieked and scattered, trying to dodge the flying debris.

"Yo, that's not—" Jonah began, as he tried to regain his balance.

The ninjas shoved him again, knocking him back. Jonah's windmilling arms hit Alistair as well. Both of them plunged into the angry audience.

Amy grabbed Dan's arm, ready to flee, but the mysterious ninjas surrounded them.

But they just helped us! she told herself. *Maybe they're allies after all?*

Amy wanted to believe that.

"Uh, thanks for getting rid of Jonah and Isabel, uh—Hamilton?" Amy guessed.

Elizabethan ninja costumes weren't the Holts' style, and the ninja in breeches didn't seem nearly big enough to be Hamilton. And the voice hadn't sounded right. But the Holts were the only ones on the Clue hunt with two girls and a boy.

"We're not the Holt dolts!" the ninja growled. "They're over there!"

Amy looked and saw all the Holts swarming across the stage from the opposite side. The girls and Mary-Todd were in new-looking, shiny pink tracksuits. Hamilton and his dad were in Manchester United shirts. They were definitely the real Holts.

"Who *is* that?" Hamilton yelled across the stage. "Who are they working for?"

Amy thought it might be better to escape than to stick around and find out. But just then the breeches-clad ninja grabbed her arm, yanking her away from her brother. Both of the other ninjas grabbed Dan.

Then Hamilton was there, grabbing the breeches-clad ninja and tugging at the ninja's hood.

"I'll find out!" Hamilton cried. He held firm, even as the ninja screamed, "No! Stop!" and tried to squirm away.

Long auburn hair tumbled out of the ninja's hood.

Amy gawked. She'd read the expression "her eyes popped out of her head" dozens of times, but she'd never experienced it so completely before.

"Sinead Starling?" she gasped.

CHAPTER 6

Hamilton Holt dropped the boy — er, *girl* — he'd just unmasked. Hamilton was quick on his feet. Put a football or a hockey stick in his hands, and people started using words like *nimble* and *fleet-footed* to describe him. In the Clue hunt, he'd discovered that, under pressure, his brain could be pretty nimble and quick, too.

This wasn't one of those times.

Right now his eyes and ears were telling him that the kid he'd just dropped was his distant cousin Sinead Starling. But his brain couldn't catch up.

"No!" he protested. "You Starlings — you've been out of the race since Philadelphia. The second day. That explosion at the Franklin Institute . . . you were going to have to be in the hospital for ages!"

Hamilton felt a twinge of guilt — the Holts had been the ones who'd set off the Franklin Institute explosion. Hamilton's own family had caused the Starling triplets' injuries. But only by accident.

Because we were trying to hurt Amy and Dan instead, Hamilton thought bitterly. He shook his head, trying to clear it. *Nobody knows,* he told himself. *Nobody knows it was us.*

Sinead was sneering up at him.

"We're geniuses, remember?" she said. "Ted and Ned and I, lying in our hospital beds, we figured out new medical procedures to speed healing. And" — she smirked — "we read up on the clues, so we *totally* caught up in the clue hunt. I'd say we're probably even ahead. Wouldn't you, Ted?"

Hamilton was still having trouble accepting that Sinead had been the ninja in breeches. He squinted at the other two ninjas, who still had on dark masks.

"Ted and Ned are the dudes in dresses?" he asked. "I don't get it."

"You Neanderthal brain," Sinead said, rolling her eyes. "Hello? It's a disguise *and* an homage. Obviously you don't know Shakespeare."

Hamilton didn't. But the Clue hunt had taught him a lot about danger, and he could feel it around him now. If he stood here listening to Sinead, Jonah would be back up onstage, attacking again. Or Isabel would start carrying out some diabolical plan. Or . . .

Or Dan would be carried away.

That was already happening. Even as she talked, Sinead had given some signal to her brothers, and they were carrying Dan toward the balcony.

"Help!" Dan screamed. "Amy! Hamilton! Somebody!"

"I'm on it!" Hamilton yelled, running after them. Amy was right behind him.

Romeo blocked their path.

"Begone!" the actor demanded. "Get thee off our stage! Let us finish our play, meet our intended fates. . . ."

Eisenhower Holt slammed into Romeo like a tank.

"Your fate just changed, dude," Hamilton muttered.

Eisenhower took Romeo by the collar and hurled him toward the edge of the stage, where Isabel, Alistair, and Jonah were trying to climb back up. It was like watching an expert bowler pick up a nearly impossible split: As Romeo fell off the stage, he knocked all three Clue hunters back into the crowd.

"Romeo!" Juliet shrieked.

She jumped after him.

The panicked crowd screamed louder.

"Focus, Holts!" Eisenhower hollered like a coach at a halftime huddle. "No distractions! Don't think about anything but the clue hunt!"

Hamilton raced after Dan. The Starling boys had tied him to the balcony, several feet above the stage. Now they were reaching for the paper in Dan's hand. Dan was doing his best to keep it away from them, even as he squirmed and fought against the ropes.

Amy had managed to dodge Romeo and Eisenhower and reach the balcony ahead of Hamilton. She tugged on one of the Starling boys' arms, but he just flicked her away.

"Pathetic," Sinead murmured behind Hamilton. "Who let those mouth breathers stay in the clue hunt so long? It's a good thing we Starlings are back because the rest of you are losers!"

Eisenhower Holt's words still echoed in Hamilton's mind: *No distractions! Don't think about anything but the clue hunt!*

Really, Hamilton only needed to grab Dan's paper and take off. But Hamilton was already distracted. He couldn't help seeing the pain and fear on Amy's and Dan's faces—and the hope that showed up any time either of them glanced toward Hamilton.

Hamilton strode toward Ned and Ted and slammed their heads together. Then he slid one of the boys across the stage toward Sinead—just a variation on Dad's bowling-with-people technique. Sinead toppled in exactly the right way so Hamilton could scoop her up in a tight grip. He hung her by the back of her breeches beside Dan on the balcony.

"Show some respect for my buddy Dan-o," Hamilton lectured Sinead, his face a few inches from hers. "Amy, too. You've missed a lot of this clue hunt, and things have changed. Amy and Dan, they're, they're—" He remembered a term his football coach back home liked to use. "They are *worthy competitors.* Got it?"

"Ned!" Sinead gasped. "Ted! Plan B!"

Barely bothering to look, Hamilton flailed out a fist in either direction—catching one Starling boy on the right jaw and the other on the left. Both crumpled to the ground.

"Thanks, Ham!" Dan exploded. "Do you mind?"

Hamilton skillfully picked the knot the Starling boys had tied around Dan and lowered him to the floor of the stage.

"Okay, okay, get on with it!" Eisenhower screamed, even as he and the rest of the Holts guarded the edge of the stage. They shoved back everyone trying to climb up again. "Now grab the clue for Team Holt! Do it!"

Automatically, Hamilton reached his arm over Dan's shoulder. Dan belatedly tried to shift the paper from one hand to the other, to get it out of Hamilton's reach. This was pointless: Hamilton had already grabbed the tattered page. He held it up in triumph.

"All right!" Eisenhower hollered.

At the same time, Dan peered up at Hamilton in astonishment.

"Ham?" he said. He sounded . . . betrayed. "I thought, well, since we helped each other out before . . ."

Hamilton froze. He looked back and forth between his jubilant dad and forlorn Dan.

"Um," Hamilton said.

"Worthy competitors are still competitors!" Eisenhower jeered. "Sucker!"

"Oh, yeah? And some competitors aren't even worthy!" Sinead countered.

She detached her breeches from the balcony and leaped for the paper in Hamilton's hand.

Hamilton could have moved. He had time. But his brain was slowing him down again.

Team Holt, he thought. *What does that really mean anymore? Beating up little kids—is that any way to win? What's really going on here?*

Sinead ripped the page from his fingers.

The rest of the Holts abandoned the edge of the stage to run and tackle her. And then other relatives piled on, too, each of them biting, kicking, scratching, screaming. Alistair Oh's elbow was in Isabel Kabra's ear, and her hand was in Sinead Starling's mouth, and Sinead's fingers were in Madison's hair.

And the paper itself was torn to shreds.

CHAPTER 7

"Amy! Let's go!" Dan screamed.

"No! The paper! We have to—" Amy pointed toward the pile of Cahill relatives flailing about on the stage. She looked like she was about to leap into the battle.

Dan grabbed her arm. Now she was fighting *him*.

How was he supposed to play this?

"Let's just go plan our strategy," he said, in case any of the others could hear him.

Amy flashed him a baffled look.

He winked at her.

Now Amy seemed completely confused. Dan looked around quickly to make sure no one was watching, then pulled her behind the stage curtain.

"Dan, what are you doing?" Amy asked. "We've got to stay and fight—"

Dan whispered in her ear, "No, we don't. I kept part of the paper!"

Amy jerked away, stared at him, and then pulled Dan deeper into the backstage area, farther from the other relatives. They ducked into a dimly lit room marked PROPS. Amy locked the door behind them.

"We should be safe here," she whispered. "Now, tell me — what do you mean?"

"When Ned and Ted tied me to the balcony, I made sure I had both hands behind my back," Dan said. "I knew they wouldn't let me keep the paper, so I started tearing pieces off and stuffing them in my pockets."

"Dan — maybe that was a priceless document!" Amy protested. "Maybe it was an original page written by Shakespeare!"

"And maybe I got enough of it that we can figure out the next lead!" Dan countered.

Amy stopped arguing.

Dan began pulling shreds of paper out of his pocket.

"Well, it's not an original written by Shakespeare — unless he used a typewriter," Dan said, smoothing out the first one.

Amy seemed to relax a little.

"Shouldn't we wait and look at this outside?" Dan asked.

"No — we've got to see if you have enough or if we'll need to go back and fight," Amy said. It was so obvious that she was trying to be brave, battling the instinct to run. The swords and armor lining the wall cast scary shadows across her face.

Dan quickly began assembling scraps.

When they'd put everything they could together, Dan's piece of the page read:

```
A SONNET IN THE STYLE OF SHAKESPEARE
You seek a Clue? Be ye his kin? Or else
A friend            best-known Madrigal


                    upon-Avon, there
For this great man we sing was b      here.
```

"I tore off pieces from the top and the bottom both," Dan said apologetically. "Because I started thinking about how, with a lead, usually the stuff at the bottom is the most important, and since I'd never looked at the paper, I didn't really know which way was up." He touched the solitary "b" in the last line. "Sorry I didn't get the whole word there. You probably could have solved it then."

"I can solve it anyway!" Amy said. She beamed at him.

"You can?" Dan asked.

"Because guess where William Shakespeare was born?" Amy asked.

"I don't know, but I bet you're going to tell me," Dan said.

"Stratford-*upon-Avon, there*," Amy said, touching the words as she spoke them.

"So you think that one missing word in the last line is *born*," Dan said. Something like dread began to creep over him. "Oh, no, don't tell me—"

"That's right, even though it was five hundred years ago, the house where Shakespeare was born is still there," Amy said. "And we're going to go see it!"

Alistair Oh hobbled into the Tate Modern museum of art. Alistair was no fan of modern art—in his opinion, it was proof that the Janus branch of the Cahills had gone insane. But the museum was practically next door to the Globe Theatre, and right now it was a good place to hide. Nobody would expect him to come *here.*

Alistair tried to walk with his usual dignity, but that was difficult when the pocket of his cream-colored jacket flapped loose and he had blood caked on his cheek from the all-out family battle at the Globe. And—was that mud in his hair?

All that, and he still hadn't emerged with even one scrap of the paper.

I'm too old for this, he thought, even though his uncle, Bae Oh, was much older and still every bit as obsessed with the Clue hunt as Alistair.

Alistair ducked into a dark, empty alcove, which turned out to be a tiny screening room.

Lunacy, Alistair thought. *People nowadays think* video *is art?*

He eased himself down onto a bench and thought longingly of the museum his branch, the Ekats, had proudly maintained at their stronghold in Egypt. He'd always hoped that his own genius inventions would one day hold a place of honor there, amazing all visitors. But he'd been so focused on finding Clues over the years that all he'd ever really invented was the microwavable burrito. And, like so much else, many Ekat treasures from the museum had been stolen or destroyed during the Clue hunt.

Treasures destroyed, hopes destroyed, lives destroyed . . . does it ever end? he wondered, as images flickered and died on the wall before him.

The juxtaposition of three words — *hopes, lives, destroyed* — brought a flash to his mind of the lively, charming Hope Cahill, murdered years ago. Amy looked more and more like her every time he saw her.

I didn't kill Hope, Alistair thought reflexively, as he'd been thinking for the past seven years. This time there was an echo to the thought: *I'm still to blame. . . .*

Alistair closed his eyes, trying to shut out the pain. When he opened them again, he was surrounded.

"You owe us!" a surly voice snarled.

Creditors, Alistair thought. It was inevitable, with all the millions he'd wasted on the Clue hunt.

Alistair blinked, and the people jostling against him turned out to be three teenagers who'd traded their Elizabethan-ninja costumes for jeans and T-shirts: Sinead, Ned, and Ted Starling.

"I beg your pardon?" he asked, with politeness they didn't deserve.

"You're an Ekat, we're Ekats — you owe us some help

with the clue hunt," Sinead said. *"Uncle* Alistair."

That one word—*uncle*—made him wince. He could so clearly remember how he'd said that word to Bae Oh when he was a teenager . . . before he knew that Bae Oh had had Alistair's father killed over Clues.

And he could remember how Amy and Dan had said that word early on in the Clue hunt.

Back when they trusted him.

Alistair shook his head, trying to clear it, trying to focus on the kids standing around him, not the ones who'd vanished again.

"How did you know I was here?" Alistair asked.

"Simple," one of the boys—Ned?—said. "Except for the Kabra mansion, it was about the least likely place in London for you to go. So we looked here first."

Alistair had heard family gossip that Ned had earned a PhD at age ten but still couldn't tie his shoes or talk sensibly about anything but quantum physics. Alistair didn't really feel up to discussing quantum physics right now, so he turned away from Ned.

"See, we know how you think," Sinead purred. "We're just like you."

I hope not, Alistair thought sadly.

"I thought you said you were completely caught up in the clue hunt," Alistair said. "Maybe even ahead."

"Of course that's what we told *them*," Ted said. "Our *enemies.*"

"But with you, our fellow Ekat, it's like we're on the same team," Sinead said ingratiatingly. She picked a little mud out of Alistair's hair. "I'm sure if you share everything you've learned so far, we'll know *lots* more than anyone else."

She smiled, showing entirely too many teeth.

A lifetime of work, searching for clues, Alistair thought. *My life's work, really. And they want me to just give it away?*

"No," Alistair said.

Sinead recoiled.

"What—are you going to help those brats, Amy and Dan, instead?" she accused. "We know you've been helping them all along. How else would they have solved anything?"

"Integrity," Alistair said softly. "Courage. Intelligence. Daring. Hard work."

Sinead snorted.

"Yeah, right. Them?" she asked. "Before this clue hunt, they weren't even brave enough to cross the street alone. You expect me to believe they've gone all around the world on their own?"

"They've . . . grown up," Alistair said, and was surprised that the words brought a pang to his heart. *I could have been there for them all along,* he thought. *But I mostly wasn't.*

Sinead seemed to remember she was trying to sweet-talk Alistair.

"Well, anyhow," she said. "This isn't about them. It's about us. The brilliant Ekats. Our parents always told us you were the smartest one of all."

She gazed at him, a worshipful expression—clearly fake—plastered across her face. She even batted her eyelashes a little. She was trying so hard.

Like Alistair had always tried so hard.

And done so much wrong.

"Foolish," Alistair murmured. "I've been so foolish."

"But—the microwavable burrito!" Sinead said. "You *invented* that! You made millions!"

"Listen," Alistair said. "I'll share some of the wisdom I've earned over the years."

All three teenagers leaned close.

"When you near the end of your life . . . when you're a lonely old man . . . you start realizing what your accomplishments are really worth," he said. "The most brilliant clue I ever deciphered, the millions I earned—even the microwavable burrito itself— sometimes I think I'd be willing to trade all of it for a single hug from someone who truly loves me."

Sinead, Ted, and Ned froze for a moment. Then Sinead bounced up and rather gingerly put her arms around Alistair's shoulders.

"Oh, *we* love you, Uncle Alistair!" she said.

Alistair pulled away.

"No, you don't," he said.

Alistair pushed the bench back and stood up. His legs were stiff and sore, but he wanted so much to be able to make a dignified exit. He started walking away.

"Wait!" Ned cried.

Alistair kept walking.

"There's something else you might want to know," Sinead called after him. "We stole Bae Oh's clues!"

Alistair hesitated for a moment. And then, slowly, he turned back around.

CHAPTER 8

"AHHHHH!" Nellie screamed.

"AHHHHH!" Dan screamed from his place beside her in the front seat of the car.

"What is wrong with you two?" Amy asked from the backseat. She looked up from the pile of Shakespeare books she'd settled in with as soon as they'd pulled out of the rental-car lot toward Stratford.

"I forgot I'd have to drive on the wrong side of the road again!" Nellie said. "I mean, it's the right side for them—er, the left side, that's where they drive—but—"

"DO YOU SEE THAT CAR?" Dan screamed.

It seemed to be in their lane.

"Swerve right?" Nellie muttered. "No—left. Right? Left? AHHHH!"

At the last minute, she jerked the steering wheel to the left. She pulled off into the grass and sat there, shaking, while cars whizzed by them.

"I'm not sure I can do this," she said.

"What?" Amy said in amazement. "Nellie—you

already drove on the wrong side of the road before when we were in South Africa."

"You were *awesome* there, zigzagging all over the place!" Dan said. "Nellie, you're the *best* driver."

This was true only if you defined *best* as *most dangerous*. Which Dan probably did.

"Yeah, usually I am," Nellie agreed. She wiped her hand across her forehead. Her fingertips came away sweaty. "But I don't know, it's weird. It's, like, this is all real now. Back in South Africa, I kind of felt like I was just driving in a video game. But now—now I know what the clue hunt is for, and how much it matters. It's like, whoa, *responsibility.*"

"If you'd crashed us into another car in South Africa—or anywhere else—you would have been responsible for killing us," Dan said. "Even when you didn't know what the clue hunt was about."

"Thanks. That makes me feel *so* much better," Nellie said sarcastically. She rubbed the snake nose ring she'd insisted on repairing before they left Jamaica.

She made no move to pull back onto the road.

Amy remembered how shaken Nellie had looked when they met up with her after sneaking out the back of the Globe.

Does Nellie *think this is all impossible now?* Amy wondered. *Is it just hitting her a day late?*

"We can't let Isabel win, remember?" Amy reminded her. "Not Isabel . . . or Eisenhower . . . or Cora . . . or Alistair . . ."

It was no accident that Amy named people who'd been there the night her parents died.

Nellie clutched the steering wheel.

"You're right," she said, resolutely setting her jaw. "I have to do this. Just—don't watch, okay? It makes me nervous."

"I'll be reading," Amy said quickly.

"This is what long-life computer batteries are for," Dan said, opening his laptop.

Amy even stacked books next to Saladin's cat carrier so he wouldn't watch, either.

At first Amy was very aware of the car's motion. But then she lost herself reading about Shakespeare. She loved the man. In his writing he could be so funny, so wise, so . . . human.

And it was so clear that he was a Madrigal.

He hadn't been born rich and famous. The experts weren't even sure his parents knew how to read and write. His father had had money problems when William was a teenager, and so experts thought William had probably dropped out of school. He definitely hadn't been able to go to university. When he'd started out writing plays in London, some of the other writers had made fun of him for being uneducated.

He was like Dan and me, Amy thought. *An underdog.*

Then there'd been Shakespeare's Lost Years, the time when he'd seemed to vanish from the historical record.

Obviously he was off doing Madrigal business, Amy thought. *Searching for clues, maybe negotiating with Lucians and Ekats, secretly keeping the balance of power between the branches.*

She and Dan had been in the Clue hunt for so long, it was like they barely had to glance at something to see the Cahill fingerprints all over history.

"Oh, man!" Dan burst out from the front seat. "How could this dude be one of us? William Shakespeare — a Madrigal? No way!"

Once again, Dan's mind was running in a totally different direction from Amy's.

"Are you kidding?" Amy shrieked. The car swerved, then corrected itself. Amy looked sheepishly at Nellie. "Sorry, Nellie. Didn't mean to distract you."

"S'okay," Nellie said, staring fixedly at the road before them. "You can talk now that I'm on the highway. It's much easier. No cars coming straight at me."

Amy turned her attention back to Dan.

"Let me guess," she said. "You think Shakespeare should have been a Janus because his writing was great art. Or — you're jealous that Madrigals don't have kung fu artists or mountain climbers or sword fighters as their famous 'dude,' like some of the other branches. Pretty much everybody says Shakespeare was the greatest writer ever. Isn't that enough for you?"

"Oh, come on," Dan said. "He did all his work with a quill pen."

Amy could feel her head getting ready to explode.

"But," Dan went on, "I agree that Shakespeare was a great writer."

Everything Amy had planned to yell at him fizzled.

"You . . . you do?" she managed to say.

"Oh, yeah," Dan said. "Didn't you see that list of Shakespeare insult stickers back at the Globe gift shop? That made me curious, so I've been checking out some things online. This dude really knew how to insult people. 'You muddy conger'? 'Thy tongue outvenoms all the worms of Nile'? 'Thou art a boil, a plague-sore, an embossed carbuncle'? I'm so going to use these the next time I see Isabel Kabra! Or the Starlings!"

"So you think Shakespeare was great just because of his insults," Amy said faintly.

"Oh, that, and—did you know he couldn't spell?" Dan pointed to something on his computer screen. "There are six copies left of his signature, and none of them are spelled the same way. He's the greatest writer in history, and he couldn't even spell his own name!"

"There wasn't standardized spelling in his time," Amy said defensively. "*Nobody* spelled things the same way all the time. It was really confusing."

Dan chuckled.

"Yeah, but if Shakespeare were alive today, I bet he'd be wearing this great T-shirt I saw once: 'Bad Spellers of the World—Untie!'" he said.

Amy rolled her eyes.

"You're losing me," she said. "Are you saying you don't think Shakespeare could have been a Madrigal because he didn't spell well enough?"

"No," Dan said impatiently. "I'm saying he was too great to be a Madrigal."

Amy felt her face go blank.

"Totally lost now," she said. "Not even on the same continent with whatever it is you're trying to say."

"Listen," Dan said. "Think about what the man in black—er, Great-uncle Fiske—told us back in Jamaica. The original Cahill dude, Gideon, invented some amazing serum that was supposed to make him great at everything. Four of his kids got some part of the serum, and when they took it, it even changed their DNA. So everyone on Katherine's side was smarter than normal people, and Thomas's side was stronger and more athletic, and—"

"Yeah, yeah, I know this part," Amy interrupted. "Jane's family got the artistic, creative gene. Luke's family got strategy and leadership. Leading to the Ekats, Tomas, Janus, and Lucians we know and love today." She made a face. "What's that got to do with Shakespeare? If he's a Madrigal, he wasn't part of any of those branches."

"Right," Dan said. "Our ancestor, Madeleine, came along after the serum was gone and the family broke up. So Madeleine never took any serum. And neither did her kids or their kids. Her branch—our branch—we're not *enhanced*."

Amy felt a little pang—her own brother had just admitted they were completely ordinary. Talentless. Dull. Everything she'd always suspected about herself.

But Dan wasn't done talking.

"So without any serum—how'd Shakespeare get to be the greatest writer ever?" he asked. "Better than all those Janus writers who did have the miracle serum in their DNA?"

"I don't know," Amy admitted. "Do you think he just tried really, really hard?"

She felt dazed, like she did any time she thought about the serum. It just seemed so much like cheating. Not that Cahills were above cheating: She'd seen enough in the Clue hunt to know that cheating was practically a family trait. But the serum—that was like drugs. Something really, really dangerous.

Secretly, when she'd learned the truth about the Madrigals' place in the family, she'd actually felt a little relieved that there wasn't any serum in her DNA. But before she'd understood anything, she'd struggled to get that vial of the Lucian serum back in Paris. She'd gone all the way to the top of Mount Everest hoping to find the Janus serum.

And it sounds like the master serum is the final prize in the clue hunt, Amy thought. *Somehow.*

Anxiety stabbed in her gut. This was something she'd been trying not to think about. She remembered Dan's argument back in the hotel room, about how winning would mean that they'd get enough power to knock everyone else into shape, to achieve all their goals. But was that really the Madrigal way to solve things? Had Grace really set the entire Clue hunt in motion, just so Amy and Dan could get access to something that might change them completely?

Didn't she think we were good enough just the way we are? Amy wondered.

She realized she'd begun to whimper.

"Amy," Dan said. "Are you freaking out again?"

"Everything's so complicated," Amy complained. "I was feeling good that we could decode the Shakespeare leads, and that Hamilton called us 'worthy competitors'—things really have changed since the clue hunt started. So maybe there is hope. But there are still so many things I don't understand. How did the Starlings catch up with us so easily? How did all the other teams know to be at the Globe the same time as us? What are we really supposed to do to win? What do the Madrigals expect from us? And then—"

"Amy," Dan said very solemnly. "I know exactly what you need."

"What?" Amy asked.

"A snack break," Dan said. "And—even if it doesn't help you, it will help me. Nellie, can you *please* pull over? I'm starving!"

"I wouldn't mind getting off the road for a little bit," Nellie said. She veered around two Volvos and a BMW. All three of them honked at her.

When they stopped at a service station, Dan ran through the aisles, marveling at all the great British snack foods.

"They have something called Mega Monster Munch?" he cried. "I've got to have some of that! And BBQ Beef Hula Hoops! And . . ." He began grabbing bags off the shelves.

"Dan, you've had junk food on practically every continent now," Nellie said. "Why is this so exciting?"

"Because just about everywhere else, it's been the same old stuff we have at home, or labeled in some language I don't understand," Dan said. "This"—he picked up a bag of Crispy Bacon Frazzles—"it's like something I've always dreamed of. Wouldn't it be sad if I'd never come here? This is why people should travel!"

Amy wandered away from Dan and Nellie. This was so typical. Dan refusing to worry, her worrying enough for both of them.

She heard a voice say, "Globe Theatre." She turned quickly.

The voice came from a TV set near the cash register.

"It appears that a riot broke out in the famous theater this afternoon," the BBC announcer was saying.

Amy stepped closer and angled so she could see the screen. But there was no video rolling, just a woman talking.

"International hip-hop and reality TV star Jonah

Wizard was detained for questioning about his part in the riot, which caused hundreds of pounds worth of damages," the announcer continued. "Performances at the Globe have been suspended indefinitely. Police are considering whether to charge Wizard—and possibly others—with willful destruction of property."

Amy threw a wad of pound notes down on the counter.

"That's for everything," she said, pointing at the bags Dan and Nellie were carrying. She knew she'd overpaid, but she didn't care.

She pulled Dan and Nellie outside.

"Whoa, whoa, what's going on?" Nellie demanded as they hustled into the car.

Quickly, Amy told the other two what she'd heard on the TV.

"What?" Dan said. "That doesn't make sense. During this clue hunt, Cahills have destroyed historic sites all over the planet, and it's never made the news!"

"It gets hushed up," Nellie agreed. "Each branch pays for its own. The Madrigals have always paid for the damages you two caused."

Amy hadn't known that.

"Well, we didn't hurt anything except in Venice," she said. "And, okay, Vienna, too . . ."

"Jonah's family has tons of money to hush things up," Dan protested. "He broke all those terra-cotta statues back in China—well, to rescue me, after he set me up. But I know his dad paid off the Chinese officials, and nobody else ever heard anything about it. All Jonah did at the Globe was break a barrel, and it's all over the news?"

"Something else has changed," Amy said slowly. "Something big . . ."

CHAPTER 9

Jonah Wizard stood very, very still. He was posing at Madame Tussauds, where everyone who'd been anyone for the past two hundred years had been immortalized as a wax statue. Actually, Jonah was impersonating a wax statue, since the one they were making of him wasn't quite finished yet. Madame Tussauds had just opened for the day, and the room was beginning to fill up with people exclaiming, "They look so real!"

In a few minutes, Jonah would move. He'd start with something small, maybe a raised eyebrow. Then he'd segue into some sweet dance move. Music would fill the room, and he'd start singing. Everyone would scream with delight and crowd around. Maybe some of the girls would even faint.

Normally, this was the kind of thing Jonah loved. The music, the adoring fans—it was what he lived for. But today . . . today, he hated it.

Today, he wasn't doing this just to thrill his fans or to promote his music, TV show, energy drinks, pop-up books, or clothing line. Or anything else in the vast, sprawling Jonah Wizard entertainment empire. Today he was just a distraction — a sideshow. While he was singing and dancing and sucking up all the attention in the entire building, his mother planned to pluck out a hint she believed was hidden in the shoe of the William Shakespeare wax statue only a few rooms away. And, just in case that didn't work, she had canisters of poison gas with her. She had grenades. She had a gun.

Someone could get hurt, Jonah thought. *Someone could be killed. Maybe even some of my fans, because of me.*

And there was nothing Jonah could do about it.

Jonah's mother was blackmailing him. Blackmailing him to stay in the Clue hunt — and do it her way.

She'd been livid that he hadn't emerged from the Globe with any leads.

"Apparently, you don't care enough about winning the biggest prize in history," she'd said, glaring at him. "Apparently, you need more incentive."

"No, Mom, I *tried* at the Globe," he'd protested. "It's just — we're not Lucians. I thought of a better way to win, a more *Janus* way — I could tell you —"

"It didn't work, did it? I don't want to hear anything about plans like that," Cora said. She favored him with a thin, heartless smile. "I know what *will* work."

And then she'd called the police herself. She'd driven Jonah to the police station to stand in a lineup and be picked out by witnesses from the Globe.

"You see your choices now, don't you?" she'd asked. "You do what I want. Or you go to prison."

Thinking about it now, Jonah had to work very hard to keep still.

He couldn't really imagine being sent to prison. But Jonah's dad had spelled out exactly what a little bad PR, uncorrected, could do to Jonah's life:

TV show—canceled.

Concert dates—canceled.

Recording contract—canceled.

Trademark T-shirts—put on the 75 percent off sale racks. Maybe even yanked off the shelves and burned because nobody wanted them.

Jonah couldn't bear the thought of nobody wanting his T-shirts, his music, his TV show . . . not wanting him.

But if Jonah did what his mother said, his parents would fix everything. Prevent all those possible disasters.

Across the room, Jonah's mother winked at him— his cue.

Jonah raised an eyebrow, and a girl staring him right in the face jumped back and shrieked. Jonah started dancing and singing, and everything went exactly as he expected: the screams, the fans' delight, the instant enormous crowd, even the fainting girls.

So bizarre. It all felt wrong. Even without Mom having to resort to the poison gas, the grenades, the gun.

Afterward, Jonah slid into the limo waiting outside

Madame Tussauds. For perhaps the first time in his life, he didn't even glance out at the crowd as the car pulled away from the curb.

"I know Mom called you. Did you take care of everything?" he asked his dad.

Broderick kept his head bent over his BlackBerry.

"Little problem," he said. "One witness won't recant. Won't change her story at all."

"Pay her off," Jonah said.

Finally, Broderick looked at his son.

"She says she doesn't want our money," he said.

"Everybody wants money," Jonah replied, a bit of his old confidence returning. "Offer her more."

For a moment, he almost felt close to his father because he knew they would be thinking the same thing: Neither of them had ever met anybody who didn't want money.

But Broderick was shaking his head. "She won't take anything," he said. "But—she said she would meet with you if we wanted. To talk about it."

"Oh—one of those," Jonah said. He laughed, and he didn't even have to try to make it sound normal. "Yo, why didn't you say so?" It was just another fan, someone who thought the chance to meet him was worth more than any amount of money.

He could respect that. Right now, that was exactly what he needed.

Half an hour later, they pulled up in front of a drab hotel.

"You might want to really turn on the charm," Broderick said, with a look Jonah couldn't quite identify.

"I *know*," Jonah said coldly. "It'll be off the chain. Like always."

He strode out of the car, up the cracked sidewalk. At the front desk, Broderick said, "My son is supposed to be meeting one of your guests in, ah, your sitting room?"

The worker pointed to a broken-down collection of chairs.

Jonah whirled around.

"Yo, yo, yo, my homie—"

And then he stopped.

The woman sitting before him was old.

She had white hair.

She had wrinkles all over her face—like she'd never heard of plastic surgery.

She was clutching a handbag in her lap—a really, really cheap knockoff, maybe, of the one Queen Elizabeth had been carrying that time Jonah had met her.

And she was wearing a brown polyester . . . what would you call it? A pantsuit?

"Jonah, um, this is Gertrude Pluderbottom," Broderick said.

The old lady pursed her lips.

"You may call me Miss Pluderbottom," she said in a strict, scratchy old-lady voice.

Her eyes seemed to bore into Jonah and his dad, both at once. How did she do that?

"I believe we agreed that I would be meeting with Jonah alone?" she said to Broderick.

"Um, er, yes, uh—Jonah, I'll be waiting out in the car," Broderick said, and escaped.

Jonah sagged into one of the chairs opposite Miss Pluderbottom.

"Yo," he said, rather feebly. "Wassup?"

Miss Pluderbottom narrowed her eyes at him. It made her look even scarier.

"In the interest of carrying on a cordial conversation," she said, "I will interpret that slurred collection of syllables to mean that you are pleased to make my acquaintance, and that you wish to inquire about my thoughts and concerns. Is that correct?"

Jonah heard his own voice say, weakly, "Yes, ma'am."

Jonah was certain that he had never before in his life called anyone "ma'am."

He hadn't even realized he knew the word.

Miss Pluderbottom sniffed.

"That's better," she said. "Now, I did try to speak with you yesterday at the Globe."

"You did?" Jonah said.

"You don't remember anything I said?" Miss Pluderbottom said.

Jonah barely managed to stop himself from saying, *I don't pay attention to people like you.* Had some old lady talked to him there? Miss Pluderbottom wasn't young and fly. She wasn't A-list. She couldn't do anything to help his career or the Clue hunt.

Today she can, he reminded himself.

"I'm sorry," Jonah apologized, pumping a full level of sincerity into his words.

Miss Pluderbottom didn't look like she believed him. She picked a tiny piece of lint off her brown polyester vest.

Jonah found himself feeling sorry for the lint.

"Why were you at the play yesterday, Jonah?" Miss Pluderbottom asked, her eyes still narrowed and suspicious.

"Oh, I am such a fan of Shakespeare," Jonah said. "He's my homie, Billy S.!"

"Hmm," Miss Pluderbottom said.

She waited.

Jonah's mouth went dry.

"And—it was for my mom," he added.

"Of course," Miss Pluderbottom said. She leaned forward slightly. "But I'm inclined to believe that your mother wanted you to *absorb* some culture, not destroy it."

Jonah's brain swam with panic.

"Most mothers, yeah," he said. "But mine . . . see, there's kind of a treasure hunt in my family."

Why had he said that? Jonah knew the unspoken rule: You didn't tell outsiders about the Clue hunt.

And yet Jonah kept talking.

"There's a big prize at the end," he said. "My parents — well, my mom — it's all she cares about. Winning."

"Indeed," Miss Pluderbottom said. She was still watching him.

Jonah was used to people watching him. Practically his whole life had been recorded and broadcast worldwide. *Everybody* watched him. But he wasn't used to being watched like this. It was like Miss Pluderbottom could see right through him, like she could read his mind, like she knew about every single bad thing he'd ever done.

Did she know he'd abandoned Dan and Amy on a crocodile-infested island in Egypt?

That he'd set up Dan to be murdered in China?

I knew nothing would really happen in Egypt! he wanted to tell Miss Pluderbottom. *And I changed my mind in China! I risked my own life to go back and rescue Dan! See, I'm not so bad!*

"And this big prize," Miss Pluderbottom said slowly. "Was it worth ruining the play for hundreds of other people? Worth ruining your reputation? Worth lying about?"

Jonah squirmed in his seat.

"My mother thinks so," he said. "It's, like, some huge family treasure."

"A family legacy, then," Miss Pluderbottom said. "Don't you know that 'No legacy is so rich as honesty'?"

"Um," Jonah said.

"That's Shakespeare. Your 'homie' Billy S.," she said. "From *All's Well That Ends Well*."

It should have been really funny to watch Miss Pluderbottom's pruny lips say "homie" and "Billy S." But Jonah couldn't laugh.

"Let me tell you why I was at the play yesterday," Miss Pluderbottom said.

Jonah listened.

"I'm a teacher," Miss Pluderbottom said. "I've been teaching Shakespeare to high school students in Cedar Grove, Iowa, for the past forty-nine years. And I've been saving money for this trip the whole time. I packed my lunch every day—even when the school cafeteria was serving Meatloaf Surprise. And I do love their Meatloaf Surprise. I clipped coupons. I stopped buying new clothes."

Jonah guessed that must have happened about 1972.

"All I wanted to do was see where the Bard was born, walk where he walked," Miss Pluderbottom was saying. "Then the Globe opened, and I realized I could also see Shakespeare performed the way it would have been in his lifetime, when all his plays were new. . . ."

"So come back the next time the Globe does *Romeo and Juliet*," Jonah said.

"Look at me. Do you think I have another forty-nine years left to save up for another trip?" Miss Pluderbottom asked.

Jonah realized his father was an idiot. This *was* about money.

"I'll pay for your next trip," Jonah said. "Change your story, and I'll even pay the Globe to reopen as fast as they can. You help me, I help you—everyone wins."

"No," Miss Pluderbottom said. "Everybody loses. I would be selling out my integrity. You would start thinking you could get away with anything."

Was she nuts? He *could* get away with anything.

Or—he'd always been able to before.

"No, no, it'd be like you were schooling me," Jonah argued frantically. "Your trip might cost a lot of money." He flicked his eyes toward the gaping hole in his chair where the stuffing was coming out. "I'd put you up in a real hotel. Five star."

"Even if my trip cost a million dollars, you wouldn't even notice it was gone," Miss Pluderbottom said, and somehow her eyes seemed to get steelier. "And if I wanted to 'school' you—not that *I* would ever use that word as a verb—I'd want you to do something that made an impression. Promise to read all of Shakespeare's plays, maybe. Send me a report on each one of them."

"I could do that," Jonah said softly.

He waited for her to argue that he could easily get someone else to do that for him. They could draw up papers working out those details. That's what lawyers were for.

This was almost over.

But Miss Pluderbottom's eyes suddenly went soft.

"Why, Jonah," she said. "Oh, my." She clutched her heart. "Every other fifteen-year-old boy I've ever met would moan and groan and act like that assignment was torture. But you—you really do like Shakespeare. I can tell."

Jonah bolted straight up in his chair.

"I do not!" he said. "That's a lie!"

Miss Pluderbottom was studying him again.

"No, you're lying now," she said. "You are a *huge* Shakespeare fan."

Jonah dropped to his knees on the floor in front of Miss Pluderbottom.

"Please!" he said. "Don't tell anyone! I'll do anything! I'll send you to every Shakespeare performance at every recreated Globe Theatre in the world! You'd love the Tokyo one! And Dallas! And Rome! And—"

"Jonah." Miss Pluderbottom actually laughed. "It's not a crime to love Shakespeare."

"But it would ruin my rep!" Jonah said. "All my street cred—gone!"

Sure, around other Janus he could admit that he loved Shakespeare. And Mozart, Rembrandt, Beethoven, Bach . . . all the old dudes. Back in China he'd even slipped and said too much to Dan. But he figured he could deny that if he had to.

He could never let his fans see this side of him.

"It's *okay*," Miss Pluderbottom said. "Truly, Shakespeare has a lot in common with hip-hop artists."

Jonah stared at her.

"That's . . . that's what I always thought," he whispered.

"That's why I always use 'Gotta Live the Gangsta Life' to introduce my Shakespeare sonnet unit. Really gets my students listening for the rhythm of the words," Miss Pluderbottom said.

Jonah fell over backward onto the floor. When he could sit up again, he stammered, "You—you know my work?"

"Get out!" Miss Pluderbottom said. "Can't a seventy-year-old spinster schoolteacher from Iowa like hip-hop? That new song you just posted online, 'How the Feuding Hurts'—I think that might be your best work yet!"

So Miss Pluderbottom *was* just another fan. Everything was going to work out.

"Then you'll tell the police and the media you were wrong," Jonah said confidently. "Say you just mistook some other kid at the Globe for me. Tell them I wasn't even there!"

"I can't do that. Didn't you hear anything I said about integrity and honesty?" Miss Pluderbottom said.

"But—you're a fan!"

"And that's another reason I'm not going to lie for you," she said. "Telling the truth is good for your character and mine. 'To thine own self be true, /And it must follow, as the night the day, /Thou canst not then be false to any man.' From—"

"*Hamlet*," Jonah said glumly.

Jonah felt like Hamlet: doomed. Miss Pluderbottom would never recant. Jonah would be charged with vandalism. His career would be ruined. And the Clue hunt would only get worse and worse—until he really did have to kill someone.

"Jonah, those aren't just empty words," Miss Pluderbottom said gently. "I think *you* need to be true to your own self."

She was probably just talking about admitting to the world that he loved Shakespeare. But Jonah heard so much more in her voice.

Is my true self the kid who set Dan up to be murdered—or the kid who rescued him? Jonah wondered. *The kid who obeys his mom or the one who sees a better way?*

Who am I?

CHAPTER 10

Dan peeked into a cradle. It held a doll, meant to represent the infant William Shakespeare.

Maybe the next clue is hidden on that doll somehow, Dan thought. *Under its clothes? In its stuffing?*

Dan reached toward the doll—

And felt his whole body jerked backward. Someone had grabbed him by his collar.

"Young man!" It was the guide, a woman who had looked deceptively friendly when he, Amy, and Nellie had first walked into the room that was supposedly where Shakespeare had been born.

Now she glared down at him.

"No touching the artifacts!" she said sternly.

"But you just said none of the furniture was original, so—"

"It's still hundreds of years old!" the guide said.

Would it be pushing his luck if Dan said, "Not the doll. The doll looks plastic"?

Before Dan had a chance to decide, the guide shoved him toward the next room.

"Out!" she commanded.

Amy and Nellie hung back, pretending they didn't know him. Maybe they'd find a lead without him.

But when they rejoined him in the garden behind the Shakespeare Birthplace, Amy shook her head glumly.

"That guide was a rising bollard!" Dan complained.

"Is that another one of the Shakespeare insults?" Nellie asked.

"No—it's just something I saw on a road sign a few blocks back," Dan admitted. "'Beware rising bollards'—it must mean speed bumps or something like that. But it *sounds* like a great insult, doesn't it?"

Amy shrugged off her backpack and let it drop to the ground. She'd been carrying around about a dozen Shakespeare books, "just in case." She seemed to be aiming the backpack at Dan's toes, but he dodged it.

"Really, Dan," Amy said. "Did you think you could just grab whatever you wanted with the guide right there? Use your brain!"

"I *was* using my brain," Dan insisted. "I thought that the guide wasn't looking. And that the doll would be the best place to hide a lead. And that we don't have much time. What if somebody else gets the next clue before us?"

Amy put her hands on her hips.

"Do you see any of the other teams lurking around?" Amy demanded.

"No, but—"

Dan stopped because Amy was no longer listening. She was glancing around the deserted garden, a baffled look on her face. She walked over to the fence and peered up and down the street.

"What are you looking for?" Dan asked.

Amy came back, grimacing.

"Cahills," she said. "Isn't it weird that none of the others are here?"

It was surprising, Dan realized. The other teams had had eighteen hours to catch up with Amy and Dan and Nellie. The Shakespeare Birthplace was already closed when they arrived in Stratford last night—and the house had been locked up tight, with serious-looking bars on every window. So the three of them had had to check into a hotel and wait for morning.

"I bet nobody else got as much of the poem back at the Globe as I did," Dan said proudly. "They couldn't figure it out."

"Yeah, but coming to Stratford-upon-Avon is pretty obvious if you're looking for something about Shakespeare," Amy argued. "And all of them know about Shakespeare, or they wouldn't have been at the Globe. Maybe we missed something. Maybe the others are at one of the other Shakespeare houses."

"Wait—how many Shakespeare birthplaces are there?" Dan asked. He tried not to sound panicked. "The dude was only born once. And that was here. Right?"

Amy laughed. "Right, as far as anyone knows. But there are four other Shakespeare houses around Stratford," she said. She pulled a book out of her backpack and began leafing through it. "The houses where his wife grew up, where his mother grew up, where his daughter and son-in-law lived, where his granddaughter lived . . ."

"Jeez, why didn't they just save every house the man ever stepped in?" Dan muttered.

"Oh, I wish they had!" Amy said wistfully.

"Joking, Amy," Dan said. "Big-time joking."

"Well, I think we should go to all the other Shakespeare houses, just to be sure," Amy said, looking through the book. "We could start with—"

"Oh, no," Dan said, shaking his head. "Remember the poem?" He dug into his pocket and pulled out the scraps they'd brought back from the Globe. They'd carefully taped everything together last night at their hotel. "See this line?" He stabbed his finger at the paper. "'For this great man we sing was bo-orn here.' You said that word had to be 'born.' We wrote it in! So that's where we have to look. Just where Shakespeare was born. Just. This. One. Old. House."

"Where he was bo-orn," Nellie mocked.

"Well, I had to say it that way," Dan said. "It's like the words forced me."

Nellie started to laugh. Then she stopped and gaped at him.

"Give me that," she said, snatching the paper from

Dan. She seemed to be reading it to herself. Her lips moved. Her head bounced up and down, just like it did when she was listening to her iPod. "Iambic pentameter," she muttered. "It's supposed to be iambic pentameter, isn't it?" She bent over and began digging through Amy's backpack. "Got any books analyzing Shakespeare's sonnets?" she asked.

"No," Amy said apologetically. "I couldn't buy everything. I only had so much room in my backpack."

Nellie sprang up. She looked toward the gift shop, shook her head, and then dashed back into the Shakespeare Birthplace.

Amy and Dan exchanged glances and ran after her.

By the time they caught up with her, she was on the second floor again, back in the Shakespeare birthroom—and talking to the guide who'd yelled at Dan.

Dan tried to hide behind Amy.

"Shakespeare's sonnets," Nellie was saying to the guide. "Iambic pentameter, right?"

"Oh, yes," the woman said. "Almost always. Iambic pentameter, fourteen lines, rhyme scheme a-b-a-b—"

"C-d-c-d-e-f-e-f-g-g," Nellie finished, as if she was agreeing with the woman.

Dan thought this was like the times when Nellie jabbered away in some foreign language—French, Spanish, even the Italian she'd picked up so quickly. Once again, Dan had no clue what she was talking about.

Oh! He suddenly realized. *She's distracting the guide so I can search the doll!*

He wished she'd said she was planning to do that. He poked Amy. If he could just get her to step to the right, he could bend down over the cradle and the guide wouldn't see him. Amy glanced at him, and Dan motioned with his hands.

Amy frowned and shook her head—and stepped closer to the guide and Nellie.

Okay, maybe that would work instead.

"Pentameter?" Amy asked the guide. "That means five something per line?"

"Feet," the guide said.

Were they still talking about poetry? Since when did poetry have feet?

"Maybe it's easier to think of it as five beats per line," the guide said. "It's easiest to hear if you say it out loud like, oh, let's try Sonnet Eighteen: 'Shall I com*pare* thee *to a sum*mer's *day?*' See? Five syllables emphasized, each one coming after one unstressed syllable. Iambic pentameter."

"I thought so!" Nellie exclaimed.

She was really laying it on thick. She made it sound like this was exciting, like iambic whatchamacallit really mattered.

The guide looked toward Dan. Quickly, he ducked behind Amy again.

Nellie was fumbling with the taped-together paper.

"A, uh, friend of mine is trying to write a poem about Shakespeare in the same style as his sonnets," she said, holding out the page for the guide to see. She folded it over, so the only part that showed was the ending. "This last line doesn't really work, does it?"

"'For *this* great *man* we *sing* was *bo*-orn *here*'?" the guide read aloud.

Hey! Dan thought. *The words forced her to say it that way, too.*

While the guide's head was bent over the paper, Dan dipped toward the cradle. Amy yanked him back up just as the guide lifted her head.

Cover for me! Dan wanted to scream. But maybe it didn't matter. Maybe Dan should just dive at the cradle, grab the doll, and run away so fast no one could catch him.

Dan waited for the guide to look at the paper again.

"Are you sure this is a 'friend's' poetry?" the guide asked suspiciously. "Not your own?"

"Oh, yeah," Nellie said. "I wouldn't write like that."

Her hand shot out, and she grabbed Dan by the arm, holding him in place.

Now Dan was completely confused. How was he supposed to snatch the doll and run away with Nellie holding on to him? What did she expect him to do?

"This line's not that bad," the guide was saying.

"Not bad enough to be torn up. Can you think of a two-syllable word that means 'born'? That's what's throwing everything off."

Dan froze.

What the others were talking about—it *was* important. All this talk of syllables and beats meant that the word Amy had been so certain about was wrong. The doll Dan had been planning to steal didn't matter. They weren't supposed to look for their next lead at the place where Shakespeare had been born. They were supposed to look in a place where he'd been . . . something else.

The guide was still studying the paper.

"Are you sure your friend doesn't want to write about Shakespeare's death instead of his birth?" she asked. "'Buried' would fit perfectly here."

Buried, Dan thought. *"For this great man we sing was buried here." Yes.*

Nellie grabbed the paper back from the guide.

"You're right!" she said. "Thank you! Thank you!"

With her hand still on Dan's arm, she began dragging him toward the door.

"You're welcome but—where are you going?" the guide asked.

"Burst of poetic inspiration. Gotta follow it," Nellie explained.

"Where was Shakespeare buried?" Dan asked. He thought it was safe to let the guide notice him, now that he was leaving.

"Holy Trinity Church, over by the river," the guide said. "You just go—"

But Dan missed the rest. He, Amy, and Nellie were already through the next room and racing down the stairs, leaping down three steps at a time.

CHAPTER 11

Sinead Starling crouched out of sight in a pew at Holy Trinity Church. She and Alistair were the advance scouting team. Her brothers were on guard duty outside. At least, that's what she'd told Alistair the boys would do.

He can't tell, can he? she wondered. *He hasn't noticed that my brothers are . . .*

There were certain words that Sinead didn't let herself think. She hugged her arms around her torso. Even through her sweatshirt, she could feel the ridges of scar tissue that crisscrossed her rib cage—just one of her souvenirs from the explosion at the Franklin Institute. She shivered, the horrible memories crashing down on her yet again:

The flash of light, the rumble of what seemed to be the whole world falling in on her and her brothers . . . the pain . . . the screaming. How many times did she shout her brothers' names before anyone answered? How many times did Sinead beg, "Save them! Please save them!"

Sinead gritted her teeth and tried to shut down the flow of memories.

We just have to win, she reminded herself. *No matter what. That's the only thing we can think about.*

She and her brother had already had two lucky breaks, getting mysterious tips about the Globe yesterday and the church today. Not that Sinead had exactly told Alistair she was getting help with her brilliant deductions.

"Psst." Alistair's whisper came through the tiny communications device hidden in Sinead's headband. Sinead might not trust Alistair, but this was one point in his favor: He loved gadgets as much as Sinead and her brothers did. Or as much as they always *had.*

"I'm in," Sinead whispered back. "Nothing to report yet."

Not that she intended to report anything truly worthwhile to Alistair.

"I think we can call your brothers off guard duty," Alistair whispered from his position on the other side of the church. "It appears we are latecomers to this party."

"What? What's that mean?" Sinead hissed.

She raised her head so fast she cracked it against the side of the pew.

Oh, Sinead realized, the pain in her head growing. *He means that the other clue-hunting teams are already here.*

A cluster of Holts was striding down the aisle near

the front of the church in what looked to be a military formation.

Jonah Wizard was skulking along the wall, running his fingers over the stones.

And two of those nasty Kabras, Natalie and Ian, were closing in on Alistair. Trapping him in the corner.

We're Ekats, you're an Ekat. . . . It's really like we're on the same team, Sinead had said to Alistair only yesterday when she was trying to get him to tell his secrets. Had he believed her? Would she expect her to come to his assistance now?

Sinead started to stand up — she really did. But the memory of the Franklin Institute explosion hovered at the edge of her mind. Sinead still didn't know which of the other Clue-hunting teams had caused it. What if it had been the Kabras?

Ian was reaching into his pocket.

For a gun? Sinead wondered. *Or something worse — a hand grenade? A detonator?*

Sinead's flashback was starting again. If there was another explosion, could Sinead get out to her brothers in time to make sure they were safe?

Ian pulled out . . . a piece of paper.

"How many clues do you have, Uncle Alistair?" he asked in an ingratiating voice as he glanced down at the paper. "Just confidentially, you can tell me. Brag. Tell me how much smarter you Ekats are than we Lucians."

He gave Alistair a smile that was probably meant to

be charming. Sinead thought it looked desperate.

Desperation was something she understood.

"Appealing to my vanity, are you?" Alistair asked. "Please. Give me credit for being smarter than that."

"You have fourteen clues, don't you?" Natalie asked. "Fifteen, if you count the clue the Starlings stole from Bae Oh and shared with you. And six of them are clues that no one but Ekats have. Right?"

Alistair blinked.

Uncle Alistair! Sinead thought. *Can't you fake them out any better than that? You just confirmed everything!*

"No!" Alistair said, a bit too emphatically. "You're wrong!"

Ian scribbled something on his piece of paper.

Quickly, Sinead popped a contact into her eye — one of the telescopic-vision contacts she and her brothers had designed. She focused as quickly as she could on the paper in Ian's hand. It was a welter of initials and numbers and question marks. Most people wouldn't have been able to make heads or tails of it. But Sinead had always been good with numbers. She zeroed in on the column where Ian had written the numeral 6. She added numbers in her head and double-checked twice.

All three times she came up with the same number: thirty-eight. And she knew what it meant: Ian Kabra thought that the Clue-hunting teams all together had found thirty-eight Clues.

We're even further behind than I thought, Sinead realized, despair sweeping over her. *There's only one clue left.*

The scars on her torso ached. Her head throbbed. She popped out the telescopic contact and peeked out the door behind her, catching a glimpse of her brothers huddled behind a tombstone in the church cemetery.

I don't care what we have to do, Sinead thought. *Lie, cheat, steal, betray every relative we have . . . We Starlings have to get that last clue.*

Hamilton patrolled the front section of the church while his mother and sisters peered down at Shakespeare's tombstone. It was inside rather than out in the cemetery — part of the floor, really, in a roped-off section not far from the altar.

Hamilton saw Ian and Natalie Kabra edging too close.

"Scram," Hamilton commanded. "This is Holt territory right now."

In a fair fight, Hamilton knew he could take both Kabra kids, no contest. But Kabras didn't fight fair. And Dad wasn't here for backup. Eisenhower had left early that morning for a top secret mission elsewhere in Stratford. Right before he walked out the door, he'd clapped his ham-size hand on Hamilton's shoulder and said, "I'm counting on you to take care of things here, son."

Did that mean pummeling Ian before he took another breath?

Ian held up his hand in a gesture of innocence. Faked, of course.

"Just a simple question," Ian asked. "You've found eleven clues, right?"

Hamilton squinted at Ian, trying to figure him out.

"Why would I tell you?" Hamilton asked. Should he start the pummeling now?

Mary-Todd stepped up beside them.

"Are you perhaps suggesting an exchange of information?" she asked Ian quietly. "A moment of cooperation?"

"No," Ian said, backing away. He pulled his sister with him. "No. Not that. Not—I don't think—"

Now Hamilton looked at his own mother in amazement. *Exchange of information? Moment of cooperation? Where had* that *come from?*

Mary-Todd Holt was anxiously watching the other Clue-hunting teams. Sinead was conferring with Alistair over by the far wall. Ian and Natalie glided toward Jonah, like a pair of snakes slithering toward prey.

"Should we worry about the ones who aren't here?" Mary-Todd murmured.

"What?" Hamilton asked. "Everyone's here but Dad. And . . ."

And Amy and Dan. And Isabel Kabra.

Hamilton whirled away from his mother and strode after the Kabra kids. He grabbed Ian by the neck and lifted him off the ground, pinning his head against the stone wall. It felt so good to do *something*.

"Where are they?" he demanded. "What did your evil mother do with Dan and Amy?"

Natalie tugged uselessly on Hamilton's arm.

"Let him go!" she whined. "Mum didn't do anything with Dan and Amy. She's not even here!"

"Right," Hamilton said. "She's not here, Dan and Amy aren't here. . . . It all adds up. Everyone knows what your mom's like. She tried to feed Amy to the sharks. Dan said she dropped poisonous spiders and snakes on them. She tried to burn them alive. She told you to explode a cave on them. What's she up to now? What's she doing to my little buddy and Amy?"

"*Erp—ulp—uth!*" Ian choked.

"There they are!" Natalie cried. "Amy and Dan just walked into the church!"

Hamilton figured this was just a ploy—like an opponent in a fight saying, "Look! Your shoe's untied!" so he could sneak in a punch when you were stupid enough to look. But Hamilton wasn't too worried about little Natalie Kabra punching him. He looked.

Amy and Dan and their crazy-haired au pair were rushing in the side door. Their faces were flushed, like they'd run a long way.

Hamilton dropped Ian, and the boy sprawled help-lessly on the ground.

"Catch you later," Hamilton said. He started to walk away, then changed his mind. He leaned close, his nose only inches from Ian's. Hamilton sincerely hoped that the smelly English cheese he'd had with breakfast was still lingering on his breath. "But tell your 'mummy' — she better not try to hurt Amy and Dan ever again. Or else."

Ian flinched.

"You won't have to worry about our mum doing any-thing else to anybody," Natalie said. She glanced at a frilly bracelet-watch on her wrist. It was the kind of thing Madison and Reagan wouldn't be caught dead wearing. "Mum's taken care of. As long as we finish this clue hunt in time." She glanced at her watch again, even though it couldn't have been more than ten seconds since the last time she'd looked. "We have to hurry."

"Do you . . . do you think Amy and Dan would help us try to figure out what to look for here?" Ian asked weakly.

"Maybe — if you'd never tried to *kill* them," Hamilton said.

"Yeah," Ian murmured sadly. "That's what I thought."

Hamilton had never thought he'd find himself feel-ing sorry for a Kabra.

Why were there so many surprises in this Clue hunt that had nothing to do with Clues?

CHAPTER 12

We're the last ones here, Amy thought, gasping for breath as she stepped into the church. *It's like we're in last place all over again.*

Ned and Ted Starling had been out in the cemetery, lurking behind tombstones. Jonah Wizard was crouched down in a pew—oddly without his ever-present, BlackBerry-obsessed dad. Hamilton and the Kabra kids were huddled together against the wall. Mary-Todd, Reagan, and Madison Holt were at the front of the church, staring down at the floor. Sinead Starling and Alistair were whispering together near the altar.

They've all teamed up in different ways, leaving us out, Amy thought. *They're all solving the clue, and we haven't even seen Shakespeare's tomb yet.*

"Oh, good!" Dan said cheerfully. "None of the teams have left yet!"

"Are you nuts?" Amy asked. "You *like* seeing our enemies again after yesterday? After everything that's happened in the clue hunt?"

INTO THE GAUNTLET

"No," Dan said. "But if they're all still here, that means nobody else has figured out where we're supposed to go next."

He had a point.

"So where's Isabel Kabra?" Amy asked.

"And where's Eisenhower Holt?" Nellie asked.

Dan shrugged.

For all Amy knew, both Isabel and Eisenhower could be out hunting for the next Clue—the Kabras and Holts still at the church might be decoys.

But this way, Amy thought, *we don't have to face the worst people who were there the night our parents died.*

Amy drew in a ragged breath. They still had to face everyone else.

Can't let any of the others win, she reminded herself. *Can't let any of these terrible people become the most powerful in the world. Because then, even more innocent people will die. . . .*

She flashed to remembering Lester's kind, smiling face back in Jamaica. She remembered how completely his smile had been erased.

We have to go on for Lester, she thought. *For Mom and Dad. For Grace . . .*

Amy took one step closer to her enemies, who stood between her and Shakespeare's tomb. This wasn't like back at the Globe, where her enemies had popped up right and left, and all she and Dan could do was run and run. This was harder. Amy had time to think between steps, to remember how much destruction the people in this church had caused, how close so many of them had come to killing her and Dan.

And the Madrigals want us all to be friends? she marveled.

"Yo! My homies! Amy and Li'l Dan! What's good?"

It was Jonah Wizard's famous voice, booming out from across the church. Amy looked down at her brother, who'd palled around with Jonah so happily back in China.

Dan was staring straight ahead, his face pale.

"Yo! Come *on*, fam, don't hate," Jonah called out. He rushed toward them, speaking more quietly. "Look, maybe I should apologi—"

Nellie stepped out to block Jonah's path and threw her arms protectively in front of Amy and Dan.

"Shouldn't you be in police custody?" she asked Jonah. "Under arrest for what happened at the Globe? Or—in China? Or Egypt?"

She glared at him, her gaze laserlike in its intensity. Amy found herself rethinking her view of Nellie as an "anything goes" au pair.

Jonah took a step back.

"No, no, those were all . . . misunderstandings," he gasped. He recovered enough to flash his famous grin. "And the Globe scene—my parents are taking care of that." His grin widened. "What did you expect? I'm Jonah Wizard!"

Was it Amy's imagination or were the corners of his grin trembling? Something unusual showed in his eyes, too—worry? Doubt? Fear?

From the great Jonah Wizard? Amy thought. *Never.*

"I thought you said you were quitting the clue hunt," Dan said, speaking up bravely. He stepped out from behind Nellie's protective stance. "Isn't that what you told your mom back in China?"

"Word," Jonah said, nodding. "The truth is — yes and no. I have embarked on a new endeavor. A different way of hunting clues, you could say."

This didn't even sound like Jonah. Granted, nothing he said had ever made much sense. *That* was typical. But *embarked? Endeavor?* That wasn't hip-hop talk.

Jonah must have noticed Amy staring at him in amazement because he added, rather halfheartedly, "Yo, yo, yo. Word."

Amy didn't have time to figure out Jonah Wizard. She turned away from him — and immediately bumped into Ian Kabra instead.

"Amy!" Ian said, his face lighting up. "I'm so glad to see that you didn't get hurt at the Globe yesterday!"

Ian's amber eyes did seem full of concern for her well-being.

Oh, no, Amy thought. *Those eyes will never fool me again.*

Amy narrowed her own eyes, trying to channel some of the same cold fury that Nellie had just used on Jonah. Fury was a much better emotion than fear.

"Get out of my way," Amy told Ian.

"No, please, just listen —" Ian begged. He looked around frantically, wincing slightly at the sight of

Nellie and Dan and Jonah standing so close by. "If you'd come with me, so we can talk privately—"

"You mean, so you can lure me off to your evil mother? To some trap?" Amy challenged. "How stupid do you think I am?"

"This isn't about Mum," Natalie piped up beside Ian. "We're not . . . I mean, she's not even here. We know how many clues you have, and—"

Amy stepped past them. Her heart thudded—she expected Ian to hit her, to grab her, to start another round of nightmarish Kabra torture.

Nothing happened.

Amy took another step and dared to quickly glance back over her shoulder. Ian wasn't chasing her. He and Natalie had turned the other way, toward the door.

And . . . now they were leaving.

Amy's heart began thudding even faster. Panic made her stumble.

Had the Kabras already found the next Clue?

By the time Dan and Amy and Nellie reached the front of the church, all of the other Clue hunters were heading for the exit.

"Later, dude," Hamilton said, waving awkwardly.

"Wait—did you find something here?" Dan asked. "Or are you giving up?"

"Oh, uh, just going to lunch early," Hamilton said, almost sounding embarrassed.

He stepped out the door.

"Did they *all* find the clue before us?" Amy asked despairingly.

"I believe it'd help to sketch a picture of Shakespeare's statue over there," Nellie said in an unusually loud voice. "Do either of you have a notebook I could borrow?"

Amy pulled one out of her backpack. Dan just flashed Nellie a startled look. What was wrong with *her*?

Nellie spent about two seconds scrawling in the notebook and then held it out to Amy and Dan.

"Isn't this a good drawing?" she asked, so loudly that the attendant glared at her.

Dan glanced at the notebook.

Nellie hadn't drawn Shakespeare on the paper. She'd scrawled three words: I SEE CAMERAS.

"Well, sure, Shakespeare is, like, England's most famous dude," Dan said. "Of course they'd have security. . . ."

He stopped and looked around. Nellie didn't mean security cameras. She meant spy cameras. Like the one hidden in the crook of the Shakespeare statue's arm. And the one hidden by the altar. And the one hidden in the choir loft. And the one hidden in the front pew.

The others hadn't left because they'd found a Clue. They'd left because they couldn't. And they wanted to know right away if Amy and Dan did.

Amy reached over and took the pen out of Nellie's hand.

"I think you need to make the eyes bigger," she said. "Like this."

She didn't draw any eyes. She wrote: SHOULD WE DESTROY THEM?

"Oh, I see," Nellie said, taking the pen back. She wrote, NO, THEN EVERYONE WILL JUST COME BACK. ACT!!!!

Dan walked toward the life-size Shakespeare statue. It was part of a memorial shrine mounted on the wall near the altar. Shakespeare was shown just from the waist up, posing with a quill pen and a piece of paper.

"I bet the clue's in there!" Dan exclaimed.

Secretly, he was thinking that it might be important that Shakespeare was gazing out rather than down at his paper. Maybe the Clue was really in the stone on the opposite wall?

"Or in the words below," Amy suggested.

There was something in Latin under the Shakespeare statue, and then a poem, which Nellie began reading out loud.

"'Stay passenger, why goest thou by so fast?/Read if thou canst, whom envious death hath plast . . .'" Nellie wrinkled her nose. "Wow. That's really bad poetry."

Dan was pretty sure she meant that for real—she wasn't just acting.

"Maybe the clue's in the misspelled words," Dan said. Maybe the other teams wouldn't know that no one in Shakespeare's time could spell. "'Tomb' with an 'e' at the end, 'wit' with two 't's . . . I think I'll copy this down."

He took the notebook from Nellie and wrote what he was really thinking: THEY USE A "V" EVERY TIME IT SHOULD BE "U." CODE?

"Here. I'll do that," Amy offered. She wrote: ONLY 24 LETTERS IN ALPHABET IN WS's TIME. ALL U's = V. ALL J's = I.

Wow, Dan thought. *Shakespeare only had twenty-four letters to work with and he* still *couldn't spell?*

Aloud, he said, "Well, we know the clue wouldn't be by his actual tomb, but I'll look and see if words are misspelled there, too."

Dan was certain that would throw off anyone watching by way of the cameras. He moved over to look at the tombstone itself. It was so plain and flat anyone could easily overlook it.

But it had a threat carved into the top of it:

GOOD FREND FOR IESVS SAKE FOREBEARE,
TO DIGG ͓HE DVST ENCLOASED HEARE.
BLESE BE Ẏ MAN Ẏ SPARES ͓HES STONES,
AND CVRST BE HE Ẏ MOVES MY BONES.

"I think those weird 'Y's with the 'T's over them mean 'that,'" Amy said. "And the 'E' over the 'Y' is 'ye.'"

And "IESUS" was "JESUS"; "CVRST" was "CURST"; "DVST" was "DUST."

SHAKESPEARE HIMSELF WROTE THIS AND WANTED IT ON TOMB, Amy wrote in the notebook. She raised an eyebrow, and Dan knew she meant, *Why would he be so worried about people moving his bones that he'd curse them?*

Madrigal business, Dan thought. *This* has *to be the lead.*

He began looking for anagrams in the bizarrely spelled words.

Nothing. Nothing good, anyway.

Maybe it was another problem with the number of syllables?

Dan tried to count the number of syllables per line, but he wasn't sure if "encloased" would be read as two syllables or three. Even "blese" might really be said "bless-y."

Amy and Nellie will figure it out if it's another iambic pentagon-o-meter-type problem, Dan thought.

Amy and Nellie looked as puzzled as Dan felt.

He was pretty sure they weren't just acting.

Curst be us, Amy thought.

They'd been hanging out near Shakespeare's tomb for hours. Amy had read the poem in the stone so many times it was practically engraved in her eyelids. She felt like she would never solve it.

Nellie had left the church once, to sneak in food for all of them to eat. The cookies iced to resemble William

Shakespeare's face had not inspired them the way she'd hoped. And Dan had just left to use the public restrooms outside. But Amy felt like she'd been sentenced to sit by Shakespeare's tomb for all eternity.

I never even got to sit by Grace's tombstone, Amy thought. *And Aunt Beatrice would never take us to Mom and Dad's.*

Had Miss Alice already erected a tombstone for Lester? Would anybody put one up for Irina Spasky?

Don't think about any of that right now, Amy told herself. She could tell that Nellie, beside her, had begun silently rereading the tombstone for the umpteenth time, and Amy did the same. *Good friend for Jesus' sake forbear . . .*

Footsteps approached—a strangely happy-sounding clatter.

"Look what I found!" Dan cried out behind them.

Amy and Nellie both whirled around, Amy with a finger on her lips, Nellie gesturing toward the collection of spy cameras around them.

"Oh, sorry—it's nothing to do with the clue hunt," Dan said, but with such excitement in his voice that Amy suspected he was lying. She started to hand him the notebook they'd been exchanging notes in, but he shook his head.

"No, really!" he exclaimed. He held out a huge sack. "I just found this great place called the Stratford Brass Rubbing Centre, right by the public restrooms. Well, I had to go down a little path, but still. . . . Look what I bought!"

He opened the bag.

Amy remembered that back in their normal lives, one of Dan's wacky fascinations had been grave rubbings. Many Saturdays back home in Boston he'd take the bus to a cemetery, pick out his favorite tombstones, and make a copy by rubbing a pencil over paper on top of the inscriptions. Even on the way to their grandmother's funeral, Amy knew, he'd been hoping to get a rubbing of her gravestone. Amy guessed brass rubbings were pretty much the same thing, except on a grander scale. Dan was pulling out banners of black paper and figures of knights and kings and dragons to use for the rubbings.

"Isn't this the coolest stuff you've ever seen?" Dan asked, beaming. He looked from Amy to Nellie, and his shoulders slumped. He began putting everything back into the sack. "Of course, I just bought it to do later, after we finish the clue hunt."

He sank down beside the two girls.

This is like a curse, Amy thought, and went back to reading the poem.

Time passed. Dan went out again and came back with more snacks. Nellie left to go feed Saladin back at the hotel. And then the church attendant was standing over them, saying, "I'm sorry. I'll have to ask you to leave. We're closing in five minutes."

They'd lost an entire day. And they still didn't have a clue.

"We can't leave!" Dan protested. He glanced down at Shakespeare's tomb, the same stupid slab of stone he and Amy and Nellie had been studying for most of the day. "Not yet!"

The attendant stared at him.

"I've been volunteering here for twenty years," the old man said. "And I've seen lots of people obsessed with Shakespeare. But I've never seen quite such devotion to his grave site. You've been here all day, haven't you?" He shook his head in disbelief.

"What can I say—we're fans," Dan mumbled.

"Then perhaps you can come back another time," the attendant said. "But you'll have to say your farewells to the Bard for now."

Dan reluctantly stood up and started moving toward the door. He exchanged glances with Amy. Her face twisted in anguish, and he could tell she was thinking, *But we can't leave without a clue! And—what if everybody else really did figure it out already?*

Desperately, Dan whirled around.

"Please, sir," he said to the attendant. "I know this probably isn't usually allowed but—could I make a rubbing of the words on Shakespeare's tomb?"

He hoped Amy was proud of him for not just running up there. He held up one of the large sheets of black paper he'd gotten from the Brass Rubbing

Centre and put on his most innocent, pitiful-looking expression.

The old man hesitated.

"Oh, all right," he finally said. "It's good to see a young lad like yourself already so interested in great literature."

The man went over to his desk for a moment—Dan tried to watch to see if he was turning off any sort of security system, but it was impossible to tell. Then the man lifted the rope to let Dan actually step onto Shakespeare's tomb. He had to move a bouquet of flowers to kneel down and start the rubbing.

Dan put the paper over the inscription and began rubbing a silver-colored wax stick across the surface.

appeared on Dan's page. He shifted to do the middle section of the poem, working the wax up and down across the paper.

"Hey! Whatcha doing? Some kind of artwork?"

a voice cried out, and Dan jumped, his wax stick skittering across the page.

It was Hamilton Holt.

Of course, Dan thought. *If the Holts were watching everything on camera, naturally they'd think I was copying over a lead. Stupid me.*

Fortunately, Amy was already answering for him.

"Oh, Dan has this weird hobby, doing grave rubbings," she said, shrugging. "That's all."

"Cool," Hamilton said. "Will you do one for me?"

"And me?" Jonah appeared behind him.

"And me?" That was Sinead.

"Really, guys. It's nothing," Dan protested, looking up as he continued to color.

"Then you won't mind sharing." Now it was Ian speaking, even as he palmed the camera that had been on the altar.

So maybe they didn't all come back just because they saw me kneeling on the tombstone, Dan thought. *They came back to pick up their cameras, so the church attendant wouldn't find them when he closes up.*

That didn't make Dan feel any less nervous.

What's the big deal? he told himself. *I haven't found a lead. I'm just getting a copy of this poem so Amy, Nellie, and I can stare at it for another six or seven hours. Why shouldn't I ruin everybody else's night, too?*

"Sure, I'll make a copy for all of you," Dan said, faking a generous tone. "Each team."

He looked back at his paper. His rubbing had gotten

sloppy while he was looking away. He'd started coloring his paper below the last line of the poem, over a section of the tombstone that had been covered by the flowers.

So this is a bad copy, Dan thought. *So what? I'll just give it to one of the other teams.*

Then he realized more words were appearing on his paper, words that were carved into the tombstone so lightly that they couldn't be seen in the stone. They showed up only in the rubbing. But they were definitely there. Shakespeare's tombstone poem didn't just have four lines—it also had a secret second verse.

And the secret fifth line, the only one Dan could read so far, began:

BUT IF A MADRIGAL KIN Y BE . . .

CHAPTER 13

Dan froze.

No! he told himself. *You can't let anyone see that you've noticed anything new. . . .*

He forced his arm to start moving again, to keep rubbing the wax stick across the paper. But he was careful to keep the wax stick in the area away from the secret words. He scooted forward onto the paper, as if he was just trying to reach the farthest word, "FOREBEARE." But he was really trying to cover the secret line of poetry with his knees.

Was it just his imagination, or was everyone standing too close? Claustrophobically close? Who would catch on first—would Ian over on the one side see the words *But if* not quite covered by his left knee? Or would it be Jonah on the other side seeing the *ye be* not quite covered by his right knee? Why hadn't Dan spent his whole life up to this point eating constantly so he'd have really, really fat knees?

Dan's wax stick careened almost off the paper. He hadn't been this bad at coloring since kindergarten.

No, wait, he told himself. *Use it!*

He whipped the paper away from the tombstone and began tearing the page into pieces.

"Messed up," he said, trying to sound matter-of-fact. "Sorry."

He tucked the torn papers facedown under his foot.

"Amy?" he said. "Want to hand me another sheet of paper?"

Amy's eyes met his. He could tell she knew he'd found something. She understood he was trying to hide it from the others.

"Sure," she said, and gave him the paper.

As he very, very carefully started another rubbing of only the top four lines of the poem, Amy started talking.

"Did anybody else get to see Shakespeare's birthplace?" she asked, clearly trying to distract everyone from Dan. "The wallpaper in some of the rooms is painted cloth — kind of like cheap tapestry is how the guide described it. But it's really gaudy looking. And back in the 1800s when tourists visited the house, they wrote their names on the walls and windows. There was a fight over who controlled the house, and the names on the walls were whitewashed over, but there are still some windowpanes with names on them, even of famous people like Sir Walter Scott. . . . Oh, and John Adams and Thomas Jefferson visited the birthplace together in 1786, I think, and both of them signed the guestbook. . . ."

Obviously, Amy was trying to bore everyone to the point that they all just fell asleep.

Dan finished two rubbings and handed them out. Hamilton drifted toward the door. So did Ian.

But Sinead leaned closer.

"I read about that!" she said to Amy.

"And did you know that P. T. Barnum tried to buy Shakespeare's birthplace in 1847?" Amy added. "He wanted to ship it to the United States and put it on wheels, to be displayed all over the country. Like it was part of his circus."

"That's awful!" Sinead said.

Dan thrust a rubbing into Sinead's hand. Then he did one for Jonah, too.

Okay, Amy, he thought, hoping she could read his mind again. *Start moving everyone else toward the door so I can do a rubbing for us with all the secret lines.*

"Perhaps you would be so good as to do another rubbing just for me?" Alistair said, leaning in close.

Dan jumped. He'd been so focused on Amy and Sinead that he hadn't even noticed that Alistair had arrived, too.

"I — I thought you were teamed up with the Starlings now," Dan said. "I'm just doing one per team."

"Ah, but what is a team, really?" Alistair asked cryptically. "Shakespeare said a rose by any other name would smell as sweet. Is that also true of the word *team*? Or — *family*? What do the words really mean?"

Alistair was definitely losing it.

Just to get rid of him, Dan did another quick rubbing and handed it to him.

Now it was only the attendant standing over Dan.

"Young man," the attendant said. "It's past six."

"Last one," Dan said frantically. "I promise."

He did the top part of the rubbing in a flash, getting only the barest hint of each word. Then he shifted positions. He filled in the last part, the secret part, upside down, with his back toward the attendant. Dan just hoped the old man wasn't craning his neck and looking over Dan's shoulder. Dan actually got goose bumps thinking about what could happen — what if the attendant saw the words appearing on Dan's paper and cried out loudly enough for everyone to hear, "Great Bard in Heaven! I never knew it said *that* on Shakespeare's tomb!"

Dan was trying so hard to keep the attendant from seeing the secret lines of poetry that he didn't look at them himself. He reached the bottom of the tombstone and dropped his wax stick. Then he rolled up the paper as quickly as he could.

"Thanks," Dan told the attendant.

As soon as he got outside, Dan pulled Amy aside. The others were just ahead of them, but Dan couldn't wait. He unrolled the paper and held it so only Amy could see.

"Didn't I do a good job on this one?" he asked, trying to make it sound like he was only bragging, showing off his work.

The silver rubbing glowed in the fading sunlight.

And finally Dan got to read the entire poem from Shakespeare's grave, secret lines and all:

GOOD FREND FOR IESVS SAKE FOREBEARE
TO DIGG HE DVST ENCLOASED HEARE
BLESE BE Y MAN Y SPARES HES STONES
AND CVRST BE HE Y MOVES MY BONES

BUT IF A MADRIGAL KIN Y BE
HEN PLEES MINE WISH REVERSE, FOR ME
AND DIGG AWEIGH AT HIS STONE SITE
Y Y MAY SOLVE OVR FAMILY PLIGHTE

Sweet, Dan thought. *This is actually poetry I understand right away. And something that will be fun to do!*

Shakespeare was asking them to dig up his grave.

CHAPTER 14

This is terrible! Amy thought, staring at Dan's tombstone rubbing. *We can't dig up Shakespeare's grave! We can't!*

It wasn't like the Clue hunt hadn't forced them to be grave diggers before. But this was *William Shakespeare. . . .*

"Amy," Dan said very, very softly, so no one else could hear. "If we don't do this, one of the others will. Eventually, they'll find the rest of the poem or just start digging because they can't think of anything else to try."

Amy looked around. Just ahead of them, Jonah was saying into his cell phone, probably to one of his parents, "Yeah, saw the tomb. Even got a drawing of it from Dan. And I've got a report ready to send you."

If Jonah Wizard decided to dig up Shakespeare's grave, he'd probably buy the church first, have it torn down, hire a bunch of bulldozers and backhoes to do the digging . . . and then just throw away Shakespeare's body when he was done.

If the Holts dug up Shakespeare's grave, they'd probably use his skull for football practice. Oh, they wouldn't plan to. But with the Holts, everything ended up being about sports.

If . . .

Amy couldn't go on imagining dire possibilities.

"Why do so many things in the clue hunt come down to deciding between bad choices?" she asked Dan.

"I knew you'd agree to do this!" Dan said, beaming.

"We'll be respectful about it," Amy said. "We won't disturb anything we don't have to. We'll put everything back the way we found it—"

"Except the next clue," Dan said.

Fiske Cahill and William McIntyre sat in a private room in a restaurant on the banks of the river Avon. The view was lovely—the trees, the sky, the boats bobbing gently in the water—but neither man was paying attention. Mr. McIntyre was talking on his cell phone. Fiske Cahill was wishing that his bold, decisive sister Grace were still alive. This was not a new wish for Fiske—he'd missed his sister desperately ever since she died. But the Clue hunt was winding toward its most dangerous moments. Fiske himself would have to make judgments that could help save or ruin everything.

"You were always better than me at that kind of thing, sis," he whispered.

He reminded himself that so much more depended on Dan and Amy than on him. But how was that fair?

Mr. McIntyre said, "Yes, thank you. Good-bye," and shut his phone.

"Our friend at the church says everyone has departed now," Mr. McIntyre reported. "He believes that master Dan was the only one who found the lead. But someone from each of the other teams was there. And no one was fighting."

Fiske nodded once, curtly, accepting this.

"So it was not too risky tipping off each team to go to the church," Mr. McIntyre added, almost sounding cheerful.

Fiske stood and went over to stand by the window. He wished he could have seen how Amy and Dan had looked, coming out of the church. Were they happy? Confident? Excited? Or was the Clue hunt wearing on them?

Could their bright young lives be destroyed as their parents' had been destroyed?

"This round isn't over yet," Fiske said. "Look what happened when we handed out all those tickets to the Globe."

"You know we have to keep forcing the branches together," Mr. McIntyre said. "There's no other choice. What's the Shakespeare quote? 'There is a tide in the affairs of men/Which, taken at the flood, leads on to fortune.' We had to memorize that whole speech in school. This clue hunt—it's like that tide for the

Madrigals. This is our best shot in five hundred years for reuniting the Cahills. And, as you know, it's more important than ever that we succeed." His expression turned grim again. "It's our last chance."

Fiske had never done well in school. He'd been too shy and awkward to feel comfortable sitting in class, or even just with a private tutor.

But he was pretty sure that Shakespeare's next line after 'leads on to fortune' was something about miserable failure.

"You do know the play that that line's from — *Julius Caesar* — you do know that it all ends in tragedy," Fiske said. "Don't you?"

"We've got to tell Nellie," Amy whispered.

"And get some supplies back at the hotel," Dan whispered back.

"And by then it will be dark and we can sneak back into the church," Amy said, finishing their plans.

They waited for the others to get far ahead of them and then they took a circuitous route back to the hotel. The whole village of Stratford seemed to be closing up for the night.

A block from their hotel, they rounded a corner — and saw Nellie on the sidewalk, talking to Alistair.

"Well, that's very kind of you to invite us to join you for bangers and mash for dinner tonight," Nellie was saying.

Amy and Dan began frantically shaking their heads at Nellie, behind Alistair's back.

"But we're all really tired," Nellie said, without changing her expression. "I think we'll just order room service and go to bed early."

Amy and Dan nodded and darted back around the corner. They walked all the way around the block to get to the hotel. At each corner they flattened themselves against the wall and looked first, just in case.

In the room, Saladin let out an angry *Mrrp!* that clearly meant, *What? You left me alone all day and now you're going to abandon me again?*

Dan grabbed a flashlight. Amy grabbed the best tool she could find in a rush: a metal nail file. As they started to leave the hotel, she pulled out her phone to call Nellie.

"Didn't you see how close Alistair was standing to her?" Dan asked.

"Right," Amy said unhappily as she put the phone away.

"We'll be back before she has a chance to miss us," Dan said.

But it was slow going, heading back to the church. They tiptoed and crept around corners. Whenever they passed a window, they stopped and peeked in to make sure no one from the other Clue-hunting teams was inside watching. As it grew darker and darker, the shadows around them lengthened, seeming to hide threatening shapes.

Once they reached the cemetery that surrounded the church, Dan switched on the flashlight. The weak light just made the darkness around them seem thicker, more menacing. Eerie sounds echoed in the trees above them — from owls? Bats?

It's just your imagination, Amy told herself firmly.

They reached the side door of the church. A huge sign warned potential trespassers about the church's excellent security system. Amy stared in dismay at the heavy chains looped around the door handle.

"Dan — even if we can get in, the police will be here before we have a chance to dig up the grave," she said.

"We'll dig fast," Dan said stubbornly.

He touched a link of the chain, and the whole thing began coming unwrapped. The huge links made an awful clatter rattling against one another and then crashing down.

Finally, there was silence. The entire chain lay in a heap on the ground.

"Why would anyone put a chain on a door without locking the ends?" Dan asked. "Why just make it *look* like a door is locked?"

"Someone from another team got here first," Amy said numbly.

They'd been so foolish — anybody could have driven back to the church faster than they'd walked. Or Isabel or Eisenhower could have crept in the minute everyone else left.

The full weight of their failure crushed down on Amy.

"Somebody beat us," she moaned. "They already got the next clue and left."

Dan pushed against the door.

"No," he corrected his sister. "Then they would have locked the chain again. Covered their tracks."

The door creaked open.

"See?" Dan said. "Whoever it is—they're still here."

CHAPTER 15

Amy, the coward, started babbling about how they'd have to be really, really careful now.

"Whoever's in there had to have heard that chain fall, so they'll be on alert," she whispered. In the dim light from the flashlight, her face looked ghostly and terrified. "They're probably laying a trap for us. We should go back and get Nellie to help. Maybe Hamilton, too—Hamilton's helped us before, he'll help us now. We'll have to make plans, set our own trap—"

"What? And let whoever it is escape with the clue? While we're sitting around talking? No way," Dan said.

He stepped in through the door and was instantly engulfed in darkness. A plan came to him in that one step. Amy was right about the chain being too loud. Dan might as well use that to his own advantage.

He swung the beam of the flashlight toward the front of the church.

"Police!" he shouted. "Freeze!"

Nobody was there.

Quickly, he flashed the light around the entire

church. He listened for panicky breaths from someone hiding in the pews. He poked his head back out the door and said to Amy, "Come on in. The coast is clear."

"You *idiot*," Amy muttered. "Moron."

But Dan noticed that she walked into the church. Dan pulled the door shut behind her.

"You forgot 'poisonous bunch-back'd toad,' 'knotty-pated fool' and 'vile standing tuck,'" Dan said. "But at least I'm not 'pigeon-livered and lacking gall' like you."

"More Shakespeare insults?" Amy asked.

"Want me to go on?" Dan asked cheerfully. "I know dozens of them now."

"No," Amy said. "I want you to be quiet so we can hear if anyone comes."

This actually struck Dan as a good idea. He shut up, and they both tiptoed toward Shakespeare's grave. Dan held the flashlight low to the ground to light the uneven stone floor. But all sorts of dangers seemed to lurk in the darkness just beyond the flashlight beam.

If one of the other teams isn't here digging up Shakespeare's grave, then — who did leave that door unlocked? Dan wondered. Is *this a trap?*

There was nothing he could do but keep walking toward the grave.

"Shakespeare died in 1616," Amy whispered. "I hope no one's replaced the mortar around his tombstone since then. Four-hundred-year-old mortar should be crumbly and easy to dig through. But if it's newer than that . . ."

"We'll be fine," Dan whispered back.

They were at the gravestone now. Dan bent down and moved the bouquet of flowers once again. His fingers brushed the secret carved words that had shown up on the grave rubbing—vague, random-seeming lines in the stone. It wasn't surprising that they could have gone undetected for almost four hundred years.

Amy bit her lip.

"Don't break the stone or anything," she said.

"Amy, it's a *stone*," Dan said. "How would I break it?"

"Superpowers?" Amy said. For her, that was a really, really good attempt at a joke.

Not that it was actually funny.

Dan moved his hand to feel along the crack between Shakespeare's gravestone and the one beside it. He touched the mortar in the crack—and then jerked his hand back.

"Amy!" he whispered. "That's not mortar! It's fake!"

"What?" Amy said.

Dan pulled her hand toward the fake mortar so she could feel it, too.

"It's just—rubber?" she asked. "Made to look like crumbly mortar?"

Dan began pulling on the rubbery fake mortar. It came up in one long strip.

"Careful," Amy said. "One of the other clue-hunting

teams might have put it there to cover their tracks. It might be set to explode—"

"Or someone's making this really easy for us," Dan said. He pointed to a set of hinges that had been hidden under the fake mortar. He used the nail file like a lever. One side of the stone began to creak upward, moving under its own power now.

Dan shone the flashlight beam down into the grave.

He was braced for some horrifying decaying skeleton. But all he could see was a coffin.

Something gleamed on top of the coffin: an irregularly shaped metal pole. Words ran around the pole, circling it again and again and again. Dan rolled the pole to the side and realized that there were only five words, repeating over and over: Madrigal Stronghold • Cahill Ancestral Home • Madrigal Stronghold • Cahill Ancestral Home . . .

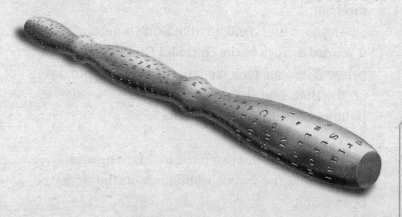

"It's telling us where to go next!" Dan whispered.

"The Madrigal stronghold," Amy said. "Of course."

The Clue hunt had taken them to strongholds for all the other branches: for the Lucians in Paris; the Janus in Venice; the Ekats in Egypt; and the Tomas in South Africa. It made so much sense that they'd have to go to the Madrigals' headquarters, too.

"'Cahill Ancestral Home' — think that means where Gideon and Olivia Cahill lived?" Dan asked.

"Yeah — the last place the Cahill family was all together," Amy said sadly. "Of course the Madrigals would build their headquarters there."

Dan rolled the pole again, scanning the words looping down its side.

"Okay, great," he said. "All very symbolic. Like poetry. Whatever. But where *is* this Madrigal stronghold-ancestral home? They forgot to write down directions!"

Amy took the flashlight from Dan's hand and aimed it toward a crack in the coffin lid Dan hadn't noticed before. Then she took the nail file Dan had put down on the floor and she pried at the crack. No, she was pulling something out of the crack:

A ribbon.

"I think there are two parts to this," she said.

They laid the fragile ribbon out on the floor and peered at it:

"And I thought Shakespeare's spelling was bad before," Dan muttered.

"See any patterns?" Amy asked. "Any anagrams or—"

"In that mess? You've got to kidding," Dan said, then groaned. "Couldn't we have a nice, easy numbers clue? Thanks a lot, Shakespeare."

"No, thank *you*, Dan and Amy," a voice said behind them.

Both kids whirled around. It *wasn't* someone from one of the other teams. It was the old man who'd volunteered at the church, the one who'd given Dan permission to do the grave rubbing.

"We can explain everything," Dan said quickly. He hoped Amy would be able to, anyway.

The old man lifted his hands in a forgiving gesture.

"No, no, I know the explanations already," he said. "I'm just so grateful to the two of you for . . ." He stopped and looked around, bafflement spreading over his face. "Where are the others?"

"Others?" Amy repeated stupidly.

The old man was gazing far down the aisle. Even in the dim light, Dan could see the blood draining from the man's face. The man began backing away.

"This isn't what I thought," he said. "I thought . . . I thought . . ."

He faded back into the shadows.

Dan stood up and stared off toward the spot where the man had been looking. Years ago, one time when they were between au pairs, Dan had gone through a phase where he'd watched a lot of horror movies—the kind shown on cable TV in the middle of the night. The kind any kid Dan's age with actual, living parents was never allowed to watch. The kind where there was always some angry mob of villagers showing up with pitchforks and torches, ready to kill someone.

Dan felt like he was watching that same kind of angry mob, down at the opposite end of the aisle.

The other Clue-hunting teams had arrived.

CHAPTER 16

For Amy, it was like seeing all her least favorite Shakespeare villains come to life. With their faces shadowed, Mary-Todd, Reagan, and Madison Holt reminded her of the three witches from *Macbeth*. Alistair was like mad King Lear, who punished the child who loved him best. Hamilton was like Brutus from *Julius Caesar*, the supposed friend who joined in the murder plot. Jonah was like the two-faced Richard III, who pretended to be a good guy but killed off one relative after another. Sinead was like . . .

Amy remembered this wasn't English class. She didn't have time to come up with analogies for everyone.

Did she and Dan have time to save their own lives?

Amy threw the flashlight down on the floor, so the beam of light pointed out toward the other teams. She and Dan were in total darkness.

"Amy, Dan—we don't want to hurt you," Alistair called.

"Of course not," Amy yelled back. "Did you want to hurt our parents seven years ago?"

Shouting that made her voice shake. And it made her ears ring, so she couldn't hear what, if anything, Alistair said in reply.

No time to think about that, Amy told herself. *No time to feel. Just . . . plan.*

Amy bent down and picked up the delicate ribbon from the floor. The end of the ribbon was already coming unraveled.

"Dan!" she whispered. "Did you get a good look at this? Enough to memorize the letters?"

"I think so," he whispered back. "I'm pretty sure."

"Sure enough that it's okay if I destroy it?" Amy asked.

Dan glanced at the ribbon quickly.

"Go ahead," he whispered.

Amy put one end of the ribbon under the vase holding the bouquet of flowers. She grabbed the metal pole from the coffin top and handed it to Dan.

"Swing it at them if you have to," she told him grimly.

Then she picked up the flashlight and directed the beam of light toward the end of the ribbon she still held in her hand.

"This is the next lead," she called out to her relatives. "If you get up here in time, maybe you can stop me from unraveling all of it!"

She pulled on the ribbon end that wasn't under

the vase. It obligingly separated out into individual threads. She kept her end of the unraveling ribbon firmly between her fingers. Then she dropped the flashlight and grabbed Dan's hand.

"Run!" she yelled at him.

Dan was halfway down the side aisle of the church before he figured out what Amy was trying to do. He knew she was unraveling the ribbon, leaving a trail of thread behind them as they ran. But why?

Oh, yeah, he thought. *She's trying to get everyone to run up to the front of the church to save what's left of the ribbon, instead of chasing us. She's buying us time to get away.*

Was it working?

Dan and Amy reached the door without Dan having to swing the metal pole even once.

All right, Amy! Dan thought. He almost regretted calling her pigeon-livered.

"Let's hide in the cemetery," Dan hissed to her.

"No—keep running," Amy whispered. "We've got to get back to Nellie. We've got to get out of Stratford."

Dan couldn't see how that would work. Sure, the other Clue hunters hadn't caught them yet. But any of the Holts could run faster than Dan and Amy. Probably Ian and Jonah and the Starlings could, too. If this turned into a flat-out race, Dan and Amy would lose.

They sprinted through the cemetery and burst out the gate to the street outside. Dan could already hear footsteps behind them, getting closer and closer.

"Turn left!" Dan whispered to Amy. "Everyone would expect us to turn right, so we've got to fool them!"

Amy cast a quick glance over her shoulder.

"But if anyone's close enough to see—"

A car down the street suddenly turned on its headlights, pinning Amy and Dan in the bright beams.

"Oh, no—get out of the light!" Amy yelled.

A figure stepped out of the car.

"Amy! Dan! Over here!"

It was Nellie.

The old man sat beside the open grave, his face buried in his hands.

Fifteen generations.

That was how long his family had been working at Holy Trinity Church. His father, his grandmother, his great-grandmother, his great-great-grandfather . . . all the way back to the 1600s. All of them had watched over Shakespeare's grave and watched over his Madrigal secrets.

As Cahill accomplishments went, it wasn't much. Their tiny offshoot branch of Madrigals had produced no Shakespeares of their own. But the old man's family, generation after generation, had been loyal and hardworking and true. They took their pride in that.

Every five years they would replace a decaying old

ribbon with a newer one, after meticulously copying down a string of letters. Once or twice they had made strategic decisions to modernize, updating even what was printed on the ribbon.

But mostly, for fifteen generations, they had waited.

The old man had been so sure that this would be the night everyone was waiting for.

He picked up a wisp of thread still lingering by the grave.

Ruin, he thought. *All our hopes in ruin.*

But his family had had their hopes dashed before. They had learned the value of backup plans. He went to the church gift shop and reached under the desk to pull out a very precise length of satin ribbon. Then he went to a secret hiding place of his own and retrieved a computer disk containing one file: a photo of an old ribbon, the one that had been destroyed. He had a tedious job ahead of him, but by morning, Shakespeare's grave would once again contain part of a lead toward the most important of all the 39 Clues. Recovering or reproducing the metal pole would take only a little longer.

A shadow fell across the old man's shoulder.

"I'll take that," a voice said behind him.

And then a hand reached out to grab the computer disk.

CHAPTER 17

Nellie squealed the tires as she rounded the corner.

"Left! Left! Drive on the left side!" Dan yelled at her.

"Oh, right," Nellie said. She swerved back into her lane, barely missing a parked car.

"How'd you know where to find us?" Amy asked.

"I've been hanging around you two goobers practically twenty-four/seven for more than a month," Nellie said. "I can tell when you're trying to keep a secret. You had 'We're planning to sneak back into the church' written all over your faces."

Amy slumped in her seat.

"*Everybody* knew we were planning to sneak back into the church," she muttered. "They were just pretending not to."

"As Shakespeare himself would say, 'All the world's a stage,'" Nellie said. She peered into her rearview mirror. "Wow. I have to hand it to Hamilton. He's practically keeping up."

Amy whirled around in her seat. Hamilton was running behind their car, only four or five lengths back. If Nellie had to stop for a red light or a stop sign, he'd catch them.

"Should I wait for him?" Nellie asked, slowing slightly.

Amy saw another hulking figure striding alongside Hamilton.

"No! His dad's with him!" she shrieked.

Nellie whipped around another corner.

"So," she said. "You got a destination in mind or do you just want me to keep going with the evasive driving?"

"Back to the hotel to pick up our stuff," Amy said. "And then—"

"Been there, done that," Nellie said.

She took a hand off the steering wheel to point at the backseat and floor. For the first time, Amy noticed that Saladin's cat carrier and Nellie's bag were right beside her.

"As soon as I got away from Alistair, I packed up and checked out," Nellie said. "Then I headed toward the church. I thought my timing was pretty good, didn't you?" Nellie sounded amazingly casual given that she was practically driving a slalom course around cars parked on either side of the narrow street. "Oh, this is crazy! Eisenhower's waving at us like he thinks we're going to stop!"

"Get on the highway," Amy said.

"Toward . . . ?" Nellie asked.

"Not sure yet. Got any scissors?" Amy asked.

"On my Swiss Army knife," Nellie said. "Bottom pocket in my bag, right-hand side."

Amy pulled out the knife. Then she reached into her own bag for a Boston College T-shirt that had gotten kind of ragged during the Clue hunt. She began cutting off a spiral strip of the shirt from the bottom up. She made the strip extra long, just in case. Then she leaned over the front seat and handed the cloth and a thin marker to Dan.

"Start writing," she said.

Dan let out a deep breath.

That's why he wasn't talking, Amy thought. *He was holding his breath, trying so hard not to forget.*

She'd noticed on the Clue hunt that Dan's photographic memory wasn't completely effortless. He just acted like it was.

"Done," Dan said a few minutes later.

He held up the strip. Its edges curled up because of the way it'd been cut.

Curled, Amy thought. *A spiral. Like . . .*

"I still don't get it," Dan said. "I can remember the letters from the ribbon. I'm even pretty sure I got the wacko spacing right, all the gaps between the letters. But I can't figure out what any of it means."

"Wrap the cloth around the pole," Amy said. "Because back in Shakespeare's time, English villages always had these huge midsummer parties where girls would dance and wrap ribbons around a maypole in particular patterns. The midsummer festival would have been a big deal in Stratford, something Shakespeare probably missed when he moved to London. Something that reminded him of home."

Home, Amy thought. *That's what this clue is about. It's calling Cahills back home. Like in the hint we got in London: "Everything can come full circle."*

"One of Shakespeare's plays is called *A Midsummer Night's Dream*," Nellie said as she jerked the steering wheel left and right. "It's kind of bizarre, with—"

"Stop it!" Dan yelled. "Both of you—stop trying to tell me stuff!"

"I just thought it might help you solve that," Nellie said, sounding offended.

"But I already have," Dan said, holding up the pole. "It's numbers, after all. Just spelled out as words!"

Amy hung over the front seat so she could see. Dan had lined up the edges of the strip of cloth with the words spiraling around the pole: MADRIGAL STRONGHOLD * CAHILL ANCESTRAL HOME * MADRIGAL STRONGHOLD * CAHILL ANCESTRAL HOME . . .

With the strip of cloth wrapped all the way around the pole, the nonsensical list of letters did indeed spell out words on one side.

"'Fifty-three oN Six oW'?" Amy said. "What's that mean? Oh—"

"That's not 'oN' and 'oW,'" Nellie said, glancing toward the pole. "That's—"

"Degrees north," Dan said.

"And degrees west," Amy said.

"Latitude and longitude," Nellie finished.

They'd all figured it out at the same time. The ribbon gave them the precise coordinates of the Madrigal stronghold.

Nellie yanked the portable GPS unit off the dashboard and tossed it back to Amy.

"Good thing I sprang for the deluxe rental package, now that you both know we're spending Madrigal money," Nellie said as Amy punched in the coordinates. "Where to?"

Amy stared at the glowing screen.

"Somewhere that might take a lot more Madrigal money," Amy muttered. She shifted to dialing Nellie's cell phone. "Hello, Mr. McIntyre? We need to rent a helicopter."

CHAPTER 18

Fiske paced while Mr. McIntyre talked on the phone.

"Amy and Dan know where they need to go," Mr. McIntyre reported, his hand cupped over the phone. "They're in a hurry. They want to rent a helicopter."

"But we haven't heard from our man at the church about how things went there?" Fiske asked.

Mr. McIntyre shook his head and went back to talking on the phone. "Do you feel that you and the other teams have reached a proper, ah, *rapprochement*?" he asked. "You believe that your actions in Stratford—and from this point forward—will lead to the achievement of all our goals?"

Fiske could always tell when Mr. McIntyre was nervous. He started sounding more and more like a lawyer.

"Yes," Mr. McIntyre continued. "I am talking about the reunification of the Cahill family, and the end of five hundred years of hostility, enmity, and outright war."

Fiske passed close enough in his pacing that he could hear Amy's voice coming through the cell phone.

"Mr. McIntyre, we're doing the best we can," she said. "Dan kind of has a plan."

Grace had told Fiske once that Amy reminded her of him. Because of that, Fiske had spent the entire Clue hunt trying to imagine himself in Dan's and Amy's shoes.

They're braver than I am, he'd thought, again and again. *They're always so sure of themselves.*

But now, hearing the worry and fear in Amy's voice, he knew that wasn't true. Amy was terrified. She had no certainty of success. But she and Dan had always tried their hardest, done their best, from the very beginning.

Could Fiske say the same about himself?

He would have to do his best now.

Fiske grabbed the phone from Mr. McIntyre's hand.

"We trust you, Amy," he said hoarsely into it. "You won't be able to contact us once you get there, but — we'll trust your judgment. It's all up to you."

Mr. McIntyre was staring daggers at him. McIntyre was a cautious man. He didn't like having to trust people — especially not children who were too young and erratic to be predictable.

"Don't worry about the expense," Fiske found himself saying into the phone. "Don't worry that you'll tip off the others that you're connected to us. This is the final stop. It's almost time for everything to be revealed."

On the other end of the phone, Amy gasped.

Fiske wanted to keep talking. This was strange—he wasn't used to wanting to explain, to comfort, to encourage. But he couldn't think of anything comforting or encouraging to say. All he could think of were warnings.

Hastily, he shut off the phone and dropped it onto the table. Mr. McIntyre watched him.

"We'll need to make our own travel arrangements," Mr. McIntyre said.

Fiske just stood there, staring out at the darkness that had enveloped the river Avon.

The phone rang again, rattling against the table. Mr. McIntyre answered it.

He was silent for a few moments, then he cried, "*What* happened? *Who* stole the lead?"

The phone slipped from his hand and fell to the floor.

Fiske reached for it.

"This is too dangerous!" he said. "We have to stop—"

"We can't stop anything," Mr. McIntyre said. Now he was the one staring out into darkness. "It's out of our control."

CHAPTER 19

"I'm telling you," the pilot insisted. "There's not going to be anything there!"

"And *I'm* telling *you*," Nellie said, standing almost nose to nose with him. "We're paying you tons of money to take us there anyway!"

The pilot pointed at the computer screen.

"Let me explain again," he said with exaggerated patience. "The map reading of fifty-three north, six west is in the water." He zoomed in on the computer, so the screen showed nothing but blue. "It's off the coast of Ireland, yes, but there's not an island there. There's not even a big rock. There's nothing to land on!"

"We'll take parachutes," Nellie said.

The pilot snorted.

"Do you know what kind of trouble I could get into, dropping two kids and a teenager off in the middle of the Irish Sea?" he asked. "I could lose my license!"

"I am not a teenager!" Nellie said furiously. "I am twenty years old!"

It felt like the two of them had been arguing forever,

back and forth, while Dan and Amy ate a very late improvised dinner from the heliport vending machine. Dan crumpled the last bag of Crispy Bacon Frazzles.

"What if we throw in an extra two thousand dollars for you to take us there?" he suggested.

Everyone turned and looked at him.

What? Dan wondered. *Can't I be the calm, reasonable one in the room?*

He realized that he never would have been before the Clue hunt.

Of course, before the Clue hunt, he'd also never had access to huge sums of money he could use to bribe people to do what he wanted.

"Fine," the helicopter pilot snapped. "I will take you on this crazy mission. Just to look. We will not land on the waves. You will not jump out in parachutes. You will not even unlatch a window unless I say it's safe!"

It was a tense flight. Nellie told Amy and Dan to sleep if they could, but every time Dan closed his eyes he saw the mob of his enemies back at the church. He kept dozing off and jerking awake from nightmares about the other Clue hunters chasing him with pitchforks and torches, or nightmares about the coffin from Shakespeare's grave rising up and zooming after him, or nightmares about Isabel Kabra suddenly showing up to . . . to . . .

"There it is!" Nellie shrieked.

Dan jerked upright. He blinked at the sudden light: The sun was just coming up over the sea. And down below in the bouncing waves there was a small black dot.

"See? What did I tell you? There *is* an island," Nellie said, grinning triumphantly.

"Oh, no, no, no," the pilot said. "That's just—" He glanced down at his instrument panel. He flicked one of the dials. He glared at a screen that seemed to be the helicopter version of GPS. "This is impossible! There isn't an island there on any map!"

"Typical Cahill setup," Amy muttered beside Dan. She was speaking too softly for the pilot to hear her over the whir of the helicopter blades. "They've probably been bribing mapmakers for five hundred years to keep that island secret. Wonder how many ships have crashed into it because of that?"

"It's like with Lester," Dan said softly.

Staring out at the roiling water, Dan could imagine shipwreck victims reaching up desperately from the waves, just as Lester had reached from the quicksand back in Jamaica.

"This is why we have to win," Amy whispered back.

She'd said the same thing the day Lester died: That they had to finish the hunt on behalf of all the ordinary people who'd been hurt or killed by Cahills fighting to take over the world. Dan agreed, but . . . he didn't want to be ordinary himself. It was more fun to be in control, to have thousands of dollars to throw around to get his own way.

It was easier not to think about any of it.

And, Dan told himself, it didn't matter what their reasons were — for Lester, for the Madrigals, for the memory of Grace or Dan and Amy's parents, just to keep the other teams from getting too much power. . . . No matter what, Amy and Dan had to win.

"And look, the island is big enough to land on." Nellie was gloating in the front seat.

Without saying a word, the pilot let the helicopter drop toward the island. Dan's stomach lurched upward — he had a feeling the pilot could have made a much smoother descent if he'd wanted.

"Wait!" Dan yelled. "There! That's where we need to land!"

The island consisted of a broad, flat, pebbled beach leading up to a field of tall grasses, and then one huge, sheer cliff with only a narrow flat space at the top. Dan couldn't begin to imagine what weird natural forces could have created that setup — maybe it wasn't anything natural. Maybe the layout of the island was a Cahill invention. Dan knew that what he'd seen wasn't natural: a metal-framed doorway at the top of the cliff. And, beside the doorway, a metal panel with push-button numbers.

"Land beside that door!" Dan yelled.

The pilot let out an exasperated burst of air.

"Do you know nothing about helicopters?" he asked. "If I try to land there, my blades will hit the door and we will topple off the cliff and die."

"Then lower us down to the door on one of those little rope-ladder things people always use in the movies," Amy said.

Dan couldn't believe it was *Amy* suggesting this.

"Don't you know how long people have to train to do that?" the pilot asked. "Someone like you, without experience, you would be caught in the draft and blow away and die."

"If we don't hit the cliff and die that way instead," Dan muttered under his breath. This guy was just a bundle of laughs.

"Then the idea of parachutes—" Nellie began.

"You would be blown out to sea," the pilot said. "And you would expect me to come and rescue you."

"With the rope ladder, and then we'd get blown off the cliff and die," Dan muttered again.

Amy frowned at him and shook her head.

"Please," she said, leaning forward. "Isn't there some way—"

"I will land on the beach. Nowhere else," the pilot said emphatically. "That is much more than I originally promised."

There was nothing they could do.

The helicopter landed. Dan walked toward the bottom of the cliff. The grasses whipped against his legs and chest. Then his foot struck something hard.

"Ow! Oh!"

He jumped back and saw what he'd hit: a tall, thin stone that had been hidden by the grass.

Beside him, Amy had brushed back grasses from a similar stone.

"Dan, these are *tombstones,*" she said. "This is another cemetery." The color drained from her face. "Oh, no. Oh, no. When Fiske said this was our final stop did he mean . . ."

Dan's head spun, and for a moment he couldn't hear anything Amy said. Now he could see regular breaks in the grasses — signs of a whole row of tombstones.

Death, he thought. *This whole clue hunt's been about death. Dead parents, dead grandmother, dead ancestors, all those clues in graves and tombs and crypts . . .*

He shook his head, as if that could drive all the death-thoughts away.

"Get a grip," he told Amy harshly. "Stop acting like you've never been in a cemetery before. When Fiske said this was our final stop, he meant this is where we're going to find the last clue. Where we're going to *win.*"

He reached out and touched the tombstone before him, which was so weathered and ancient it was impossible to read. But Dan could feel what was left of the inscription; he could make out dates with his fingertips.

"Amy, this is from, like, 1432 or 1482 — something like that," he said.

"Then it's the original Cahill family cemetery," Amy said. She stepped back, looking at the tombstones, then looking at the expanse of empty grasses just beyond. "Gideon and Olivia Cahill's house was over there.

There was a fence around it. I saw pictures in those family history books Alistair had back in Korea."

"But the house burned down five hundred years ago," Dan said. "So you think the last clue is somewhere over in all those grasses?"

"No," Amy said. "There were always arrows pointing up in all the pictures. I didn't understand it then, but now . . . Remember how Fiske said, 'It's all up to you'? The way he said 'up'? That was a hint, too."

She turned her gaze to the cliff, looking up and up and up. The cliff was as tall as a skyscraper — the top blocked out the sun.

"We're going to have to find some way to get up to that door," Dan said.

Amy nodded.

"I guess we'll have to go back for climbing equipment," she said. She grimaced. "Or a pilot who will drop us off on a rope ladder without telling us we're going to die."

"That'll take forever!" Dan objected.

Amy looked out at the empty water surrounding the island.

"Maybe we've got time," she said. "None of the other teams saw that ribbon."

Dan shook his head — not disagreeing, just impatient. He wanted to finish the Clue hunt *now*. He looked over at the helicopter, where Nellie and the pilot were arguing again. How long would it take to get the pilot to agree to a new plan?

Just then Dan heard the putt-putt of a motor.

He squinted off into the distance. The water around them wasn't empty anymore. Something was moving toward them.

A boat.

Amy peered off in the same direction.

"That's probably just a fishing boat," she said. "It probably doesn't have anything to do with us or this island or the clue hunt."

Dan squinted harder. The boat got closer.

"Is that why Hamilton Holt is hanging out one of the windows, waving at us?" he asked.

CHAPTER 20

The Holts had come with climbing equipment. They swarmed out onto the pebble beach carrying ropes, carabiner clips, even pickaxes.

"How?" Amy asked, standing there flabbergasted. It was torture to watch the other team move so efficiently toward the cliff.

"How what, Amy?" Hamilton asked. He paused for a second in the midst of checking knots in his rope.

"How did you solve the puzzle so fast when you didn't have anything but thread?" Amy asked. "And how did you know to bring the ropes and everything?"

"Amy, we didn't solve any puzzle," Hamilton said. "We just followed you."

"We put a tracking device on Nellie's rental car," Madison said, leering.

"And then it was easy to check your flight plan at the heliport," Reagan gloated.

No, Amy wanted to protest. *That's not fair! This was our lead!*

But they'd been in too much of a hurry leaving

Stratford to look for tracking devices. They never would have been able to convince the safety-obsessed pilot not to file a flight plan.

They hadn't had a chance.

"Anyhow, we take climbing gear pretty much everywhere we go," Hamilton added. "Doesn't everyone?"

He seemed to take in the stunned look on both Amy's and Dan's faces.

"Oh, guess not," he muttered, turning back to his ropes. "Too bad for you."

"It's like that famous Shakespeare quote," Eisenhower added, hovering nearby. He squinted, as if thinking hard. Then his face lit up. "Shakespeare always said, 'Be prepared.'"

"That's not a Shakespeare quote!" Dan protested. "It's the Boy Scout motto!"

"And the Girl Scouts'!" Amy added.

Eisenhower's smug expression didn't change.

"Yeah, well, what good is all that fancy knowledge doing you?" he asked. "We Holts are going to leave you down here in the dust. And us—we're going to be up there!" He pointed to the top of the cliff like it was heaven itself. "Claiming the final prize. Holts are going to rule the world forever!" He stuck his ax into the first crack in the side of the cliff. "Who's laughing at us now?"

He knows, Amy thought. *He knows this is the final stop. The final chance to win. Which . . . Dan and I aren't going to do.*

"So what if you can climb better than us!" Dan yelled as all five Holts began ascending the cliff. "The prize isn't just sitting up there waiting for you to claim it! There's a door and a keypad! Bet you anything the door is locked! Bet it's going to take a math puzzle to solve the keypad code! Bet you're just going to have to climb right back down here to beg for my help!"

The Holts just kept climbing.

This is the greatest day of my life, Eisenhower Holt thought.

He was dangling from a rope thousands of feet above the ground, the fresh sea air in his face, his wife and children by his side. With the exertion, the family togetherness, the adrenaline coursing through his veins—with all that, the climb itself was enough to make this a wonderful day.

But this climb would be the best of his life. He'd had a horrible day yesterday, but at least it'd given him valuable information. And now he knew that ultimate victory awaited him at the top of the cliff. His family was about to win the biggest prize they could ever win—the biggest prize *anyone* could ever win.

True, Eisenhower hadn't quite figured out what the final prize in the Clue hunt would be. But he knew it would be something so great it would outweigh everything he'd ever failed at. It would make up for getting kicked out of West Point. It would make up for losing that security guard job when he'd accidentally Tasered his own rear end. It would make up for the other Tomas laughing at him—for *everyone* laughing at him.

And it proved that one of his favorite quotations in the whole wide world was true: "It's not whether you get knocked down; it's whether you get up."

The great football coach Vince Lombardi had said that. Eisenhower wished that there'd been something in the hunt requiring Vince Lombardi quotes because Eisenhower knew them all: "Winning isn't everything; it's the only thing." "If winning isn't everything, why do they keep score?" And . . .

"Dad," Hamilton said softly beside him. "Look."

Eisenhower planted his foot as firmly as he could on a three-inch spike and turned his head. Surprise almost made him lose his grip on the rope: Jonah Wizard was stepping out onto the beach from a yacht. The Kabra kids were parachuting down from a small plane. And Alistair Oh had just surfaced on the beach in something that looked vaguely like a submarine.

The competition had arrived.

"Guess we weren't the only ones who used a tracking device," Hamilton muttered.

"The girls and I will go down and hold off our opponents," Mary-Todd volunteered. "Eisenhower, honeybun, you and Hamilton go claim the prize for all of us."

Eisenhower spared a second to gaze lovingly at his wife as she and the girls began their descent.

"See, that's teamwork," Eisenhower told Hamilton. "Your mother knew what had to be done, and she did it. It's all about the team. And in this family, the family is the team. I mean, the team is the family. I mean . . ."

"I know what you mean, Dad," Hamilton said, which was a big relief for Eisenhower because he'd kind of lost track himself.

Hamilton was quiet for a minute. With just about any other kid—any non-Holt—Eisenhower might have thought it was because the boy was inching up a sheer rock face with little more than a rope and a few carabiner clips between him and death. But Hamilton could climb a little old cliff like this in his sleep.

"Get moving!" Eisenhower barked, because that was the only way to deal with mopey kids.

But Hamilton hung for a second too long by the point of his ax. He sighed.

"Do you remember when I was little, and you'd come to my games?" Hamilton asked. "Do you remember what the other parents said?"

"You mean—'Holt, your kid's the best one on the whole team'?" Eisenhower asked. Actually, what the parents had mostly said was, "Holt, make your kid stop beating up my kid!" Or, "Holt, you'll be paying my kid's medical bills for the rest of your life!" But Eisenhower knew what the parents had really meant.

"No," Hamilton said. "That other thing. Something

like . . . 'It's not whether you win or lose. It's how you play the game.'"

"Oooh," Eisenhower said. "You mean, what the *losers'* parents said. To make them think it's okay to lose. How else would winners like us ever have people to play against if losers didn't think that?"

"What if that's not what that saying really means?" Hamilton asked. "What if it means that . . . winning doesn't mean anything . . . if you cheat?"

A feather could have knocked Eisenhower off the cliff face at that moment.

Does . . . does my son think I cheat? Eisenhower wondered.

This was the worst day of Eisenhower's life.

"*Et tu,* Hamilton?" Eisenhower gasped.

"Dad?" Hamilton said in a strangled voice. "You're quoting Shakespeare?"

Eisenhower guessed he was. He almost let himself feel a burst of pride that he knew any Shakespeare—even if it was just two syllables. But what was pride worth if his own son was ashamed of him?

No matter what the Clue-hunt prize turned out to be, it wouldn't be worth anything if Hamilton wasn't proud, too. Hamilton and the girls—that's who Eisenhower wanted to win *for*.

"In the clue hunt," Eisenhower managed to gasp. "You think we're not winning . . . fair and square?"

"Amy and Dan figured out how to get here," Hamilton said. "And all along, things you thought I was figuring out . . . lots of it was stuff Amy and Dan told me. We don't deserve the prize. They do."

For a moment, Eisenhower felt like he was dangling over a huge void, held up only by the thinnest of threads, a cold wind at his back. Actually, that was a fairly accurate description of Eisenhower's position, vis-à-vis the cliff and all. But Eisenhower hadn't even felt the chill in the wind until just now; the void below him hadn't felt so empty and vast.

Then he realized where his son had gotten confused.

"Ham, Ham, Ham," Eisenhower chuckled. "You've been seeing this clue hunt like it's just another game. I do that with most things, too. But there's a big difference. Games have rules. The clue hunt doesn't. It's not cheating if there aren't rules."

"What about the rules you're just supposed to follow in life?" Hamilton asked. "The ones that make you a decent person?"

Eisenhower stared at his son. He'd heard other parents say they didn't understand their kids, but Eisenhower himself had never known what that was like.

Now he did.

"I'm not saying we should just give Amy and Dan the win," Hamilton said quickly, shifting his feet against the mountainside. "I'm just saying we should . . . share."

"You mean—have a tie?" Eisenhower asked incredulously. "My own son wants to settle for a tie?"

"It's not like that," Hamilton said. "It's like . . . you know how baseball teams get new players every year in the draft? Or through trades?" For some reason, he'd completely stopped climbing and was just hanging on to the cliff face. "Think of it like we're drafting Amy and Dan."

"But our team is our family," Eisenhower countered. "We don't have trades! We don't do a draft!"

Hamilton peered deep into his father's eyes.

"We could if we wanted to," he said. "Amy and Dan are our family, too."

"No," Eisenhower said stubbornly. "No. You're wrong." He was shaking his head so hard he could barely hold on to the cliff. "They're not *Holts*! I'm the team captain! I'm your father! Nobody's on our team unless I say so!"

This was awful. His own son was almost sounding like those men in the shadowy room yesterday—the men who'd lured him away from his family with the promise of extra Clues, extra help, if he cooperated. Those men had practically kidnapped him, held him hostage. They'd talked about the number of Clues, and which teams were ahead, and how nobody had enough Clues to win alone.

Eisenhower knew what all that talk really meant: The Clue hunt was almost over, and the men were upset because the Holts were winning.

So why had they just let him go at the end? Why hadn't they beaten him up—even killed him—instead of only warning, "We'll be watching"?

"Dad, *think*," Hamilton said, which was cruel, after what Eisenhower had told him at the Manchester United game. "If we don't team up with Dan and Amy, we could still lose. What if everybody else teams up against us? You didn't see how the others were acting yesterday at that church. Nobody was even fighting! I mean, not until last night."

"Anybody can pretend," Eisenhower sneered.

Pretend . . .

It was a good thought. No, it was a brilliant thought.

Especially if anyone really was watching.

Madison Holt bent her head back, staring straight up the cliff.

"Mom!" she called. "Why are Daddy and Hamilton coming back down? Was the prize only halfway up the cliff?"

Hamilton will understand in the end, Eisenhower told himself as he climbed. For a moment he couldn't remember if he was going up or down. Then he went back to moving automatically. *After we win, he'll see why Dan and Amy could never* really *be part of our team. He'll be proud of the way I'm faking everyone out.*

Even him.

CHAPTER 21

"Don't trust them."

Amy's last words still echoed in Dan's ears. Everything had happened so fast: Hamilton and Eisenhower jumping down from the cliff, Hamilton grabbing Dan, Eisenhower waving his ax at the others and proclaiming, "We're taking Dan with us to get the prize. Everyone else—stay back."

Amy had run to Dan's side, crying, "Let me kiss my brother good-bye!"—*ewww*—and Dan had known she was going to whisper something in his ear. He expected one last attempt to cram Shakespeare info into his head or something about being careful climbing the mountain. But, "Don't trust them"?

Hamilton's carrying me up the side of a cliff. We're thousands and thousands of feet up in the air. If he lets go, I'm dead meat. And I'm not supposed to trust him?

Dan did trust Hamilton—when he wasn't around his father. But Eisenhower was just a few feet away, ascending the cliff right beside his son. Eisenhower could easily reach over and slash a knife through the ropes that held Dan on Hamilton's back. Or Eisenhower could easily tell Hamilton to cut those ropes himself.

Dan shivered.

"Do you mind not moving?" Hamilton asked. "It throws me off a little."

Below them, chunks of stone plunged down the cliff. Dan's shiver had made Hamilton lose his footing and kick away the stones. Hamilton was hanging on to the cliff by only two fingers.

Dan held his breath while Hamilton found toeholds for both his feet.

"Don't you dare do that again!" Eisenhower barked at Dan. "Don't you endanger my son!"

Dan took a very small breath. He imagined what it would be like to have a father protecting him that way.

Now was not a good time to think about stuff like that, though. Because he might slip and say something to Eisenhower like, "You know, I could be climbing this cliff with my own father right now—if you hadn't helped kill him."

Eisenhower glared harder, and for a moment Dan feared he had spoken aloud.

No, he's just straining to reach the next handhold, Dan told himself. *Chill. You're safe until you get to the top of the cliff.*

Dan figured the two Holts had come back for him because they really did think they'd need him to solve whatever puzzle waited at the top of the cliff.

But what would happen after that?

What would Eisenhower do to him then?

It was a long, slow climb.

After going halfway up, down, and then up again with Dan on his back, Hamilton had entered the zone where he could think about nothing but rock. Rock above him, rock below him, rock smashed against his face as he inched higher and higher.

Then came a moment when he reached up and touched only air. He brought his hand down flat, spreading his fingers freely for once.

They were at the top.

Now what?

The three of us will solve a puzzle, Hamilton told himself. *We'll win the prize. And—we Holts will share it with Dan and Amy. Dad promised.*

He and Eisenhower crept carefully onto the narrow rock ledge that lay before the door. They began pulling up ropes, unclipping carabiners. As soon as he was free of his own ropes, Dan scrambled toward the door and the keypad.

"G-guess I'd better start solving this thing," he said in a thin, reedy voice. His mouth must have gotten really dry on the climb. "Th-then I bet there are a lot more puzzles you'll need me to solve, after the door. You'll probably need Amy and Nellie's help, too."

Dan wobbled a little as he walked—like he had

climbers' legs, even though he hadn't been doing the climbing.

Then he tripped.

Dan fell straight toward the door and the keypad, his hands outstretched. The palm of his left hand slammed directly against the keypad, smashing it in.

The door slid open.

"Whaddya know," Hamilton grunted, looking up from his ropes. "Guess there wasn't any special trick to that. No puzzle or math skills required."

Dan jerked back from the keypad as if it'd been electrified. He whirled around, his eyes wide and terrified. He glanced once at Eisenhower, then he darted toward Hamilton.

"No!" he screamed. "You'll need me later! You still need my help!"

He grabbed Hamilton's arm and cowered behind his bulk.

Hamilton would have been fine if he hadn't been so surprised. Or if he hadn't just climbed up an entire cliff. Or if Dan hadn't been so off-kilter.

But Dan's yank was just a little too hard. Hamilton had to jerk back in the opposite direction to keep from crashing down onto the narrow rock ledge. He overcorrected. Both he and Dan lost their balance. They fell—and kept falling.

Right off the edge of the cliff.

CHAPTER 22

Dan squeezed his eyes shut because he didn't want to see this: the ground rushing toward them, death rushing toward them.

Amy will be so sad, he thought. *Nellie, too. I hope they're kind of mad at me, too, so they're not just crying all the time. . . .*

Dan realized that he seemed to have a lot of time to think for someone plunging toward the ground.

Then he realized he'd stopped falling.

"Huh," Hamilton said. "Guess it's a good thing I still had the rope attached to my climbing harness."

Dan dared to open his eyes.

They were dangling alongside the cliff again. Dan could see straight down to the cemetery, far below. He looked up: Hamilton was above him, clutching Dan's wrists every bit as tightly as Dan was holding on to Ham's arm.

But Dan wasn't wearing a climbing harness. Dan wasn't attached to any rope.

I could still fall, Dan thought. *If my hands slip, if Hamilton lets go . . .*

He didn't dare to look down again. He didn't want to see all the empty air between him and the cemetery—empty air that would be so easy to fall through.

"Didn't I tell you not to endanger my son?" Eisenhower bellowed from above them, clutching the rope that was attached to Hamilton's harness.

"Dad, why don't you pull us up before you start screaming?" Hamilton said.

He spoke calmly, but Dan could feel his hands beginning to slide. They were sweating. Slippery. Losing their grip.

"The way these ropes are, I'm not sure I can save you both," Eisenhower said frantically. He seemed to be yanking ropes around, diving for extra clips. Hamilton and Dan lurched a little lower. "I can't—"

"You're going to have to," Hamilton said. "Because I'm not letting Dan fall."

Dan's ears were ringing too much to hear what Eisenhower or Hamilton said next. But the rope jerked up. And then it was Eisenhower's hands lifting him over the rim of the cliff, pulling him back to safety. Dan scooted as far away from the ledge as he could, across the rock, through the open door in the rock wall. He wasn't thinking about where the door might lead. He wasn't even thinking about the Clue hunt anymore. He let his eyes close again.

Safe, he thought. *I'm safe. I'm not going to die. Hamilton didn't let me fall. Eisenhower didn't let me fall. He wasn't even going to hurt me before. I just got scared.*

Then Eisenhower punched him right in the face.

"You could have killed my son!" Eisenhower screamed at Dan.

Now that everyone was safe, Eisenhower let the fury flow over him. He grabbed Dan by the shoulders and shook him. Dan's head rattled against the ground. He looked groggily up at Eisenhower, like a quarterback who'd taken too many hits.

"You could have made me lose Hamilton!" Eisenhower repeated. He had to make Dan understand how awful that would have been, how close Dan had come to ruining everything.

Dan blinked.

"You mean, like I lost my mom and dad?" he asked.

"Dad, stop it!" Hamilton yelled, tackling his father and knocking him away from Dan.

Eisenhower let go.

Does Dan think it's my fault his parents died? he thought. *It wasn't, but . . . what does* Hamilton *think?*

"Dad, what's wrong with you? Dan's on our team!" Hamilton was screaming, pinning Eisenhower back against some sort of wall.

Eisenhower bit back the words, "No, he isn't! Not really!"

How had he thought he could lie to his own son?

What does Hamilton see when he looks at me? Eisenhower wondered. *Doesn't he know—everything I've done, everything I'm doing—it's so he can be proud of me?*

Now Eisenhower felt like the world around him had gone dark, and he was plunging down. Like everything he'd ever believed in was falling away, and the very ground beneath him was dropping.

Wait—it really *had* gotten dark, and the ground *was* plunging downward.

"Is this an earthquake?" Eisenhower bellowed. "A rock slide?" He grabbed Hamilton by the shoulders. "Quick—let's get someplace safe!"

"Dad, I think it's just an elevator," Hamilton said, shoving him away.

Eisenhower put together the sensations. The darkness could have been from a door closing behind them. And the falling was slow and steady.

Exactly like an elevator.

"Right," he said gruffly. "I was just testing you, son."

Everything was going to be okay. The elevator was undoubtedly taking them to the final prize. The Holts were still going to win.

The elevator stopped moving. The door slid open.

They were back at sea level.

Back by the cemetery.

CHAPTER 23

Chaos erupted around Amy.

"Look—that rock's opening!"

"There's a door!"

"Why couldn't we see that before? It was so perfectly hidden from—"

"Run!"

Amy couldn't tell who was saying what. There wasn't time to think about any of it. One minute she was sitting beside Nellie, both of them craning their necks and trying to see what was happening on top of the cliff. The next minute she was sprinting toward the open door alongside Madison and Reagan Holt. It was like her body knew what to do even before her brain registered what her eyes were seeing: *Door. Elevator. Dan. Hamilton. Eisenhower.*

The two Holts and Dan were all sprawled on the floor of the elevator, far apart from one another. Amy couldn't make sense of that, not while she was trying to run, dodging tombstones.

"Out of the way, loser," Reagan said, swinging her

elbow toward Amy's face. "Hamilton and Dad came back for *us*."

"And Dan came back for *me*," Amy muttered, ducking the elbow.

She was already down low enough — and close enough — that she decided to dive in through the elevator door. Someone landed on top of her: Reagan? No — it was Natalie. Then Reagan and Madison crammed in behind her, pushing Amy farther back.

Amy's right ear was squashed against the wall, and Natalie's hand was shoved over her left ear. But she could hear a mechanical beeping sound and then an automated voice: "Elevator will not move from this spot without at least one representative from each Cahill branch. Step to the mirror for retinal scan. Ekat?"

"If you please," Alistair said coldly from outside the elevator. There was a shuffling about — Amy caught a glimpse of Mary-Todd stepping out and Alistair stepping in.

The elevator beeped again.

"Approved. Janus?"

"Out of my way," Jonah said.

Amy couldn't see, but she thought maybe he was yanking Madison and Reagan out of the elevator and shoving himself in.

"Approved," the automated voice said. "Lucian?"

"Present," Ian said.

He must have moved over in front of the eye

scanner because the automated voice said, "Approved. Tomas?"

"Oh, no," Eisenhower objected. "There are two Lucians on this elevator right now because Natalie is over there hiding at the back. That's not fair. One of you has to leave."

"Is it fair that there are two Holts?" Alistair asked. "You and Hamilton?"

"That's different," Eisenhower said.

While Eisenhower was complaining, Hamilton stepped up to the mirror.

"Approved," the automated voice said. "Madrigal?"

"What?" Alistair exploded. "Madrigals aren't a Cahill branch!"

"Madrigals?" This was Eisenhower. "Madrigals are evil!"

"Everybody hates Madrigals!" Ian cried.

The voices blended together, the indignation and fury rising with each word. It was the most unity Cahills had shown in five hundred years.

Except when the other branches united to kill Mom and Dad, Amy thought with a shiver. She was tempted to yell, "I hate Madrigals, too!" just to throw everybody else off.

"Dan told me in China that he was a Madrigal," Jonah said, his stage voice somehow cutting through the other's screams. "Dan, you want to pretend that again? Think you can fool the elevator?"

Lie, Amy thought desperately at her brother. *Deny it. Act. It's not safe to tell the truth right now.* Smashed in the back of the elevator, Amy couldn't even see Dan. She hoped he was standing close enough to the mirror that he could rise up on his tiptoes a little and secretly set off the retinal scan.

"I am a Madrigal," Dan's voice rang out boldly from the front section of the elevator. "My whole family is Madrigal. Even Nellie's a Madrigal. But it's not what you think. We're—"

He was trying to explain. Amy thought her heart might burst, listening to her brother. He was so brave.

And so foolish.

The grumblings around them turned darker and even more menacing.

"No!" Eisenhower bellowed. His voice was louder than anyone's—he was at the front of the elevator but had turned around. "I will not be on a team with Madrigals! I refuse!"

The others cowered away from Eisenhower's fury, so Amy could see over them. She saw Eisenhower grab Dan and lift him up, ready to toss him out of the elevator.

"No!" Amy screamed, shoving forward.

But her shout got lost in the automated voice calling out, "Approved. All present and accounted for."

Eisenhower must have lifted Dan past the retinal scan at exactly the right angle.

This seemed to startle Eisenhower, who took a step back, half in and half out of the elevator.

Everything happened fast after that.

Nellie broke past Mary-Todd Holt and stabbed something into Eisenhower's right arm. Amy saw a flash of silver. Was Nellie using her snake nose ring as a weapon?

Nellie screamed, "You let go of Dan," just as the pilot tugged on Eisenhower's left arm.

"Sir, sir—" the pilot began.

Are they crazy? Amy wondered. *Thinking they can fight against Eisenhower Holt with a snake nose ring and good manners?*

But Eisenhower dropped Dan with a thud. He stepped back to face his attackers. He grabbed Nellie with his right hand and the pilot with his left and swung them toward each other, as if he intended to slam their heads together.

"Nellie!" Amy screamed, pushing forward. She had no idea how she could help, but she was going to try.

She was too late.

Not because Nellie was already injured.

Not because Nellie escaped on her own.

She was too late because, just then, the door of the elevator snapped shut.

And the elevator began to zoom upward.

CHAPTER 24

"Ow! Ooh! No—don't step on my hand!" Dan screamed in the darkness.

"Dan—Dan! Are you there?" Amy yelled behind him.

"Yeah," Dan mumbled. He managed to pull his hand out from under somebody's shoe. And then he was able to mostly stand up, even though his face was smashed against the elevator door. "I'm here."

The grumbling around him had mostly turned into whispers, but somehow that was even scarier: "Madrigals. Dan and Amy are Madrigals. . . ."

"Dad! Dad! Are you there?" Hamilton called.

No answer.

"Reagan? Madison? Mom?" he tried again, even though he'd watched all of them step out of the elevator.

Still no answer.

I'm alone, Hamilton thought. *I've lost my family. I've lost my team.*

Except for Dan and Amy. And did they still count if they were Madrigals?

"Natalie?" Ian called into the darkness.

He knew she was behind him. He expected to hear her complaining: about how the crowding in the elevator was wrinkling her designer dress, about how the sea air was terrible for her hair, about how their time was running out.

Instead, his sister reached out and held his hand.

Children, Alistair thought. *It's down to just me and a bunch of children.*

He'd begun to think that he really wasn't very good around kids. Especially after all three of the Starling triplets had vanished from Stratford without even saying good-bye. And Amy and Dan—could they really be Madrigals? Was it possible?

What else might be possible?

Chill, Jonah told himself. *Be cool.*

He tightened his grip on the backpack he'd brought, stuffed with his Clues. He knew he couldn't panic now.

Not if he was going to show Mom he could win on his own.

Just think of the others as an audience, he told himself.

But audiences were all about love. All he could feel in this elevator was hate.

The elevator stopped. The door opened.

They were back at the top of the cliff.

CHAPTER 25

"Somebody hit the button to go down again!" Amy yelled, forgetting that nobody would want to help her now. "We've got to go rescue Nellie from Eisenhower Holt!"

Amy stabbed her fingers uselessly at her cell phone, trying to call Nellie. But the lit-up screen gave her the same message she'd been getting for the whole elevator ride: NO SERVICE.

Hamilton seemed to be having the same problem with his phone. He threw it to the floor in disgust.

"Yeah! Go down! We've got to go rescue my dad from . . ." A baffled look came over Hamilton's face as if he'd just realized he couldn't say Eisenhower needed to be rescued from Nellie or the helicopter pilot. Unless he really did believe that Madrigals were the most evil people on the planet. "We've got to go back for the rest of my family!" he said instead.

Alistair was feeling around on the elevator wall.

"Yes, yes, of course some of you will want to go back down," he said in an oily voice. "I'll do everything to

help you with that, just as soon as *I* get out here. . . ."
He had one foot out the door. "Hmm. I'm not finding a control panel."

Hamilton shoved his way out of the elevator and began pounding on the keypad outside.

"Down! Down! Down!" he screamed.

The elevator didn't budge.

"Ham—your family can climb up here on their own," Dan said.

"Oh, right," Hamilton said numbly.

"Fortunately, that will take a while," Alistair muttered. "And by then . . ."

By then, somebody else will have found the prize, Amy thought.

Everybody seemed to be thinking the same thing, a distraction from being outraged about Madrigals. The whole group surged forward.

"No! Don't push! I'll fall!" Jonah screamed. "You need me! You need a Janus!"

Amy reached the front of the elevator and saw what he was screaming about: There was only a narrow rock ledge and then a straight drop, all the way down to the cemetery. Amy stepped out of the elevator and immediately moved to the side, clutching the rock wall.

"Amy?" Dan said quietly beside her.

Amy braced herself for him to make fun of her fear of heights. But when she turned, Dan looked just as white-faced and terrified as she felt.

"Maybe we should . . . hang on to each other," he whispered.

Their mind-meld was working again. Amy could tell Dan had been thinking the same thing as her: *What if the others hate Madrigals so much that they decide to throw us off the cliff?*

But Dan's thought had a second part to it: *They needed someone from every branch — even the Madrigals — to get the elevator to work. They might need a Madrigal again. But they only need one of us. So . . . we have to stick together to be safe.*

Amy grabbed her brother. She turned and saw that Ian and Natalie were clinging to each other just as desperately.

Same reason, she thought. *We only need one Lucian, too.*

Alistair was watching Jonah thoughtfully.

"Need a Janus," he murmured. "Perhaps . . ." He turned toward the keypad beside Hamilton. "Perhaps someone from each of the five branches should touch this at the same time. What would happen then?"

Nobody answered him. But suddenly everyone was pushing and shoving again, each person fighting to get to the keypad.

"Come on! Now let's jump back into the elevator!" Dan yelled, tugging on Amy's arm as soon as he'd touched the keypad.

We'll go down, Amy thought. *Not back to the cemetery, but to some other level — where the prize is . . .*

Amy tripped over Jonah's feet; Dan tumbled on top of Natalie. Alistair was the last one to climb in.

He probably planned that, Amy thought. *So he'll be the first one out. The first one to get the prize.*

But the elevator didn't move.

"Perhaps my hypothesis was wrong," Alistair said.

Just then there was a whirring sound at the back of the elevator. Amy spun around to look: The entire back wall had vanished.

CHAPTER 26

The first thing Hamilton saw was more rock. The back of the elevator led into a huge cave.

All right! he thought, staring at another sheer rock wall. *Holt skills rule here, too! Get out the climbing gear!*

But then, in the dim light filtering in from outside, Hamilton saw that there were also stairs leading down in a spiral along the wall.

Hamilton considered running ahead of everyone else. He was stronger, he was faster—surely he could beat everyone else to the prize. But how would Hamilton get the prize back out past the others without his family's help?

With Amy and Dan? Hamilton wondered. *With Madrigals?*

He glanced at the two siblings, who were already pulling out flashlights and moving toward the stairs. Dan had a streak of dirt across his cheek, and his right eye looked a little swollen where Hamilton's own father had hit him. Amy was nervously twisting a lock of hair around her finger. They didn't look like evil

Madrigals. They looked as innocent as Bambi. As the Easter Bunny. As—

Hamilton's childhood hadn't exposed him to many stories about cute, cuddly, innocent creatures, so he couldn't think of the right example. But it didn't matter. Even if Amy and Dan weren't evil, they also weren't strong enough to fend off all the others if there was a fight for the prize. For that, Hamilton needed someone with muscles.

Hamilton needed his family.

"Coming, Ham?" Dan asked hopefully, as if trying to find out, *Are we still on the same team?* He and Amy were at the top of the stairs, right behind Jonah, Ian, and Natalie.

"Um," Hamilton said. "Just a minute." He glanced over his shoulder, back toward the outdoors.

"Why don't you go out and see if your family's getting close, climbing up the cliff on the other side of the elevator?" Alistair suggested, right at Hamilton's elbow.

"If I do that, you'll find some way to close the door on me!" Hamilton protested.

"No, no, I would never do anything that underhanded," Alistair said, flashing Hamilton a completely untrustworthy smile.

Hamilton saw that Alistair already had his hand over something on the wall beside the elevator—another button?

He's playing mind games with me, Hamilton thought.

If he can't lock me outside, he wants to get me mad enough that I run ahead. And then, when I'm not watching, he'll shut the door and lock out my family.

Even in sports, Hamilton hated mind games. But he kept his mouth shut and waited for Alistair to give up on his plan and start walking down the stairs.

Alistair didn't move.

Hamilton didn't move.

Alistair didn't move.

Now Ian, Natalie, Amy, Dan, and Jonah were all far ahead of them on the stairs. For all Hamilton knew, they might already be claiming the prize.

Think! Hamilton told himself. *You can't always just out-muscle everyone!*

And then Hamilton got an idea.

He dropped down low, muttering about needing to brush mud off his shoes. It was dim down near the floor. While he was crouched over, he strung together a couple of carabiner clips from his climbing kit and jammed them in the doorway of the elevator. So even if the door closed, it wouldn't close all the way.

Then — and Hamilton thought this was the brilliant part — he stood up and waited a few more minutes.

"Okay, guess I'll catch up with the others," Hamilton said nonchalantly.

He strapped on his climbing kit and began descending the stairs, into the darkness. Once he was out of Alistair's sight, he stopped to switch on a flashlight and double-check to make sure his jacket pockets still contained eleven small silver tubes—samples of each of the Clues the Holts had found.

We'll need them if this really is the end of the clue hunt, Hamilton thought. *Won't we?*

He was still thinking "we," not "I."

They'll come! He assured himself. *My family will be here soon!*

He listened hard as he began moving forward again. He'd only taken a few steps when he heard a whirring and then a click behind him. And then Alistair's uneven footsteps sounded on the stairs.

The click has to mean the carabiner clips worked, Hamilton thought.

He let Alistair pass him. He kept listening for another whirring sound that would mean his family had gotten in.

There! Was that it? Hamilton wondered. *Or—that?*

It was so hard keeping an eye on the others while also hanging back, listening for some proof that his family was right behind him.

Was that a soft footstep? Hamilton wondered. *Someone tiptoeing?*

The Holt family wasn't known for tiptoeing or taking soft footsteps, but the Clue hunt had driven them to do lots of unlikely things.

Hamilton tried to think of some way to signal the rest of his family.

What would they know that no one else would recognize? Hamilton wondered. *Oh, yeah . . .*

Hamilton began tapping out the rhythm of the University of Wisconsin fight song on the rock railing that lined the stairs.

Jonah shot him a suspicious glance from a few steps below.

"You? Trying to make music?" he asked. His eyes narrowed and he gazed around.

Just then the first stone hit the back of Hamilton's neck.

CHAPTER 27

"Stop it! Who's doing that?" Jonah screamed as pebbles rained down on him. "I'll have you know—this face is insured!"

He automatically looked around for a bodyguard to protect him, but Jonah had left all his bodyguards behind when he'd sneaked off without telling his parents. When he'd decided to be true to his own self.

Jonah imagined his mother there, taunting him, *And you thought you could win this on your own?*

Ian and Natalie dropped to the stairs together when the first stone hit.

"It can't be her. It can't be her," Natalie chanted. "Please tell me it's not her."

"Of course not," Ian said. "That would be impossible." He glanced at his watch. "We've still got time."

Another stone clattered past them.

"It's just one of the riffraff, right?" Natalie asked anxiously.

"Absolutely," Ian agreed.

He'd never realized what a lovely word *riffraff* was. The riffraff were beneath his notice. They didn't matter. They couldn't hurt him because he was superior to the riffraff of the world in every way.

But what if the riffraff beat Natalie and him to the prize?

Dan swung his flashlight around as soon as he heard Jonah and the Kabras screaming behind him.

Stones were falling from the ledge high above, where the elevator was. Dan didn't care about stones. He was more interested in the dark figure that had dislodged the stones—a figure now swinging on a rope, past the staircase.

"No! No! He—she—whoever—they're getting ahead of us!" Dan screamed.

The black figure made a perfect arc and landed at the bottom of the spiral staircase, only a few paces from a door. Then the figure turned and raced toward it.

"No!" Dan screamed. "We! Can't! Lose!"

Hamilton blinked, confused. Why hadn't *he* thought of tying a rope somewhere and swinging down past the spiral staircase?

I couldn't see where the bottom of the staircase was, he thought. *It was too dark.*

He noticed that the figure by the door was wearing the same kind of night-vision goggles that soldiers used. He felt a burst of pride that someone in his family, someone on his team—Reagan? Madison? His mom?—had been so prepared.

"Hold on! I'm coming with you!" Hamilton hollered. "I'm on your team!"

He shoved past Alistair, who was still looking back.

Ian, Natalie, and Jonah were easy to jump past, since they were crouched down on the stairs.

"I'm coming, too!" Dan screamed.

"Not while there are stones falling," Hamilton said, leaping past both Cahill kids. Hamilton didn't stop to think if he was protecting Dan or just delaying him.

Five huge steps later, Hamilton was close enough to grab the dark figure's arm.

"Reagan? Madison?" he asked. "Wait! It's me! Where are the others?"

Hamilton had probably grabbed his sisters' arms a thousand times apiece during their childhood, even if you only counted games where he held them down until they promised to do what he wanted. As he squeezed his hand tighter and tighter around the dark figure's arm, he thought, *Not enough muscle to be Reagan or Madison.* Then he thought, *Or Mom. Or certainly not Dad.*

This arm was scrawny. And—scarred.

"You're not a Holt!" Hamilton accused.

"Sure, I am!" the figure whispered. "Hammy, uh . . . bro! Let go! I'll run ahead. You hold off the others."

She was trying to pull away. Hamilton tightened his grip.

"No, you're not. You're—you're—" In his mind, Hamilton ran through the hundreds of scrawny arms he'd grabbed over the years, mostly belonging to little kids back home in Wisconsin who'd proved to be incredibly eager to give him their lunch money. Somehow, he didn't like thinking about that now. He narrowed his mental search to scrawny arms he'd grabbed during the Clue hunt. *At the Globe Theatre, the ninja in breeches* . . . "You're Sinead Starling!"

Suddenly, Hamilton understood why he could feel scars through the girl's sleeve.

She really did get hurt in that Franklin Institute explosion, Hamilton thought guiltily. *The one my family caused* . . .

His grip on Sinead's arm faltered.

CHAPTER 28

Sinead pulled away from Hamilton, but then the whole group surrounded her. Dan snatched the night-vision goggles from her head and peered through them toward the ledge Sinead had swung from.

"Her brothers," he gasped. "If they're right behind her—"

"Oh, no," Sinead said, trying for a carefree tone. "I left Ned and Ted back in Stratford. It only takes one Starling to outsmart you losers."

She hoped no one could hear the way her voice trembled, the way she had to hold herself back from saying, *I left them where they'd be safe. I knew this would be the most dangerous part of the clue hunt.*

She could feel the danger in everyone's cold stares.

"Let's tie her up and leave her behind," Ian said.

"But if her brothers do come and rescue her . . ." Natalie began.

"You don't know if I'm lying or not, do you?" Sinead challenged.

She waited for everyone to break out fighting, as

they had back at the Globe. That way, she could just slip past them. But the rest of the group just stood frozen, gazing suspiciously at her and each other.

At least they're too suspicious of each other to gang up on me, Sinead thought.

"How'd you get here, anyhow?" Dan challenged.

"I solved the hint from the Stratford church," Sinead said. "Unlike the rest of you, who just followed Amy and Dan." Everyone except Amy and Dan looked away guiltily. "Then I invented an ultralight plane to fly out here and land on the top of the cliff. I just had an intuition that I might need to include new technology for landing in such a tight space. After that, it was no big deal to reprogram the doorway to let me in."

She decided not to mention that even though she was the one who'd stolen the computer disk in Stratford, Ted had figured it out. And Ned had invented the ultralight airplane long before the Clue hunt. And the bit about reprogramming the doorway was a complete lie, meant only to flush out whoever had left the carabiner clips there.

Hamilton's face turned slightly red—*Aha,* Sinead thought.

"Really, you're going to need my help going the rest of the way toward the prize," Sinead bragged. "Just look. There's a riddle right on that door that I bet none of the rest of you are going to be able to solve."

She pointed to a sign she was sure no one else had noticed.

It read:

> # ON THIS ISLAND
> ## A FAMILY SPLIT APART.
>
> # ON THIS ISLAND
> ## A FAMILY CAN REUNITE.

"There's an extra syllable in the second line, if that's supposed to be poetry," Sinead said. "And an anagram of 'reunite' is 'uni-tree,' which is undoubtedly a botanical reference. And—"

"Sinead, that's not a *riddle*," Amy said. "It's the truth. It's—it's what the Madrigals are hoping for."

She pushed past Sinead and shoved the door open.

"See?"

CHAPTER 29

Amy's hands shook as she held the door. She dared to glance back over her shoulder at the others.

"Madrigals have wanted to get the family back together since the very beginning," she said softly. "We're descended from Madeleine, the fifth child of Gideon and Olivia Cahill. And—"

"They didn't have five children!" Hamilton protested. "They had four!"

The others nodded and grumbled, agreeing with Hamilton, not Amy.

She swallowed hard and forced herself to go on.

"Olivia was pregnant when Gideon died. Madeleine was born after the others fought and scattered. And then it wasn't safe to tell." Amy didn't feel safe now. She tried to finish. "So the Madrigals just want to stop the fighting. They want harmony. Peace. For . . . for . . ."

She couldn't quite speak the word *forgiveness* in front of Alistair, who'd helped kill her parents, and Jonah and Ian and Natalie, who'd tried to kill her and

Dan. Or even Sinead, who'd never been anything but mean.

"Turns out we're the good guys," Dan chipped in.

"Oh, right," Ian sneered. "And that's why Madrigals are always stealing other branches' clues, destroying all their plans—"

"To keep any one branch from having too much power," Dan explained. "For balance."

Amy couldn't tell if anyone believed him. She swung her flashlight forward, through the doorway. The light illuminated another door and another keypad, with a very obvious purpose this time. This keypad held five buttons in a circle, each one labeled:

"Look at that," Amy said. "Doesn't that prove the Madrigals want everyone to get along? Because someone from each branch needs to be here before anyone can go on?"

Nobody answered. They were too busy surging forward to press the buttons. Alistair and Sinead each seemed to be trying to elbow past the other to get to the Ekat button first. Alistair was also watching Ian and Natalie, and Amy and Dan.

Amy's heart sank.

He thinks the keypad could backfire, dividing people within each branch, instead of uniting anyone, Amy thought. *And he's right. It could. Not with me and Dan, but the others . . .*

The door clicked open and everyone scrambled through, casting suspicious glances at one another.

Amy sagged against a wall. She must have accidentally hit some sort of switch because the room was suddenly bathed in light.

"Another museum?" Dan groaned.

It was.

Just like at the other branches' strongholds, Amy thought.

Looking at the roomful of display cases steadied her. Unlike the Janus museum, with its amazing art, or the Ekat museum, with its dazzling and horrifying inventions, these exhibits were fairly plain. An ordinary-looking wooden table stood in the very center of the room, as if occupying the place of honor.

Amy drifted toward it.

The table had a display case on top, containing two sheets of paper: one, clearly ancient, was covered with old-fashioned writing in an indecipherable language —

Gaelic, maybe? The other page was crisp and white and typewritten, with a label at the top:

A TRANSLATION FROM
OLIVIA CAHILL'S
ORIGINAL ACCOUNTS

Amy gasped and began reading:

Our family dining table was one of the few items saved from that awful fire in 1507. This was due to mere happenstance, as I had had Thomas and Luke carry it outside earlier in the day so that I might clean and polish it in the bright sunlight. I did not know the darkness that was to come. I look at the table now and can still remember happier times: my husband, my children, myself, all whole and alive, laughing and talking over bean soup or porridge. . . . I sit at this table with only Madeleine now, her with her bread and jam, me with my sorrows, and I tell her, "Bring them back. Gather them here again." I will not see Gideon again on this earth, but my dearest wish would be to see Luke and Katherine, Thomas and Jane—and Madeleine and me!—all sitting around this table together. Please, Madeleine, please . . .

The words trailed off, and then there was more, clearly written at a later time:

My dearest wish will never be fulfilled. Madeleine's searches bring her news only of deaths, scattered around the globe. I cannot recount them all—the pain is too great. I cannot accept that my children have died so far from me and from one another, in such estrangement. Madeleine tries to comfort me with the notion that now there will be many waiting for me in the next world—happier versions of themselves, more forgiving, less contentious. And, in truth, I long for that. I am an old woman; I am not far from the next world myself. But I still have hopes and fears in this one. I know that my husband's ambitions and aspirations unleashed devastation and horror on our family; it is my greatest fear that my family might—nay, has already begun to—unleash even more devastation on the world at large. I believe this can be stopped only if my family comes together again and forgives the past. It is too late for Luke and Katherine and Thomas and Jane, but perhaps their children, or their children's children . . . I have a new dearest wish. It is that someday a descendant of each of my children—even Madeleine's—will sit at this table together. They will let bygones be bygones. They will carry from the past only that which can be helpful to the future. And then the Cahill family will be at peace.

Amy had tears in her eyes when she stopped reading. She trailed her fingertips along the tabletop—the tabletop a happy family had eaten at for many years before tragedy and betrayal shattered their lives. She remembered how upset her own mother had always been when Amy and Dan squabbled when they were little.

Olivia Cahill had been that kind of mother, too. All she wanted was for her children—or their descendants—to get along.

On this island a family split apart. On this island a family can reunite, Amy thought. *Can it be as simple as everyone sitting down at a table together?*

She hastily brushed her tears away. She turned around, ready to suggest this to everyone else. But something stopped her.

The worst thing Dan and I ever did as little kids was fight over toys, Amy thought. *It wasn't that big a deal that Mom always got us to make up. But Olivia Cahill—and the Madrigals—expect everyone to "let bygones be bygones" when the "bygones" are murder?*

She could feel her heart hardening a little, the pain of her parents' deaths outweighing anything she felt about Olivia Cahill's wishes.

It just isn't possible, she told herself, the thought she'd kept returning to ever since Jamaica.

Just then there was a rumble overhead, a sound like thunder. The floor itself seemed to shudder.

And boulders began plummeting down from the ceiling.

CHAPTER 30

Amy dived under Olivia Cahill's table.

"Dan! Over here!" she screamed. "Hamilton!"

The lights snapped off, plunging the room into total darkness. Now Amy could only hear the falling rocks, not see them.

This was worse.

"Dan! Dan! Dan!" she screamed.

She could hear Dan and Hamilton calling out to her, Ian and Natalie calling out to each other.

"Everyone under the table!" Amy called out to all of them. "It's the safest place!"

Then she heard something hit hard on the table above her. The table leg she was clutching cracked.

What if no place was safe?

Dan grabbed Hamilton's arm and took off running toward his sister's voice.

"This way!" he screamed.

The falling rocks cracked and exploded around them, throwing up rock dust.

Dan couldn't breathe.

"Go on without—" He tried to scream.

Hamilton didn't listen. Hamilton lifted him up and carried him.

"It's her!" Natalie screamed hysterically. "It's her!"

"Just run!" Ian screamed back to his sister.

He heard Amy calling out something about a safe place.

He started running toward her voice.

Alistair staggered and fell, his cane knocked out of his hand. He checked quickly to make sure none of the secret compartments in the cane had sprung open, nothing had spilled out. But he was disoriented—it felt like the rocky ground had jumped up and hit him.

And was still hitting him.

Maybe that was because the air was full of rocks, too.

"Can't," he murmured. "Can't move."

He'd faked his own death in a cave-in back in Korea, tricking Amy and Dan and Bae. Was this fate's way of laughing at him? Could he die in a cave-in for real, so close to the final prize?

"Can't . . . die . . . now," he whispered.

"Oh, no," a voice said above him. Hands started tugging on his shoulders, pulling him away from the rocks. "I'm not going to let you die."

It was Sinead.

Now a new word formed on Alistair's lips: *Why?*

Why would anyone save him?

Jonah was alone, ahead of everyone else.

When the world began to collapse around him, he could hear the others calling out names: "Dan!" "Amy!" "Hamilton!" "Ian!"

No one called out for him.

A rock hit his shoulder, knocking him down.

Hundreds of thousands of people call out my name every night, he told himself. *"Jonah! Jonah! JONAH!"*

He could hear the rhythm of his fans' screams in the rocks hitting the ground around him.

Another rock hit his leg, pinning him to the ground.

I'm one of the biggest stars in the world, he told himself. More rocks fell down on him. *And . . . I'm going to die in a place where nobody cares.*

CHAPTER 31

Hamilton still had a flashlight. As soon as the rocks stopped falling, he pulled it out and shone it down at Dan.

Dan was gasping for breath.

"He needs . . . he needs . . ." Hamilton began.

"His inhaler," Amy said.

Frantically, she searched her brother's pockets. The dust in the air was bothering her, too. It made her eyes water, her lungs seize up, her throat close over.

Or was that her own fear, her own panic?

"Not Dan," she whispered. "Please not Dan."

"Is this it?" Hamilton asked, holding up the inhaler, which had fallen out just a few inches away.

Amy snatched it from Hamilton's hand and shoved the inhaler into her brother's mouth.

"Breathe," she whispered.

Dan began taking in air.

Amy slumped back against the table leg. *When did Dan start carrying his own inhaler instead of relying on Nellie?* she wondered. She resisted the urge to dive down and hug him and scream out, "Thank you for being responsible!"

He would hate that.

Amy felt too light-headed to think straight. She forced herself to calm down and look around. Olivia's table had proved to be a safe place. It was only splintered a little, with jagged bits of wood jutting out here and there. But all around it lay huge rocks — rocks that could have killed any one of them.

She drew in a ragged breath and looked at Hamilton.

"You saved Dan's life," she said. "Like you saved mine back in Australia."

She expected Hamilton to go all macho on her, maybe even brag about how he could have lifted five-hundred-pound boulders out of the way if he'd had to. But Hamilton was breathing raggedly, too.

"I owed you," Hamilton said. "Both of you. Because of all those times my family tried to hurt you early in the clue hunt. And . . ." His face twisted. "And I think maybe those rocks fell because of my family. Because they were trying to explode their way into the elevator shaft. The shock waves would have traveled here."

Amy stared at Hamilton, who looked as anguished as Dan.

Exploding the elevator shaft was the kind of thing the Holts would have done early on. But they'd pretty much stopped being so violent.

Oh, Amy realized. *Because of Hamilton's influence? And now he's not with them, so . . .*

"Maybe it was just a regular old earthquake," Amy said. It was funny how blaming an earthquake could be soothing. "They happen."

"Not in Ireland," Sinead said. She was huddled under the table just past Hamilton. "Not usually."

She seemed to be trying to sound as scornful as ever, but her voice trembled, almost sliding over into sobs.

"Madrigals," Alistair mumbled. He was lying on the floor beside Sinead. Even in the weak glow of the flashlight Amy could tell that his face was clammy and his breathing was as shallow as Dan's. "Madrigals are punishing us."

"No." Amy shook her head stubbornly. "That's not what the Madrigals are about. I know it's hard for all of you to believe, but Madrigals really are trying to make peace."

Alistair's expression didn't change.

"It had to be someone who's after the prize," Natalie said, her voice high-pitched and panicky.

Amy realized that Ian and Natalie were huddled together just past Alistair, right at the edge of the table.

Would this be good enough for Olivia Cahill? Amy wondered. *Her descendants didn't sit at the table together, but we are cowering together under it: Madrigals, Tomas, Ekats, Lucians, and, and . . .*

Amy looked around, squinting into darkness.

"Maybe Sinead's brothers set off the explosion," Ian

suggested in a tight voice. "Or Cora Wizard. Maybe she doesn't trust Jonah anymore."

"Oh, no. Oh, no," Amy said. She grabbed the flashlight from Hamilton's grip and directed the beam out into the rubble and rocks. "Where's Jonah?"

They found him under a pile of rocks, the top half of his body wedged partially under a huge display case labeled THE MADRIGALS' QUEST FOR PEACE.

Lester, Dan thought weakly, his head still woozy from the asthma attack. Or maybe it would be woozy regardless. *Lester, Irina, Mom and Dad. And now . . .*

"He's still breathing!" Hamilton announced, easing rocks away.

"He is?" Dan said, astonished.

"Barely," Sinead said, bending over Jonah. She began poking and prodding. "He's going to be in a lot of pain when he wakes up. Both legs are definitely broken, and probably a couple ribs and—"

"Patch him up enough to keep him from dying and let's get going," Ian said tensely.

"What?" Amy gasped. "Didn't you hear what Sinead said? He needs help! Medical treatment! Someone needs to take him back!"

"Who would do that?" Ian asked mockingly. "And how?" He pointed. "The door we came through—it's completely blocked."

Dan hadn't noticed this before. He'd been too busy

trying to get his breath back, then looking for Jonah. But now Hamilton turned their one working flashlight toward the original door. It wasn't even visible through the pile of rock surrounding it.

"There's only one way out of here," Ian said, pointing now toward the opposite end of the room, where the floor began to slant. "Down to the end."

"So why aren't you running ahead?" Alistair taunted. "Leaving the bleeding hearts behind to take care of Jonah while you win the prize?"

"Because the *Madrigals* won't let me," Ian said, glaring at Amy and Dan. "They're the ones who designed this place, right?"

Dan saw Amy give a barely perceptible nod.

"I looked at the door ahead of us, too," Ian said. "It's another one that requires fingerprints from all five branches." He looked bleakly down at Jonah's unconscious body. "Do you think Jonah's fingerprint will still work if he dies?"

"You're making the others hate us," Natalie whispered in Ian's ear. "They think you might kill Jonah on purpose. And that you might kill them. Don't you remember Mum always says it's best to be charming right up until—"

"Don't quote Mum to me," Ian growled.

Natalie blinked back tears.

Don't you think I hear her voice in my head, too? Ian

wanted to yell at his little sister. It was so hard to step back from everything his mother had taught him, to even consider what he might think on his own.

He glanced back over his shoulder to where the others were bracing Jonah's broken legs with his own backpack. Then they pulled Jonah into a sling improvised from a United Nations flag from one of the display cases. Evidently, the Madrigals claimed to have helped found the UN — and every other peace-related organization in the past five hundred years.

More lies, Ian thought. *Whatever. It's not important now.*

"Hurry!" he urged the others.

Dan, Amy, and Hamilton had started searching through the rubble, looking for another working flashlight. Sinead and Alistair were assembling an odd assortment of items — wire, ropes, batteries, display case frames, the shattered night-vision goggles. Maybe they were trying to *build* another flashlight.

"There isn't time for that!" Ian insisted. "Come on!"

Alistair looked up from his own search through one of the display cases.

"So eager to move along . . ." he murmured. "Are you herding us toward some trap laid by your mother?"

"No! Away from her!" Ian exploded.

Natalie shook her head frantically, trying to signal her brother.

"We have to tell," Ian said. "They won't listen otherwise."

Natalie gulped.

"We tricked Mum," she said in a wobbly voice. "Before we went to Stratford, we told her the next clue was at the Folger Shakespeare Library. In Washington, DC."

"She would have taken you with her," Hamilton accused.

"She tried to!" Natalie said. "But she booked her ticket in first class and just put Ian and me in . . . *economy*."

She whispered the last word, as if it were too embarrassing to speak aloud.

"So we got on the plane, but then we sneaked out and up to Stratford," Ian explained. "We knew we would have only as much time as it would take for her to fly to DC, find out we'd tricked her, and fly back."

"Back to England, sure, but she wouldn't know you're *here*," Dan offered.

"Oh, she'd find out," Natalie said. "She's scary that way."

"We checked the flight schedules," Ian said. "We didn't think she could be here yet but . . ."

"She's scary that way," Amy whispered.

Everyone was silent, their faces dark in the dim glow of the single flashlight.

"So what?" Hamilton said, his booming jock voice so loud it made Ian flinch. "Even if she gets to the island, how's she going to get through *that*?"

He pointed to the pile of rubble that blocked the door.

"She'll use explosives," Ian said. "Again."

Ian saw the others catching on: *Isabel caused the first explosion.*

She wouldn't care whom she hurt or killed with more explosions.

It wouldn't be safe in this room if she tried to explode her way in.

"Hamilton, you and Ian carry Jonah," Amy said. "You two are the strongest. Dan, you carry the flashlight. Hold it high."

Ian didn't want to carry Jonah. He wanted to be unencumbered so he could dash off and leave everyone else behind when they reached the final prize. But right now, it was more important to get moving.

He lifted one end of the UN flag while Hamilton hoisted up the other. They stumbled forward, tripping every few steps. At the door out, Ian was even the one who held Jonah's finger up to the Janus button.

Of course there was another door after the first one. It was covered with a large sign. Dan held the flashlight close so they could all read it:

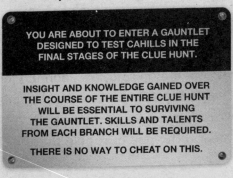

YOU ARE ABOUT TO ENTER A GAUNTLET DESIGNED TO TEST CAHILLS IN THE FINAL STAGES OF THE CLUE HUNT.

INSIGHT AND KNOWLEDGE GAINED OVER THE COURSE OF THE ENTIRE CLUE HUNT WILL BE ESSENTIAL TO SURVIVING THE GAUNTLET. SKILLS AND TALENTS FROM EACH BRANCH WILL BE REQUIRED.

THERE IS NO WAY TO CHEAT ON THIS.

Ian smirked.

There's always a way to cheat, he thought.

His smirk faded. Were those just words his mother had taught him? Or was it what he truly believed?

"Do you trust Ian?" Dan whispered to Amy.

"Of course not," Amy whispered back. "But for now . . . we sort of have to, don't we?"

Ahead of them, Dan could see Ian and Hamilton working together to lift Jonah over a particularly large boulder. They were in a narrow tunnel now, with nothing but rock all around them. Dan's flashlight cast eerie shadows everywhere.

Dan turned a corner, and another door loomed before them with more signs:

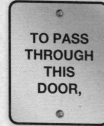  

TO PASS THROUGH THIS DOOR, **YOU MUST ANSWER THIS QUESTION:** **WHAT WAS MOZART'S SISTER'S NAME?**

But the door was already open, hanging half off its hinges.

Nobody bothered even to whisper "Nannerl" as they went through.

The group reached another door, with another keypad labeled with the names of the five branches.

This door was also hanging open.

"I'm sure there will be more doors coming up that are locked," Amy said shrilly. "That we'll need everyone for, even Jonah—"

Dan tried to catch his sister's eye.

We could run ahead, he thought at her. *I'm holding the only flashlight. If all the doors are going to be hanging open, we could leave the others behind in the dark, and—*

Just then, the ground began to shake again, and stones began to fall from the ceiling.

This time there was no table to shelter them.

CHAPTER 32

Dan instinctively crouched down, his hands clutched over his head, the flashlight tucked under his arm.

Someone tapped him on the back.

"No! Stand up!" Alistair screamed in his ear. "Less surface area for the rocks to hit!"

It made sense.

Dan scrambled to his feet as the rocks kept plunging down.

"Flat against the wall is safest!" Alistair shouted.

Dan pressed himself back against the hard rock wall. He swung his flashlight around and saw the others standing tight against the wall, too. Jonah couldn't, of course, but Ian and Hamilton held his sling as close as possible.

Dan saw a huge stone fall inches from Amy's face. Even with the thundering rocks, he could hear Sinead screaming, "Not again! Not again!"

And he could feel Alistair's hand on his shoulder. Steadying him.

"Keep the flashlight away from the falling rocks!"

Alistair shouted at him. He leaned closer. "Want me to hold it for you?"

"No, thanks!" Dan said, transferring the flashlight to the opposite hand. He held it behind his back.

And he flinched away from Alistair's hand.

He wasn't trying to save my life or protect me, Dan thought furiously. *He was getting into position to steal the flashlight as soon as this is over! He wants to run ahead, too!*

The falling rocks slowed to a trickle, then stopped entirely.

"Is—is everybody okay?" Amy asked shakily.

Ian looked appraisingly at the others.

"We've got scrapes and cuts, but that's it," he said. "Let's move on."

But there was a pile of rubble in their path. Hamilton and Ian had to work together to move some of the biggest rocks just so they could advance.

Ergh! We all need to stay together because of the explosions! Dan thought.

At least Alistair seemed to realize that, too.

He patted Dan's back and didn't try to move his hand toward the flashlight.

"I knew I could get us safely through that one!" Alistair said. "You know, I once promised your parents—"

Dan whirled on Alistair.

"Don't you *ever* talk to me about promises!" he hissed. "You don't even know what they are!"

> **WHO
> WAS
> SHAKA
> ZULU?**

> **WHY DOES
> A MÖBIUS
> STRIP SEEM
> IMPOSSIBLE?**

> **OF THE SMALL NUMBER
> OF FEMALE PHARAOHS
> IN ANCIENT EGYPT,
> WHICH ONE HAD
> THE LONGEST REIGN?**

They stepped through broken door after broken door in between explosions. Even Amy barely bothered to read the questions anymore. Dimly, she saw that the Madrigals must have been trying to bond the branches together with the questions.

Yeah, maybe a normal family would bond playing Trivial Pursuit, she thought. *But Cahills? Never.*

They reached another door with another sign:

> **AS A PRINTER, BENJAMIN FRANKLIN
> COULD ORDER LARGE AMOUNTS
> OF THIS SUBSTANCE WITHOUT RAISING
> SUSPICIONS. BUT CLUE HUNTERS WHO
> FOLLOWED HIM KNOW THAT HE WAS
> ACTUALLY TRYING TO REPLICATE THE
> WORK OF HIS ANCESTOR GIDEON CAHILL.**
>
> **WHAT IS THIS INGREDIENT?**

Iron solute, Amy thought automatically. *That was the first clue we found.*

So the Madrigals expected the Clue hunters to be so friendly by this point that they'd be sharing Clues?

Never in a million years, Amy thought.

Thirty-six, Ian thought. *Thirty-seven. Thirty-eight.*

He'd been counting the doors with questions ever since they'd entered the gauntlet. He was certain that the thirty-ninth door would be the last one.

Keeping one hand on Jonah's sling, he dodged away from the beam of the flashlight and, in the near-darkness, brushed his fingers against Natalie's arm.

She looked up at him, her eyes huge and questioning.

Will she understand? he wondered. *As soon as I step through this doorway, I'm going to roll Jonah backward to knock down everybody else. She should grab the flashlight from Dan and we'll take off running. Then we'll be the first ones to reach the prize.*

He couldn't be certain she'd know what to do. He had to whisper in her ear, which made the others gaze at him suspiciously.

Never mind. They won't have time to react, Ian thought.

He reached out to push aside the last door.

This door was firmly locked.

And it held a question Ian couldn't answer.

CHAPTER 33

OUTSIDERS BELIEVE THAT
THIS LOST PLAY OF SHAKESPEARE'S
IS A SEQUEL TO ONE OF HIS COMEDIES.
BUT MADRIGALS KNOW THAT
THE PLAY ACTUALLY DESCRIBED
MADRIGALS' HOPES FOR THE CAHILL
FAMILY TO REUNITE.

WHAT IS THE NAME OF THE PLAY?

Dan swiveled his head toward Amy, ready to hear her call out a triumphant answer.

But Amy was biting her lip.

"I don't know. Sorry," she said, her face ghostly white in the dim flashlight glow. "I only had two days to study up on Shakespeare. Do you know, Alistair? Sinead?"

"I never knew Shakespeare was a Cahill," Alistair said angrily. "How was I supposed to know anything about him?"

Sinead just shook her head.

Ian cast a frightened glance back into the darkness, where the explosions kept happening. They seemed to be getting closer.

"We've got to get this," he muttered. "We don't have much time!"

He put his end of Jonah's sling down on the ground and began typing on a keypad beside the door. It had letter keys like a cell phone.

"I'll try *Reunion*," he muttered. "No. *Peace*. No." He slammed his hand against the keys. "Stupid, useless, worthless—"

"Maybe it's *Romeo and Juliet Kiss and Make Up*," Dan suggested.

"Dan, *Romeo and Juliet* is a tragedy, not a comedy," Amy said. "And both of them die at the end of the play, so there couldn't be a sequel."

Dan hadn't known that. He kind of wished he didn't know it now.

"Pretty much the entire younger generation dies in that play," Sinead muttered.

Dan glanced around. Almost the entire younger generation of Cahills was here, trapped in this cave.

"Maybe Jonah knows the answer," Dan said, his voice raspy.

He went over and gently shook Jonah's shoulders.

Jonah moaned, his face contorted in pain.

Natalie leaned down and slapped him.

"Jonah!" she shouted. "You have to wake up and answer a question!"

Jonah's eyelids fluttered.

"Wha—wha—" he began weakly. ". . .'Sup?"

"What do you know about lost Shakespeare plays?" Natalie asked.

"Don't tell . . . fans . . . I know . . ." Jonah murmured.

"But tell us," Ian demanded. "Tell us, or you might bleed to death, right here."

Could he? Dan wondered. Even in the dim light, he could see dark spots growing on the cloths Sinead had wrapped around Jonah's legs as improvised bandages. Jonah probably had lost a lot of blood.

"*Double Falsehood,*" Jonah whispered, still wincing in pain. "*The History of Cardenio.* And *Love's Labour's—*"

"*Love's Labour's Lost* is a Shakespeare play everybody knows about," Sinead scoffed.

"Not *Lost,*" Jonah murmured. "*Won. Love's Labour's Won.*"

"We'll try it," Amy said, rushing to the keypad. She typed in the answer—and the door clicked open.

In the next second, Dan felt the flashlight being yanked from his hand.

"Hey!" he yelled.

Natalie zoomed away from him, holding up the flashlight like a prize. The beam swung crazily around, highlighting the ceiling and then the floor on the other side of the door.

Dan gasped.

"No, Natalie! Wait!" he screamed. "You'll—"

Natalie crashed forward, her first step through the doorway plunging her over the side of a cliff. Dan grabbed desperately for her, managing to grab her ankle. The momentum of her body yanked him toward the cliff as well.

Dan felt Amy's hands on his foot. But now she was sliding forward, too.

"AHHHHH!" Natalie cried.

"Help!" Dan screamed.

"Somebody! Please!" Amy begged.

Dan could see the flashlight continuing to fall, down and down and down.

And then everything went dark.

CHAPTER 34

"Natalie!" Ian screamed. "Natalie, no!"

He dived forward, aiming blindly for the spot where he'd last seen Dan and Amy and his sister. He ended up in a jumble in the doorway. Somebody's elbow was in his ear, and somebody else's knee was in his back, and somebody else's face was smashed against his arm. The only other time Ian had been in such a twisted knot of arms and legs was back at the Globe, when everyone was fighting over the next hint.

This time everyone was trying to save Natalie and Amy and Dan.

"I'm going to die!" Natalie screamed from below.

"No, no, I'm holding on to you," Dan said frantically, beneath Ian. "But I need help—"

"I'm trying!" Hamilton grunted, near Ian's ear.

A weight shifted above him—evidently Hamilton was right on top of him.

"No!" Ian screamed. "If you lean forward, we'll all slide over the cliff! You'll knock us over!"

"Then what am I supposed to do?" Hamilton grumbled.

"Hold my ankles," Ian said. "Anchor me."

To his surprise, Hamilton shifted backward and did as Ian said.

"Sinead, you hold on to Amy," Alistair instructed.

Anchored by Hamilton's firm grip, Ian reached toward the sound of his sister's voice. He got a hold on her ankle, his hand right beside Dan's. They both pulled, working in tandem.

And then Natalie was sitting with everyone else at the top of the cliff, in the doorway. She sobbed in the darkness.

"I could have died," she wailed. "I thought I was going to die. . . ."

"You're okay now," Ian said, hugging her. "You're safe."

He could feel bloody scrapes on her arms and face; he was probably getting blood all over himself. He didn't care.

Dan saved Natalie, just like Amy saved me back on Everest, he thought. He felt a slight pang of guilt about what he'd been planning to do.

And what he *still* planned to do.

He didn't want to think about that right now. All he had room for in his brain was relief.

"You're safe," he repeated to Natalie.

For now.

Amy sat in the dark, listening to the others talk. When she couldn't see their faces, they sounded different.

More scared. More battered and bruised and aching and anguished—just like Amy felt.

"What do we do now?" Dan asked, his voice shaking.

"Mum is coming," Natalie moaned. "I lost the flashlight and there's a cliff we can't even see and now we can't go on. . . . She'll catch us before—"

"Flint," Sinead said.

"What?" Hamilton said. Amy heard total confusion in his voice. "Why would you talk about a city in Michigan at a time like this?"

"Not Flint the city," Sinead said. "Flint the mineral."

"For fire," Alistair said.

Ooooh, Amy thought. *Then there's a chance . . .*

"I'm sure I saw some traces of flint in the rocks of this tunnel," Sinead said. "If we start striking rocks against the walls and hold up bits of rope against the rock as soon as we see a spark . . ."

"Then maybe we'll be able to have torches," Alistair said. "It's a pity we don't have any gasoline or lighter fluid to soak the ropes in."

"Would perfume help?" Natalie asked, shifting sideways. Amazingly, she'd kept a grip on her purse, even when she was dangling by one ankle over the cliff.

"Only you would be carrying around perfume at a time like this," Amy said.

"No, Mu—" Natalie began. She stopped. "No, I'm not."

But Amy knew what she'd been about to say: *No, Mum would, too.*

It was hard in the dark, but they all maneuvered around so that in a few moments they had strands of rope lying on the floor. Natalie began dowsing them in her perfume.

As soon as the first whiff of it hit Amy's nose, she recoiled.

"That perfume! It's—" Dan started gagging.

"I know! I know! It's the same as Mum's! I'm sorry!" Natalie wailed.

The scent was like Isabel's evil whispering all around them: *I'm coming for you. You can never win against me. I killed your parents. Don't you know I'll kill you, too?*

It was all Amy could do to force herself to take one of the perfume-soaked ropes. She began bashing a rock against the wall with extra fervor. Around her, everyone else was hitting the walls just as hard.

"You're too loud!" Ian screamed. "You'll lead Mum right to us!"

For a moment, everyone paused, the evil scent swirling around them.

"There's only one path through the tunnel," Alistair said quietly. "If what you say is true, Isabel is coming toward us no matter what."

They all went back to hitting the wall. Again and again and again and again . . .

Hamilton was the first one to get a spark—probably because he could hit the hardest. Then he tried to get a second spark to leap to the perfume-soaked rope.

"Hold it closer," Dan suggested.

"Separate the rope fibers more—down to individual strands," Alistair suggested.

"Go faster," Ian suggested.

"Every single one of you—shut up!" Hamilton commanded, pounding harder with the rocks.

Amy leaned weakly against the wall. Were those footsteps she heard in the distance or just the echo of Hamilton's pounding?

The tunnel swam with Isabel's scent. Amy felt as if she were drowning in it. Drowning in perfume and fear and darkness and Isabel's evil . . .

There's no hope, she thought.

And then Hamilton's rope strand caught fire.

Amy ignited her section of rope from Hamilton's as everyone else crowded in to do the same.

"Hey, hey, watch it," Hamilton grumbled as Dan swung his rope around. "Don't go setting me on fire."

The ropes were too limp to work well as torches. They couldn't be held aloft. Amy could only carry hers awkwardly off to the side, the flames licking up dangerously toward her hand.

Amy didn't like holding fire any more than she'd liked smelling the perfume. Each leaping flame reminded her of that awful night her parents died, that awful night Irina died.

"What good does it do to have light if there's nothing but a cliff ahead of us?" Natalie grumbled.

"There's a ledge," Alistair said, holding his own rope torch out before him. "Off to the side." He stepped out onto it but kept his burning rope down low, by the cliff. "This is such an odd pattern for a crater, if all the explosions were above us. I wonder . . ."

"What?" Ian asked, his voice thick with anxiety. "What does it mean?"

"I couldn't say," Alistair said.

Even with all the burning ropes, it was too dark for Amy to read Alistair's expression. She couldn't tell if he was honestly puzzled, or if he was holding back information, as he had so many times before.

They all inched forward along the ledge.

Don't think about the dark, gaping hole before you, Amy told herself. *Don't think about how you'll die if your foot slips. Don't think about how Dan could die if he slips. Don't think about fire and death. Think about . . .*

"Jonah?" she called out into the darkness. She wasn't even sure if he was still conscious. "How are you doing?"

"Yo, I've been better," he said weakly. Ian and Hamilton were still carrying him, but they kept

having to swing him out over the cliff to avoid knocking him against outcroppings of rock.

Now that she was listening, she could hear Jonah
gasping softly every few paces, probably because of
his broken bones being jarred.

Was it crueler to take Jonah along or to leave him
behind?

And let Isabel find him? Amy thought with a shiver.
That would be cruelest of all.

The ledge sloped sharply downward, a seemingly
endless descent. Amy wondered if they were back down
to the level of the beach and the cemetery yet. Maybe
they were even lower than that. Maybe they were
beneath the ocean.

"Here's another locked door," Alistair called from
the front of the line. "And—another keypad for five
of us to hit."

It took some shifting around to get someone from
each branch to the front of the line. They hit the buttons
on the keypad, and then there was a long pause.

"Did we do something wrong?" Dan asked. "It's
not—"

Just then the door swung open.

This time everyone was cautious stepping forward.
Even before she'd crossed the threshold, Amy could
tell that the darkness before her was a much larger
space than the narrow corridors they'd been climbing
through most of the day. Beneath her feet, rather than
endless rock, there was a stone-and-mortar patterned

floor. Dark marks stained the floor—ash? A memory of ash?

"Look," Dan breathed beside her.

He held his burning rope up so Amy could see a metal plaque on the wall:

**THIS IS ALL THAT REMAINS
OF THE LABORATORY
OF GIDEON CAHILL
1507**

CHAPTER 35

"This is where Gideon Cahill made his serum!" Dan hissed. "So this must be where the prize is!"

Belatedly, he realized that he shouldn't have spoken so loudly. But it didn't matter—everybody else was peering at the plaque, too.

"We have to be first!" Dan shouted at Amy. He grabbed her arm, pulling her deeper into the darkness. "We have to!"

Ian and Hamilton dropped Jonah's sling simultaneously, causing Jonah to scream in pain.

"Sorry, dude," Hamilton muttered. "I'll—"

What? Make it up to Jonah someday? He couldn't. Not unless he shared the prize with Jonah, too, and Hamilton had no intention of doing *that*.

Hamilton took off running, leaving Jonah behind.

"Natalie!" Ian cried out. "We have to beat everyone else! You know what to do!"

He gazed around frantically, his rope torch illuminating such a small space around him. Broken glass crunched under his feet. He was so rich, so handsome, so talented, so smart. But it was heartbreaking—none of that guaranteed that he and Natalie would win.

The pain was unbearable.

You could just let go, Jonah told himself. Already he was slipping in and out of consciousness, imagining lights dancing all around the room.

But Jonah had been battling to be the biggest star in the world ever since he could pick up a microphone. He wasn't one to give up. And this battle was even more important.

He propped himself up on his elbows and began crawling.

"This is for you, Ned and Ted," Sinead whispered.

She peered down at a rack that must once have contained test tubes—or whatever the 1507 equivalent was. Perhaps there was a trace of something important in the blobs of wax melted on the rack. Or perhaps something had seeped down into the charred table beneath the rack.

Too many possibilities, Sinead thought despairingly. *Too much to sort through too quickly.*

But she had to find the serum. It was Ned and Ted's only chance.

The children are all faster than you, Alistair reminded himself. *So you have to be craftier.*

While the others ran about desperately, Alistair watched the glow of their bobbing lights.

A table in the middle of the room, Alistair thought. *A wall to the right.*

And to the left?

No matter how far the others ventured to the left, Alistair saw no other wall, no end to the open space.

And so that's the way to go, Alistair thought.

He began tiptoeing away from the others.

"Watch where Alistair's going!" Amy called out to Dan.

Dan nodded and veered to the left. Even in the near-total darkness, Dan could tell that the room opened out—maybe becoming another room? He dodged another charred table and a fallen beam. He swung close enough to the wall to see another metal plaque:

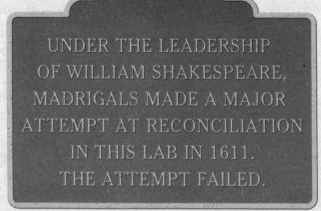

UNDER THE LEADERSHIP
OF WILLIAM SHAKESPEARE,
MADRIGALS MADE A MAJOR
ATTEMPT AT RECONCILIATION
IN THIS LAB IN 1611.
THE ATTEMPT FAILED.

Another lab, Dan thought. *The Madrigals kept trying, just like they're trying now. There could be a whole string of labs—I've got to find the newest one.*

He took off running. He was dimly aware that others were running alongside him—sometimes ahead of him, sometimes behind. Rooms flashed by, and he caught glimpses of more plaques: ATTEMPT IN 1783 . . . TRIED AGAIN IN 1848 . . . ANOTHER EFFORT IN 1914 . . . He didn't pause to read any of them thoroughly, but he could tell that each plaque ended similarly: FAILED . . . FAILURE . . . ABJECT DEFEAT . . . Each room he passed through was destroyed: charred, collapsed, exploded. The Madrigals had tried again and again and again to reunite their family, and each time they'd failed.

Soon Dan could no longer run because he had to pick his way through the wreckage of toppled walls, twisted metal beams, hulking broken machinery. The destruction and failure had just gotten bigger and more dramatic with each attempt.

We can't fail this time, Dan thought, diving frantically through the wreckage. *Amy and me—we have to win.*

Ahead of him, the wreckage seemed to end. He swung his burning rope down toward the floor and saw clean, unscarred linoleum. He lifted the rope torch higher, and off in the darkness before him something seemed to glow in response. Glass, maybe, reflecting his light.

Not just glass, Dan realized, squinting. *A vial. A huge vial. Containing . . . liquid.*

It had to be the serum.

"Is this what you're looking for?" a voice purred in the darkness.

Dan blinked, and in that moment the entire room was flooded with harsh, glaring light. Somebody had flipped a switch.

Now Dan could see who it was. He could see who'd spoken. He could see who was holding the vial.

It was Isabel.

CHAPTER 36

"No!" Amy wailed, falling in the wreckage. "No! Ian and Natalie—they said Isabel was behind us!"

"We thought she was!" Ian protested. He seemed frozen in place. Amy was surprised he wasn't trotting off to join his mother in the clean, modern lab ahead of them.

Isabel laughed, a horrible sound.

"You all proved so easy to fool," she said lightly in the cultured, confident voice that Amy had once admired. Now it hurt to listen. "Even the Madrigals didn't think about someone entering the gauntlet backward, laying explosives at strategic spots as decoys, lying in wait. . . ."

"But the explosions—you could have killed Ian and me!" Natalie complained.

"Wait—are Ian and Natalie still on Isabel's side or not?" Dan asked.

"Who cares?" Hamilton called out. "Either way, the Lucians are outnumbered. Let's tackle all of them!"

He began running forward, clearly aiming for Isabel.

Amy heard the gunshot before she even saw the gun.

One minute Hamilton was sprinting forward, getting into position for the best tackle of his life.

It's a shame Dad's not here to see this, he thought.

The next moment, he felt something being jerked from his hand—no, practically *vaporized* in his hand.

He looked down—the rope torch he'd been carrying was gone.

He looked back up, at Isabel.

"That was the warning shot," Isabel said, her eyes narrowed. "The next time I'll draw blood."

Behind Hamilton, he could hear the others shrieking. He blocked it out, just as he always blocked out crowd noise when he was preparing for a tackle. He narrowed his focus to Isabel. He saw how she'd put the vial down on a counter to pick up the gun. He saw what a large gun it was—capable of firing many shots, one after the other. He saw how expertly Isabel held it.

And he saw where she was aiming it now: directly at his heart.

Hamilton stopped running.

"The rest of you will all put your silly, primitive torches in that sink," Isabel commanded, pointing across the room. "One by one, going separately, so I can watch you. Alistair will go last and turn on the water to douse the flames."

Everyone stumbled out of the wreckage of the last ruined lab as if in a trance. Like the others, Alistair did as he was told, biding his time, watching Isabel as she watched him.

He noticed how she stopped pointing her gun directly at Hamilton's heart as soon as he looked away.

So maybe she doesn't really want to kill him, Alistair mused. *Maybe . . . she needs him? Needs the rest of us, too?*

Alistair remembered how many times in the gauntlet he'd seen five buttons in a circle, buttons requiring someone from each branch to be there.

But Isabel already has the vial, he thought. *She could have sneaked away with it before we even got here. She could have exploded the tunnel completely and killed us all way back at the beginning.*

Why hadn't she?

Amy tripped in front of Alistair. Alistair grabbed her by the arm, pulling her back up. He shook her head sternly at her.

Don't try anything yet, he wanted to advise her and all the others. *Observe. See what Isabel wants before you do anything.*

But they were terrified, impatient children. How long would it be before somebody did something stupid?

Alistair flipped through possible plans in his mind. *If we . . . No, won't work. Or if . . . Not that, either.*

Alistair could think of plenty of plans for vanquishing Isabel. But he couldn't think of any that guaranteed Alistair would be left holding the vial in the end.

"Go back to Gideon's lab and bring me Jonah," Isabel commanded Ian. "I want him here with the rest of you."

"No," Ian said. "I'm not your servant. I don't even want to be your son anymore. I—I'm emancipating myself! Natalie and I—we both are."

"We are," Natalie echoed.

Ian put his arm around his sister's shoulders. She was trembling, and Ian's legs were quaking, but Ian hoped that didn't show.

Ian had been planning what to say to Isabel ever since he and Natalie had sneaked off that plane back in London. He'd hoped to do it after finding the serum. After dethroning his parents as heads of the Lucians. After taking over.

He'd never imagined he'd have to give that speech while cowering in a position of weakness.

He'd never imagined his voice would squeak.

Isabel leveled her gun, aiming directly at Ian and Natalie.

"Mum!" Natalie cried in shock.

"You can't emancipate yourselves," Isabel hissed.

"Because I'm disowning you. Imbeciles!" She leaned in close, almost within reach. "Have you learned nothing from me? Didn't you see how I was giving you a second chance, giving you the opportunity to lie — giving you a way to come back to me?"

Something glistened in Isabel's eyes, but Ian knew it couldn't be tears. Not real ones, anyway.

"We don't want to come back to you," Ian said coldly.

He knew this was a terrible strategy. He knew she expected him to grovel and beg — to lie and say she was the best mother in the world, and Ian and Natalie had missed her.

But it felt so good to tell the truth instead.

Isabel stepped back, abandoning him and Natalie. Or just making sure that, if she needed to, she could shoot anyone there. The whole group was in range of her gun.

"Regardless," she said through gritted teeth. "Ian, you will go fetch Jonah. Now. Or I'll shoot Natalie."

"No," Ian said. "I won't. You wouldn't do that."

Too late, Ian realized he'd backed his mother into a corner.

So here's your way out, Mum, Ian thought, staring into his mother's glittering eyes. *Back down. Stop. Show everyone here that Natalie and I are more important to you than the serum. Show that . . . that you do love us after all. . . .*

Ian actually opened his mouth to say this. But he choked on the first word: "Sh-show . . ."

Because whatever trace of love he'd ever seen in Isabel's eyes was gone now. Nothing showed in her face but cruelty and resolve. Nothing else lived in her soul.

Ian saw exactly what she planned to do.

"No!" he screamed, lunging desperately forward. "No! Don't! You can't!"

He was too late.

Isabel squeezed the trigger.

CHAPTER 37

Everybody screamed.

"You shot your own daughter! You shot your own daughter!" a high-pitched voice shrieked again and again.

Dan couldn't tell if it was Amy's or Sinead's or Natalie's. His ears weren't working right. He could feel himself slipping toward the same kind of numb shock he'd fallen into after Lester's death. His vision blurred.

No, he thought, fighting against the numbness, the darkness. *That's what Isabel wants. She wants us shocked and stupid. So she can do anything she wants.*

Dan's eyes cleared a little. Now he could see Isabel, still pointing her gun. He could see Ian bent over Natalie, crumpled on the floor.

It seemed to take superhuman strength, but Dan stumbled over to Ian and Natalie.

"The rest of us can take care of Natalie," Dan muttered to Ian. "You go get Jonah before Isabel shoots again."

"That's right—and I will if you don't obey," Isabel said, her voice as cold and hard as metal. "This time it was just Natalie's foot. The next time—" She spun the gun around, pointing first at Amy's head, then at Alistair's chest, then at Natalie's back. "Who knows?"

Gasping—possibly even sobbing—Ian stumbled away.

"And don't take too long, or I *will* shoot again," Isabel threatened.

Dan crouched by Natalie's side. He could see a hole in her fancy designer shoe. Blood was seeping out.

At least it wasn't gushing.

"It doesn't hurt," Natalie whispered. "I think the bullet just grazed my foot. I'm just pretending to be in pain so we can outsmart my mum."

Dan decided not to tell Natalie that she was probably in shock, and that was why she hadn't felt any pain yet. But outsmarting Isabel—that sounded like a good idea.

Before Dan could think of a plan, he heard Hamilton call from behind him, "I'll go help Ian get Jonah. It'll be faster that way."

"No!" Isabel screamed. She fired the gun again, but this time she aimed into the space between Hamilton and Ian, keeping Hamilton back. "I won't have you plotting together back there!"

Amy dropped to her knees beside Dan.

"Does Natalie need a tourniquet to stop the bleeding? Or just a bandage?" she said loudly. Under her breath she added in a whisper, "Got a plan?"

Above them, Alistair took a step toward Isabel. He had his hands up, as if surrendering.

Dan hoped so badly that Alistair had a plan, that his surrender was fake.

But he teamed up with Isabel before, when my parents died, Dan thought. *And now . . .*

Alistair was only asking a question.

"Why?" Alistair asked Isabel. "You already have the serum. You *won*. Why do you have to torture the rest of us? Why can't you just let us go?"

"Oh, I have the serum, do I?" Isabel mocked, her face twisting hideously. "That's what the Madrigals want me to think. They want me falling for their tricks!"

"Tricks?" Alistair repeated numbly.

"Are you that much of a fool?" Isabel asked impatiently. "Or do you think that I am?"

Isabel waved the gun again, but this time she seemed to be making a decision. Selecting someone. Selecting . . .

Dan.

Isabel pointed the gun directly at him.

"Young master Cahill," she said, almost in that sticky-sweet voice that some grown-ups use with very small children. "You've proved to be quite a shining star of the Cahill family during this clue hunt. Tell me. What have you seen again and again in this silly Madrigal gauntlet? Located near so many locked doors . . . or doors the Madrigals intended to be locked before *I* intervened."

Dan couldn't think. Not with the gun pointed at him, not with Isabel staring him right in the eyes.

Amy grabbed him around the shoulders, holding him up. Protecting him.

"You mean the keypads," she said. Her voice trembled, but Dan could still hear the strength in it. He felt stronger himself. His mind cleared.

"The keypads that five people had to touch," he said. "One from each branch."

"Oh, that's right, the two of you work together," Isabel said mockingly. "You help each other. That's so touching." She winced, almost as if she regretted having no one beside her. But surely Dan was only imagining that. He blinked, and when he looked again, Isabel's gaze was as steely as ever.

It was cowardly, but Dan was so glad that Amy didn't drop her arm from around his shoulders.

"All those keypads, all along the way," Isabel mused. "All the safeguards. And then this large vial of supposed serum is just sitting here out in the open? Unprotected? Available to anyone?"

"Th-the keypads before," Amy stammered. "The Madrigals thought that was enough to pro—"

Isabel shook the vial.

"It's only colored water!" she screamed. "That's all that's in here!"

Don't shoot, Dan thought. *Please don't shoot.*

Somebody was sobbing behind him. Amy held on to Dan so tightly it hurt.

He didn't care.

Isabel moved the gun. It wasn't exactly that she'd stopped pointing it at Dan, but that she was ready to shoot anyone.

"But those tricky Madrigals can't trick me," she said. "I have been studying this vial for hours. I discovered my children's treachery much sooner than they expected. So I had time. It's such thick glass . . . and those Madrigals do so love their fingerprint proof. They want fingerprint proof here, too. But just because five people trigger a secret, that doesn't mean all five get to keep it, now, do they?"

Dimly, even with his brain swimming with terror, Dan could see what she meant. She thought the vial itself was like another keypad. If someone from each of the five Cahill branches touched it all at once, it would set off a message—a Clue.

The final Clue.

She's going to force us to help her get it, Dan thought. *And then . . .*

There were gasps around him, everyone else starting to understand, too.

Hamilton took a step forward.

"You can't make us all touch the vial for you," Hamilton argued. "You can't point a gun at five people at once. And if you kill any of us, then the fingerprints probably won't work."

"Oh, I can make you all touch the vial," Isabel said. "I can make you do anything I want."

"How?" Hamilton challenged. "*I* don't have a sister here you can threaten to shoot."

"Not *here*, exactly," Isabel said.

She took a step back and touched a button on the wall. For the first time, Dan noticed a huge flat-screen TV embedded in the wall. It came to life now, showing multiple scenes of the gauntlet they'd just left.

So she was watching us all along, Dan thought with a chill.

Isabel touched another button, and the multiple scenes were replaced by one large one: an exterior view of the island—the pebble beach and the cemetery. The helicopter, the Holts' boat, Jonah's yacht, the Kabra kids' parachutes, and Alistair's submarine all lay off to the side, abandoned. Isabel did something to make the camera zoom in closer, focusing on the tombstones.

The rest of the Holt family was tied to the tombstones.

So was the helicopter pilot.

So was Nellie.

Dan couldn't look anymore after that.

Isabel held up a remote control she'd evidently been hiding alongside the gun.

"This is hooked up to multiple explosives planted out in the cemetery," she said. "One beside each tombstone." Her lips curled up into a smile, slow and evil. "You *will* do everything I tell you. Or I will kill the people you love."

CHAPTER 38

Nellie, Amy thought, her eyes blurring with sudden tears. *We can't let Nellie die. . . .*

Nothing else mattered.

On the TV screen, Nellie sat staunchly, even bound to the tombstone. She had her head raised, her jaw jutting upward. Her nose ring glinted in the sunlight, and her spiky hair stood up like beacons.

She hadn't given up.

Think, Amy commanded herself.

"Th-the Madrigals," she blurted. "They'll never let you get away with this."

"What Madrigals?" Isabel sneered. "You mean—you *children*?" She looked down her nose at Amy and Dan, making Amy feel as helpless and insignificant as a flea. "Or—the old men I found cowering in the island control room?"

She adjusted the picture on the TV screen again, scanning down the row of tombstones.

Uncle Fiske and Mr. McIntyre were tied to the tombstones, too. Unlike Nellie, they looked completely defeated: battered and bloodied and covered in rock dust.

"I exploded my way into their control room," Isabel said carelessly. "Unfortunately, it created a bit of a crater several hundred feet up into the gauntlet."

A crater? Amy thought. *The one Natalie almost fell into? And Isabel thinks that's just 'unfortunate'?*

"They were the only Madrigals on the island," Isabel said. "And—I have hired assassins who are ready to take care of all the other Madrigals, all around the world. As soon as I give the signal." She looked Amy straight in the eye. "Shall we proceed?"

Amy saw that Isabel had just been waiting for Ian to return with Jonah. The two boys were back in sight now, Ian wearily pulling Jonah through the wreckage of the last exploded lab. Jonah barely seemed conscious.

Amy thought that it was a terrible sign that Isabel made no attempt to blindfold any of them as she gathered them around the vial.

She doesn't care what we see, Amy thought. *Because she's going to kill us all as soon as she has what she wants.*

Isabel had everyone crouch down because Jonah and Natalie couldn't stand. Dan, rather than Amy, represented the Madrigals touching the vial. But Amy leaned in close as Alistair, Hamilton, and Isabel placed their hands alongside Jonah's and Dan's. She could see the side of the vial shimmering.

And then words appeared on the glass, a hologram:

For Gideon Cahill's serum:
One portion = One ounce

Start with one portion of water.

Add 1/8 portion of each ingredient
on the list given to Luke Cahill.

Add 1/16 portion of each ingredient originally
told to Jane Cahill. Then . . .

The final Clue everybody had been searching for wasn't another ingredient in the serum.

It was the serum recipe.

CHAPTER 39

Alistair practically collapsed with relief when he saw the silvery words glowing from the glass.

There's still time, he thought.

Isabel would have to work to blackmail each one of them, individually, to find out the Clues the other branches had. She still needed them to make the serum.

Alistair thought that Hamilton would crack first. He was all but giving himself whiplash, glancing back constantly at the TV screen and muttering, "I can't let my family die. I can't let my family die. . . ."

Alistair tried to catch someone's eye—Amy's? Dan's? Sinead's?—hoping they could work together to fight Isabel. But all three of them were nearly as obsessive as Hamilton, peering toward the TV.

Alistair caught Isabel's eye by mistake.

"Tsk, tsk," she scolded playfully, as if she knew everything he was planning and it only amused her. "Surely you don't think anyone would trust *you*. It's too late for that."

She knew him too well. She knew all of them too well.

". . . thyme, bone, wormwood, tin," Hamilton finished up. He kept his voice down, so only Isabel would hear. He hoped, he hoped . . .

"Oh, very good," Isabel murmured.

Had it worked?

Isabel's face twisted and her voice turned hard.

"Very good—for getting your family killed!" she snarled, loud enough for everyone to hear.

She lifted the remote control, her finger poised over a button. She glared at Hamilton.

"The Madrigal clue your family got in New York wasn't *thyme*," she said, leering. "It was rosemary. Don't you know? You can't lie to me! I see right through you!"

You just know about the rosemary because the Lucians must have found that clue, too, Hamilton wanted to protest. But how could he be sure which Clues Isabel already had and which she didn't? Especially when the lives of his entire family depended on it?

Hamilton began sweating, more than he ever had at any athletic event.

"It's zinc at the end!" Hamilton exploded. "Zinc, not tin! And that's the only other thing I lied about! Honest! I swear! Please don't kill my family!"

Isabel smiled.

And—she didn't push the button.

"Jonah," a melodic voice purred beside Jonah's ear.

Jonah was having an awful dream. He was on a stage, but only one person had come to see him: a woman. A woman who was somehow his mother and Isabel Kabra at the same time.

"Sing your clues," the woman demanded. And then the woman split into two, Cora and Isabel becoming separate people. Cora screamed, "No! No! Don't tell her a thing! No matter what she threatens!" And Isabel was screaming, too: "Tell me your clues! Or else!"

And then Jonah awoke, and he wasn't onstage at all. He was lying on an empty, cold tile floor.

"Is the pain too bad?" the melodic voice cooed sympathetically.

The pain was a monster devouring Jonah from the inside out. The pain was a bomb blast, shattering Jonah's body every time he took a breath.

He'd never known anybody could hurt this much and stay alive.

"Perhaps this will help," the voice said.

There was a prick in his arm, and the pain began to flow away. It didn't disappear. But Jonah's mind cleared a little. He could see that it was Isabel Kabra bending over him.

His mother was nowhere in sight.

"I need your clues," Isabel said softly. "And you're going to tell them to me."

To thine own self be true, Jonah thought. *To thine own self be true.*

"I'm not like you," Jonah murmured. "Not Lucian. Janus. My mother doesn't understand. Have to win this . . . as a Janus. Artistically."

"Artistically?" Isabel sneered.

Jonah knew when he was losing an audience.

"Like at the Globe," he said, his voice a little stronger. "I just saw it—at that moment. I was going to sing. About how the Cahill feud was hurting the whole family, and how maybe if we just all, I don't know, shared the clues and the prize, maybe, maybe . . ."

Isabel began to laugh cruelly. She was like an audience who was there only to mock, to heckle, to destroy.

"Cahills don't share," she said. She grabbed Jonah's arm and twisted it—maybe some of the bones in his arm were broken, too? Because Isabel was bringing the pain monster back, full force.

"You will tell me your clues—now," Isabel commanded.

"Won't," Jonah said, drawing upon something that was beyond wanting to please his mother, beyond wanting to please his fans, even beyond being a Janus. Was there some true self inside him he hadn't even known was there?

"You will or else . . ." Isabel began.

"Jonah came to the island alone," somebody else

said—Ian, maybe, or Dan. "There's no one he loves you can threaten."

Alone, Jonah thought. *I am alone.*

"Yes, Jonah came by himself," Isabel said. "But, you know, some parents . . . When you can't do anything for yourself, and your kid's your meal ticket . . . Isn't it sweet how worthless old Broderick managed to find his way here?"

She was propping up Jonah's head, setting off more waves of pain throughout his body. Now he could see a TV screen showing his father tied to a tombstone. Broderick had tears streaming down his face and his lips were moving, saying something Jonah couldn't hear because the TV had no sound. No—Broderick was *singing* something. Jonah could even lip-read well enough to know what it was:

Jonah boy, my homie,
Jonah boy, my buddy, my son . . .

It was the first song Jonah had ever learned—a song he and Broderick had made up together.

Broderick hadn't followed Jonah to this island because Jonah was his meal ticket. He'd come because he was worried about Jonah. Because he loved him.

Why hadn't Jonah always known that? Why hadn't he trusted his father more?

"I will kill your father if you don't tell me your clues," Isabel threatened, holding a remote before his eyes.

Don't tell her a thing! No matter what! the dream Cora Wizard still screamed inside Jonah's head.

But Jonah watched his father singing. He knew his true self. He knew his father's. And he knew the choice he had to make.

"Pearl," Jonah whispered directly into Isabel's ear. "Honey, sulfur . . ."

Jonah wanted to start working together way back at the Globe, Dan thought at his sister. *What he says he wanted—it's pretty much what the Madrigals want.*

Well, he had a funny way of showing it, Amy seemed to be thinking back to him. *And he's not exactly the best partner for staging a rebellion right now, not with two broken legs.*

What about Hamilton? Dan thought. *The three of us together . . .*

But Hamilton was staring anxiously at the TV screen, mouthing the same words again and again: "Mom. Dad. Reagan. Madison." He wasn't even watching Isabel.

And Amy had gone back to staring at the TV, too, looking for Nellie.

Dan sighed. Isabel was done torturing Jonah now. She pulled Amy and Dan aside, away from the others.

Dan didn't wait.

"Mace," he said. "Lily. Copper . . ."

Each word felt like a betrayal of everything they'd worked for during the entire Clue hunt. Dan wasn't just giving up ingredients. He was giving up the trust Grace had placed in them, the hopes the Madrigals had held for them, the dreams his parents had died for. He was giving up the chance to win in honor of Lester's sacrifice, Irina's sacrifice, his parents'.

But Nellie's life was worth more than any of that.

"Which brother did you find hiding in my aircraft?" Sinead asked, squinting at the screen, at the rows of people tied to tombstones. "I can't quite tell. . . ."

"Why—do you love one brother more than the other?" Isabel cackled. "Which cripple do you prefer?"

"My brothers aren't *crippled*!" Sinead screamed, lunging toward Isabel. "Don't use that word!"

Isabel took a step back.

"No?" she said, unruffled. "What do you want me to call it? Ever since that explosion at the Franklin Institute, Ted's blind. Ted, who used to draw such intricate architectural and engineering designs . . ."

Across the room, Hamilton gasped.

"Ted's not blind!" Sinead screamed. "He's—visually impaired. He can still see light and dark!"

"Ah, yes, light and dark," Isabel murmured, shaking her head. "And Ned . . . what is it he says about those headaches he gets all the time now — 'I can't think through the pain'? And no medication helps. . . ." She clucked her tongue in a show of false sympathy. "So sad to be such a genius and not even be able to think. . . ."

"He's going to recover!" Sinead screamed. "And Ted's going to see again! When I get the serum —"

"No," Isabel said, leaning close again. "No. You're not going to get the serum. It's *mine.* Your brothers will never be cured. The only thing you can do is tell me your clues and save your brother's life. Ned or Ted — who cares which one it is?"

Sinead was sobbing too hard to say anything.

Isabel lowered her finger toward the button.

The two Starling boys were hurt that badly? Alistair marveled as he listened to Sinead and Isabel argue. *It's true? One's blind, one has disabling headaches?*

He wondered how he'd missed noticing this at the Tate museum, at Holy Trinity Church, during the handful of meals he'd shared with all three Starlings.

Ned didn't say much. Other than that, the boys seemed virtually identical, he thought.

And then he understood. Each boy had helped the other disguise his disability: Ned acting as Ted's eyes, Ted covering for Ned's mind-numbing pain.

That's why they're inseparable, Alistair thought.

And . . . that's why Sinead cares so much about which broth-er's out there tied to the tombstone.

Neither boy would have stowed away on Sinead's aircraft without the other.

So if one boy was tied up in the cemetery, another boy had managed to hide when Isabel showed up. So he was somewhere else on the island, perhaps even now climbing through the gauntlet to rescue Sinead.

Maybe it's Ned, and he won't *be having a headache,* Alistair thought. *He's a genius. He'll know what to do when he gets down here.*

Alistair realized that meant they still had a chance.

If he could stall Isabel long enough.

He saw that she still had her finger poised over the button, ready to kill one of Sinead's brothers.

"Leave Sinead alone!" Alistair screamed. "She doesn't know any clues but zinc, which she stole from Bae Oh. You've got everyone's clues but mine! And you're never going to get mine!"

"No?" Isabel asked.

"Of course not," Alistair said. He was surprised at how hard he had to work to keep his voice steady. "There's no one out there in the cemetery for me to save. Even if you brought in Bae Oh, I'd say, 'Let him die!' *Especially* if you brought in Bae Oh! There's nobody I love! Nobody who loves me!"

His voice cracked at the end.

"Not out in that cemetery," Isabel agreed. "But . . ." She lowered her remote and redirected her gun. "In here . . . should I threaten to kill Amy or Dan or Sinead? Or all three of them?"

The way she was waving the gun at all the children made Alistair's heart pound.

Isabel's a Lucian, Alistair thought. *She sees things other people don't—things she can manipulate to give her power.*

Could she possibly have seen something about Alistair that he hadn't seen about himself?

His heart sped up even faster; it felt as though it planned to break out. Or just plain break.

But—the clues, Alistair thought longingly. *I've devoted my whole life to gathering them. They're all I've ever wanted. All I've ever valued.*

He was lying to himself. He'd been deceiving himself since the Clue hunt began. Because when he imagined a bullet ripping through Amy or Dan or Sinead—or even Jonah or Hamilton, Ian or Natalie—the Clues' value faded away. If he could, he might even trade a Clue to heal the bullet wound in Natalie's foot, the shattered bones in Jonah's body.

And if there were some way to bring Hope and Arthur back? What clue wouldn't be worth that?

He saw he faced a choice, just as he had all those years ago, the night Hope and Arthur died. The difference was, this time he could see the consequences.

Isabel inched her finger closer to the trigger.

She plans to kill us all anyhow, Alistair told himself, and his own brain screamed back at him, *But for now there's still time! There's still a chance!*

"Silver," Alistair blurted. "Phosphorus. Water . . ."

CHAPTER 40

Isabel had mixed the serum. She'd found the ingredients the Madrigals knew about in the lab, hidden among dozens of decoy ingredients; she'd blackmailed the members of the other branches into giving up ingredients from their backpacks and pockets and—in Alistair's case—cane.

The others came prepared, Amy thought dejectedly. *Dan and I were never going to win.*

Now Isabel stood in the center of the lab, the huge vial clutched in her hand. She tightened a stopper in the top and shook it one last time.

When Isabel takes the stopper out, Amy thought, *she'll have to look away for a moment. Maybe she'll even put down the remote control or the gun. That's when we should attack her, all of us together.*

But Amy had no way of signaling the others. She had no way of telling them her plan, not while Isabel was watching everyone so closely.

And Amy couldn't do anything against Isabel all by herself.

Isabel's going to drink the serum, Amy thought. *Isabel is going to become the most powerful person in the world.*

Amy and Dan had failed completely.

Isabel held the vial high in the air, examining the liquid inside.

"I have been waiting for this moment my entire life," she murmured.

"Mum, don't drink that," Natalie burst out from her position huddled on the floor. "Please! It's bad for you."

"What?" Isabel exploded, lowering the vial only slightly. "Are you an even bigger fool than I thought?"

"You drank the Lucian serum and it just made you mean," Natalie said. "Mean to everyone, even me and Ian. And it made you kill Irina, and you didn't care—"

"I didn't drink the Lucian serum until after I killed Irina," Isabel said. "I've always been mean. The Lucian serum just showed me how to do it effectively—how to win. It's why I'm holding the full Cahill serum right now."

She gazed into the depths of the serum, her eyes triumphant.

She already drank the Lucian serum? Amy thought despairingly. *The partial serum I found in Paris? Then . . . she already knows everything there is to know about strategies and plotting and planning. We could never outsmart her. There's no hope.*

"And to think I once intended to share this with my worthless children . . ." Isabel muttered.

Natalie winced, but Ian only stood there stoically, glaring at his mother.

Isabel grasped the stopper in the top, preparing to pull it off. But she did this one-handed, using her other hand to keep the gun trained on all the others.

Out of the corner of her eye, Amy caught a glimpse of movement in the wreckage of the previous ruined lab. Was it just a scrap of paper—some trash blowing in the breeze?

There isn't a breeze, Amy thought.

She had to fight so hard not to crane her neck, not to turn her head—not to do anything to draw Isabel's attention to the movement.

It must be someone coming to rescue us! Amy thought jubilantly, though she had to keep all traces of hope off her face. *Whoever it is, they'll have to advance stealthily— maybe they can tackle Isabel from behind and she'll never see them coming.*

A crash sounded in the wreckage.

Now Amy had to look. She saw Ned Starling, doubled over beside a fallen rack of test tubes. He clutched his head and moaned.

And then Amy saw Isabel whirl toward him. Isabel whipped her gun into position, aiming carefully, aiming directly at Ned's heart.

Amy saw that Isabel had only been toying with them before, pretending. This was serious. This was real. This was going to happen.

Amy launched herself toward Isabel.

It didn't matter that Amy had no time to plan. It didn't matter that she couldn't defeat Isabel alone. It didn't even matter that she barely knew Ned Starling.

All that mattered was that Amy couldn't stand by while Isabel killed again.

This is how I honor my parents and Irina and Lester, Amy thought, running hard. *Even if I die, too . . .*

And then Amy realized she wasn't alone.

Beside her, Dan was lunging for Isabel, too. So were Sinead and Hamilton and Alistair and Ian and even Jonah and Natalie, though they struggled and gasped in pain. Just as four branches of Cahills had once united with Isabel, five branches now united against her. The group moved almost as one, everyone roaring, "No! Don't!"

Several of them slammed into Isabel at once. They knocked her down, jarring the gun and the remote and the vial from her grip. The gun went off, but the bullet zinged harmlessly into the darkness.

"We did it!" Amy screamed.

But then it was just Amy and Dan and Sinead holding Isabel down. The others were racing away, following the rolling vial.

Ian got to it first.

"This—must—be—destroyed!" he screamed, raising the vial of serum high over his head. "Before it causes even more evil!"

He started to smash it down toward the floor, but

Alistair and Hamilton grabbed his arms and reached for the vial themselves.

And then Sinead scrambled up, lurching toward the vial and screaming, "No! My brothers need that!"

Now it was just Amy and Dan holding down Isabel. She effortlessly shook off their grip and raised herself into a crouch. She reached for the gun and the remote.

"That's my serum!" Isabel raged.

She had the gun in her hands and was aiming it at everyone fighting over the vial.

"I'll kill all of you!" she threatened.

But everybody was screaming too loudly to hear. Hamilton knocked the vial out of Ian's grasp. It slipped through one hand after another, each person yanking it away from the last. Then the vial slid down to the ground and began to roll.

Now Isabel was reaching for it.

We can't stop her, Amy thought as she struggled to pull back Isabel's arm. *It's just Dan and me against the most evil woman in the world.*

No. That wasn't the right way to think about it. It was Dan and Amy against just Isabel — two against one.

Dan swung his fist at Isabel's face — a puny fist, yes, but enough to distract her. Isabel slammed the butt of her gun into Dan's stomach.

Dan bent over in what looked like agonizing pain.

With one hand, Amy tried to pull Isabel away from Dan. With her other hand, she felt around on the floor for something — anything — to defend her brother. Her hands grasped something round: the vial.

Amy raised it high and slammed it down as hard as she could on Isabel's head.

"Stop hurting Dan!" she screamed. "Don't hurt anyone in my family again!"

The thick vial shattered. Broken glass and serum streamed down Isabel's hair, her neck, her back.

And then Isabel fell forward, slumping harmlessly to the ground.

CHAPTER 41

For a moment nobody moved.

Then Dan heard Sinead whisper, "Amy saved us."

"And she destroyed the serum," Alistair said dazedly.

"I had to," Amy defended herself. "Isabel would have killed—"

"No, no," Alistair said, waving his hands as if trying to wave away any misunderstanding. "I'm not criticizing. You did the right thing." He stared at Isabel's body amid the broken glass, the serum trickling away. "The right thing . . ." he repeated.

"But I wanted the serum to cure my brothers," Sinead whispered, tears welling in her eyes.

"I—" Dan began, but then he stopped because he wanted to think this through.

Nobody seemed to hear Dan because Hamilton was talking, too. "Let's tie up the queen of evil before she comes to and starts attacking us all over again."

Amy carefully picked up Isabel's remote control and placed it on a counter, out of the way. Dan kicked at the handle of the gun. It slid across the floor and stopped only when it landed in the wreckage.

Nobody made any effort to grab either weapon.

That's good, isn't it? Dan thought. *And everyone wanted to save Sinead's brother. At least at first. Maybe . . .*

His brain was too numb to think. He concentrated on helping Hamilton pull rope out of his backpack, tying it tightly around Isabel's ankles and wrists.

"That's not good enough," Ian fretted. "She's going to come to. She'll figure out how to escape!"

"Desperate times call for desperate measures," Alistair said. He held up a small white pill. "Something developed by our friend Irina Spasky. This will keep Isabel unconscious for several hours. And"—he raised an eyebrow significantly—"it will ensure that she forgets what happened today."

So she won't remember how to make the serum, Dan thought, relieved.

"That means Natalie and I will get to tell her all over again that *we're* disowning *her*," Ian said in a hard voice. "I'll rather enjoy that."

He's serious, Dan thought. *He's not going to back down.*

Dan watched Alistair bend over Isabel. He put the pill in her mouth. Then he rubbed her throat to get her to swallow, just like Dan would do with Saladin.

Ned Starling stumbled out of the wreckage and toward his sister.

"The pain's worse than ever, isn't it?" Sinead asked,

gingerly touching Ned's forehead. He winced, his face twisted in agony.

"Sinead . . ." Dan tried again.

He stopped and looked at Amy.

What should we do? he thought at her. *Should we trust them? Should I tell?*

Amy tilted her head, a wry expression on her face, as if to say, *I think everybody but Sinead already knows. They're just pretending not to.*

Dan was sick of pretending.

"Sinead, I've got a photographic memory," he said. "I remember every word of that recipe on the vial. I couldn't hear all the ingredients, but everyone remembers their own. If we all worked together, we could mix up more of the serum and . . ."

Nobody reacted the way Dan expected.

Hamilton didn't slap him a high five. Jonah didn't offer a fist bump. Alistair didn't put his arm around Dan's shoulders and say confidingly, "Dan, my boy, I always knew you were a lot like your uncle."

Nobody moved at all, except that Sinead grimaced.

"Dan, I—" she began. "I don't know. What I did trying to get the serum . . . even leaving Ned's life in danger to fight for it . . . Maybe I don't just want it to help my brothers? Maybe . . . maybe I'm a little too much like her?"

She pointed down at Isabel's bound figure.

Alistair grabbed a piece of paper from a counter

and began writing a list of his Clues. Then he thrust the paper into Dan's hand.

"I trust you and Amy," he said. "I don't trust myself. You do whatever you need to with the serum."

Ian took the pen from Alistair and wrote down ingredients of his own. He, too, handed the paper to Dan.

"Natalie and I have spent our whole lives listening to our mother," Ian said. "Believing everything she ever told us . . ."

"But you stopped believing her!" Amy protested. "You changed! Or you would have helped her in here—helped her even as she killed us all!"

"Why didn't we stop helping her before, in Korea?" Ian asked. "In Australia? South Africa? Jamaica?"

"We haven't changed enough," Natalie said in a small, pained voice. "But—we're trying."

Jonah took the pen next and began writing. He had to hunch over painfully, bracing his paper against the floor.

"No, Jonah," Dan began. "You never actually—"

"If I knew how to make the serum, my mother would make me tell," he said. "And my mother . . . my mother's way too much like theirs." He pointed to Ian and Natalie.

He finished writing and flashed the famous Jonah Wizard grin as he handed his paper up.

"Besides," he said, "I'm going to be the greatest musician in the world even without the serum!"

Hamilton reached for the pen and paper after Jonah.

"What?" Dan asked in astonishment. "Hamilton, you don't have to do that! We trust you! You're on our team! You—"

"I chose the serum over Ned's life, just like everyone else," Hamilton said heavily. "Everyone except you and Amy."

He bent his head and began writing.

"Well, it's not like we're saints or anything," Dan said. "It's just that we didn't know anything about the serum until a few weeks ago. So we didn't have the *instincts* to go for it."

"Dan, that's why Grace wanted us in the clue hunt," Amy said, sounding startled, as if she'd just figured this out. "It's why nobody told us the family history until after Grace died."

"So you would have the *right* instincts," Alistair said gently. "You could win the clue hunt only by valuing human life more than the clues. Ironic, isn't it? Grace always did love irony."

"Wait a minute—we *won*?" Dan asked incredulously.

"Dude. You're holding all the clues," Hamilton said, thrusting his paper into Dan's hands. Hamilton gave Dan a pat on the back that was gentle, for a Holt. This meant that Dan pitched forward only two steps before he managed to catch his balance.

"I'm telling my dad that you and Amy won fair and

square, on your own," Hamilton said. "Because—it's the truth."

Dan was still blinking in amazement. He looked down at the lists of Clues in his hand, the ingredients that had first been assembled five hundred years earlier—and had changed human history ever since.

What could they do to the future?

"Hamilton, wait," Dan began, because he wanted more help. "Think about how many times you saved our lives. Think how you got me up that cliff. Think about—"

"How my family burned down Grace's mansion," Hamilton said. "How we almost killed Alistair in South Africa. How . . . how it's our fault the Starlings got hurt at the Franklin Institute." He looked Sinead directly in the eye. "I'm sorry," he said.

Sinead nodded once, which was not quite forgiveness. But maybe it was a first step.

"And I'm sorry," Alistair said, peering at Dan and Amy. "For everything."

"We forgive you," Amy whispered.

Dan stared at his sister, thinking, *We do?*

We need to, Amy seemed to be thinking back at him. *We can't spend the rest of our lives hating people.*

Like a little kid reaching for a security blanket, Dan searched for the anger that had propelled him for much of the Clue hunt. It was still there, but fainter somehow. Lighter.

Maybe someday it would go away completely.

"You did give up your clues to keep Isabel from kill-ing us," Dan told Alistair grudgingly.

"Yes," Alistair agreed. "But I am also too much like Isabel and Cora—and Eisenhower."

"My dad's a great *dad*," Hamilton protested. "But . . ." He looked down at his hands. "I *don't* want to be just like him."

Alistair nodded.

"Growing up, I saw how evil my uncle Bae was," he said. "And yet, I still tried to gain his approval. I still made his goals my own." He cleared his throat nois-ily. "You children are so much wiser. You're choosing a better way."

Tears sparkled in his eyes.

It's all true, Dan thought. *We really won. All of us. Together.*

He remembered how, back in London, he'd told Amy they should win and then knock everybody else into shape. But that was the kind of plan others had tried for the past five hundred years, and it had never worked. The way Amy and Dan had won was com-pletely different. They'd won because everybody else wanted them to.

He couldn't wait to tell Nellie.

"Oh—Nellie!" he cried. "We've got to rescue everyone out in the cemetery!" He began cramming the papers the others had given him into his pocket. "Everything else can wait until we do that and—"

"And get better medical treatment for Natalie and

Jonah," Alistair agreed. "And . . ." He looked down grimly at Isabel's unconscious form. "We need to turn her over to the authorities."

"People stay in prison for a long time for attempted murder, don't they?" Amy asked anxiously. "All those explosives she set off . . ."

"Oh, she's not just going to be charged with *attempted* murder," Alistair said. "I'm going to do something I was afraid to do seven years ago. I'm going to testify that Isabel murdered your parents."

"So that means . . ." Amy began.

Alistair almost smiled.

"Isabel," he said, "will be in prison for the rest of her life."

CHAPTER 42

Ned Starling led the way out through the secret passage he'd seen Isabel use. It was a slow process, since Jonah, Natalie, and Isabel had to be carried. Then Ian had to go out first, to dismiss the henchmen Isabel had left guarding the cemetery.

"Mum wants you off this island—now!" he barked, and that did the trick.

When the rest of the group emerged, everyone in the cemetery cheered.

"Amy and Dan—you survived!" Nellie screamed. "My kiddos!"

"And ours!" Uncle Fiske yelled, just a beat behind her. Then he looked sheepishly at Mr. McIntyre. "Well, they are," he said.

"I can't see—are Sinead and Ned there? Are Sinead and Ned there?" Ted hollered. Someone must have told him yes, because then he exploded, "This is even better than finding a new digit in pi!"

"Hammy! Hammy! Hammy!" the Holts cheered in unison.

"Jonah? You're hurt?" Broderick strained against the ropes binding him.

"Fo sho," Jonah said, making a pained effort to grin from his sling. "But wait till you hear the songs I'm going to write from this experience."

Alistair and Sinead insisted that, before anyone else could step into the cemetery, they had to defuse the explosives Isabel had laid.

"Quite right," the helicopter pilot said approvingly. "That's the safest way."

Hamilton stood on the beach, shouting across to his family, telling everything that had happened.

Or — almost everything.

"So, Amy and Dan won in the end, but then Amy had to destroy the prize to protect us all," Hamilton said. "And, Dad, I know you're going to be mad that I didn't win everything for Team Holt but . . ."

He waited, but Eisenhower didn't start screaming the way Hamilton expected. Eisenhower opened his mouth, winced, swallowed hard, then tried again.

"Winning isn't everything," Eisenhower said faintly. "Sometimes, just knowing your family's safe and healthy and alive is even better."

"Did Vince Lombardi say that?" Reagan asked. "Or Shakespeare?"

"No," Eisenhower said. "I did."

Once everyone was untied, Amy and Nellie hugged like

they hadn't seen each other in a million years. Dan didn't want to get involved with that, not when he really wanted to talk to Uncle Fiske and Mr. McIntyre.

Later, Dan thought. *After everyone else leaves . . .*

Frustrated, he wandered toward the Starlings.

Ted was reaching out to touch his sister's face.

"I heard what Hamilton said about the serum being destroyed," Ted was saying. "Don't worry, Sinead. It doesn't matter. Ned and I will be fine anyhow."

"Oh, but—" Sinead began.

"No, listen," Ted said. "While I was tied up here with everyone else, I started thinking about those experimental surgeries they offered Ned and me. I came up with a few new things to suggest to the doctors, so it's not so risky. Reagan Holt even drew the diagrams for me." He pulled a sheaf of papers out of his jacket pocket and held them out to her. "Look."

"But we can—" Dan began, leaning in toward the Starlings.

Sinead looked up from the diagrams and shook her head warningly.

"Ted's way is better," she said. "If the surgeries work, this helps lots of people, not just Ned and Ted. And there won't be the same . . . side effects and complications. I mean, I saw Isabel Kabra in action, and she only had *part* of the serum."

"I guess," Dan said. He was suddenly even more aware of the papers he'd tucked into his own pockets. How could paper feel so heavy?

Jonah almost passed out while the others lifted him into the helicopter. He tried to relax as they settled him into the backseat, but then he stiffened again.

"Dad!" he screamed. "The vandalism charges from the Globe—will somebody try to arrest me when we get to the hospital?"

"Oh, no," Broderick said. "I almost forgot—all the accusations were dropped. Miss Pluderbottom recanted."

"Yo! Miss 'I tell nothing but the truth' Pluderbottom *lied*?" Jonah asked, astounded. "For me?"

"No," Broderick said. "She didn't lie. She said the truth changed. She went to the authorities and said she'd discovered you were a nice young man who would never intentionally damage anything connected to the Bard."

The truth changed, Jonah thought. *And—I changed. I found my true self.*

"Miss Pluderbottom's my homie," Jonah murmured drowsily. They were taking off now, the helicopter rising into the sky. "I think I'll ask her to help me stage a hip-hop version of *Romeo and Juliet*. It can be a crossover hit. Wanna help, too? I can't be a teen sensation forever, you know. Gotta start plotting the next step, the next phase . . ."

"Whatever you want," Broderick said.

They flew higher, into clouds. Jonah's mind was getting cloudy, too. Maybe he started dreaming again.

Or maybe he really did hear his father say, over the thumping of the helicopter blades, "And we'll tell your mother whatever you want about the serum, too."

Sinead took off in her aircraft with Alistair and a still-unconscious Isabel. This left the Starling boys to go to the hospital with Ian and Natalie in Jonah's yacht.

"You know how to steer a yacht?" Mr. McIntyre asked Ian worriedly.

"I was born knowing how to steer a yacht," Ian said. Then a stricken look came over his face. "But—do you suppose Jonah prepaid the full amount for renting this? Once my dad hears what Natalie and I did, he'll cancel our credit cards."

"You mean we're . . . we're poor now?" Natalie gasped.

"Penniless," Ian said grimly.

"Actually," Mr. McIntyre said, "I should have mentioned this before the others left. Grace had an addendum to her will regarding everyone who made it through the gauntlet. There were eight of you—you will all receive double the amount you turned down to get the first clue."

"It was a million dollars originally," Ian said. "So Natalie and I each get two million dollars? I suppose we could live on that."

Natalie beamed.

"That is such a relief!" she said. "Being poor wasn't

quite as bad as I thought it would be, but still—"

"You were only poor for about two seconds!" Dan protested, rolling his eyes.

"Dan—the two million dollars apiece—that would be for us, too," Amy said dazedly.

Oh, yeah, Dan thought. *Two million apiece. Four million total . . .*

He couldn't take it in. Not while he had papers rustling in his pocket that contained a priceless secret.

Ian, Natalie, Ned, and Ted left. The Holts screamed when they heard Hamilton had won two million dollars. Then they began shrieking that that meant they could go to some world-famous soccer game that was going to be played in Ireland in just an hour. They left, too, though Hamilton kept hanging out the window of their boat holding his hand to his ear, fingers outstretched, signaling, *Call me. Let me know what happens.*

"I've still got your back!" was the last thing he shouted out to them.

And then only Madrigals were left on the island.

Dan marched right up to Uncle Fiske and Mr. McIntyre.

"Now what?" he asked. "What did Grace want us to get the serum *for?*"

CHAPTER 43

"I—I beg your pardon?" Mr. McIntyre stammered.

"Dan, Amy, please tell us—do you have the serum formula? And do you know all the ingredients?" Fiske begged. "I *think* so, because I could kind of tell you were only pretending to be disappointed when the others were here, but—"

Amy decided she had to put the poor man out of his misery.

"Yes," she said. She told the two men and Nellie the parts of the story that Hamilton had left out.

"So you accomplished everything we asked of you," Fiske marveled.

We did? Amy thought. *But—*

"We didn't reunite with *Isabel*," she pointed out. "Or Cora Wizard. Or—"

"But you reconciled with their children," Mr. McIntyre said. "And Alistair and the Starlings. Representatives from every branch. You didn't honestly think we expected you to make every single Cahill descendant get along perfectly, did you?"

Yeah, I kind of did, Amy wanted to say.

But she felt as if Mr. McIntyre had just lifted a huge burden from her shoulders.

"You reconcile with the people you can," Fiske said. "And all you can do with the rest is to bring them to justice. Which you did."

Amy could tell that, if Fiske and Mr. McIntyre had been practically anyone else, they would have begun jumping up and down and screaming like Holts and hugging Amy and Dan and Nellie. As it was, Fiske kind of flicked his eyes side to side and looked slightly less uncomfortable than usual. Mr. McIntyre almost managed a smile.

"Well," Mr. McIntyre said, leaning back against a tombstone in relief.

"Oh, no," Nellie scolded. "Uh-uh-uh. You are not getting away with such a lame response. You tell Amy and Dan they saved the world. You thank them for vanquishing the most evil woman on the planet and for reuniting the most dysfunctional family ever. You apologize for every bump, bruise, cut, heartache, and heartbreak they suffered along the way. And then," Nellie finished, "*then* you answer Dan's question."

"We do thank you. And we're sorry. And—what was the question again?" Mr. McIntyre asked, which was clearly an attorney's delaying tactic.

"What are we supposed to do now?" Dan asked. "We have the serum—what for? Are we supposed to take it and rule the world ourselves? When Olivia Cahill herself thought it was too dangerous? Are we supposed to share it with the rest of the Madrigals? With all the other Cahill branches? With everyone in the world?"

Amy gawked at her brother. Was this really *Dan* thinking through everything so carefully? If he'd found a recipe for superpowers back when the Clue hunt started, he probably would have mixed it up and drunk it down without a second thought.

And yet, here he was, still coming up with more questions.

"Why was it so important to find the clues *now*?" he asked. "Why was Grace — and I guess, all the Madrigals — so desperate that they were willing to risk letting Cora Wizard or Alistair or the Holts or even Isabel get it? Why, after all these centuries?"

"Grace was *dying*," Mr. McIntyre said. "She didn't have many choices."

But his eyes darted around; he wouldn't look directly at Amy or Dan.

"Grace could have left instructions to start the clue hunt after a delay," Amy joined in. "You could have waited until Dan and I grew up. Or until Isabel died. Or—"

"Please," Uncle Fiske pleaded, helplessly holding out his hands. "Don't you want to just celebrate your victory for now? Be happy? Bask in your impossible triumph? Not . . . ask impossible questions?"

"I like to know what I'm celebrating before I put on a party hat," Nellie said sarcastically.

Uncle Fiske and Mr. McIntyre exchanged glances.

"It's so difficult to protect these three," Mr. McIntyre muttered.

Amy began thinking about the serum. Uncle Fiske had told them back in Jamaica that Gideon Cahill hadn't originally been trying to give his family incredible powers. He'd just wanted to keep people from dying from the plague.

Amy gasped.

"The serum," she said. "The plague. Is—is there another plague coming?"

Uncle Fiske and Mr. McIntyre frowned in unison.

"Not . . . necessarily," Mr. McIntyre began uncertainly. He must have seen Nellie glaring because he sighed heavily and went on. "Another family is threatening—"

"Lucians?" Dan guessed.

"Some of the Ekats—Bae Oh?" Amy tried.

Mr. McIntyre shook his head.

"See, we've taught them that all the evil in the world lies in their own family," Fiske muttered.

"This is a completely different family," Mr. McIntyre said. "Not related at all. They're even more secretive than the Cahills, and, frankly, they make Isabel Kabra look like Mother Teresa."

Amy shivered.

"They have long been interested in acquiring Cahill powers," Fiske said. "They began trying to follow the clues years ago—you might have detected their shadowy presence during the clue hunt yourself."

Amy remembered all the times she'd felt like she and Dan were being watched, the times she'd sensed someone following them, the times she'd heard suspicious footsteps in the dark. But that had always turned out to be Irina or Isabel or even Fiske himself, back when they thought of him as the man in black.

Hadn't it?

"Right before Grace died, a Madrigal agent intercepted a top secret message from the other family," Fiske said. "A message with all sorts of threats . . . We had to be ready."

"So let's go start mixing up the serum!" Dan said, jumping up.

He wants to take it, Amy thought. *He's just been looking for an excuse. A reason that doesn't make him seem as bad as Isabel, wanting to rule the world.*

"No," Mr. McIntyre said firmly. "Merely having the full serum formula should be enough. It is too dangerous to use, unless that's our only option. And we still have other options, thanks to you. We *can* deal with this now."

Dan made a face.

"But — what does that leave for me and Amy to do?" he asked forlornly.

"Recover," Fiske said, looking at Dan's black eye and both kids' cuts and bruises.

"Wait," Mr. McIntyre said. "Be kids. Grow up."

Dan's grimace became even more extreme.

"Perhaps it's time to let Grace explain," Fiske said, nodding at Mr. McIntyre.

"*Grace?*" Amy whispered.

Dan looked around frantically. He could tell Amy was thinking the same thing as him: *Maybe even Grace's funeral was a Madrigal hoax! Maybe the clue hunt was the biggest fake-out of all! Maybe . . . maybe Grace is still alive!*

But their beloved grandmother wasn't striding across the pebble beach or sailing toward them. Mr. McIntyre was only kneeling beside a tombstone, pushing some sort of hidden lever, then reaching into the tombstone itself.

"You can't read the inscription anymore, but this is Madeleine Cahill's tombstone," Mr. McIntyre explained. "The secret vault inside was Grace's favorite place to leave messages."

He pulled out a metal box and opened it. He scanned dozens of sealed envelopes.

"No, not that one. Not that one. Not that one . . ." he murmured. "She so wanted to be able to cover every eventuality."

Finally, Mr. McIntyre handed Amy and Dan a cream-colored envelope labeled "Best-case scenario" in Grace's bold writing. Amy stood there holding the letter like it was the greatest treasure they'd found in the entire Clue hunt.

"I think Grace would want us to actually read it," Dan muttered.

"Oh. Right," Amy said.

They both sat down in the grass. Dan flipped the envelope over and slid his finger under the flap. Amy took the letter out and shook it open. They began reading together:

My beloved Amy and Dan,

If Mr. McIntyre has given you this letter, then you have fulfilled my dearest dreams.

No. That is not quite right. Let me back up.

When you were little, my dearest dream was that you would never have to know our family's complicated heritage. I never wanted it to affect you at all.

But, as you know, that was not to be. You were so young when your parents died. My dearest dream during that time of grief and devastation was to sweep in and hold you and never let you go.

I plotted escape after escape after escape. I booked trips for the three of us to the South Seas, to the Swiss Alps, to tiny villages in places that cartographers rarely put on maps. But "rarely" wasn't good enough. I knew in my heart of hearts that no matter where we tried to hide, some dangerous relative would eventually track us down. I knew my love for you was not enough to keep you safe.

And . . . I couldn't leave in that dangerous time. I had a responsibility to the world, as well as to the two of you.

And so I chose the safest—and cruelest—option. For the sake of my watching, murderous relatives, I had to pretend that the most hideous lie was true—that the two of you didn't matter very much to me. It was the only way to keep them from killing you, too; the only way to keep them from using you as pawns in their grisly games. I prevailed upon my disinterested sister, Beatrice, to adopt you, even though she

Here something was crossed out and inked over until it was impossible to read. Grace had drawn an arrow off to the side and written in the margins: "If it is wrong to speak ill of the dead, then it is probably also wrong of the dead to speak ill of the still-living. Suffice it to say that my opinion of Beatrice is no better than yours!"

The letter continued:

> I prevailed upon Beatrice to adopt you because she, with no interest in our family history, could keep you safe when I could not.
>
> But, oh, how I lived for those weekends with you!
>
> In the ongoing struggle for power within the Cahill branches, I have been forced to do many things I am not proud of. But I regret nothing so much as I regret failing you.
>
> It was to my great surprise that you did not seem to hold my failings against me. Even in grief you were both still so charming and delightful . . . and so eager to learn. I still hoped to protect you as

much as I could from the worst of your
Cahill heritage. But, perhaps selfishly,
I did want to share the best of Cahill
achievements with you. So I took you to
Shakespeare plays; I paid for piano lessons
so you could learn Mozart's music. But
I explained almost nothing about their
connections to you. My dearest dream
then was that I wouldn't have to tell you
about your family's war until the war
was over.

Oh, and that it would happen quickly, so
I could whisk you away from Beatrice and
bring you home to live with me while you
were still young.

That was not to be, either.

I learned that I had cancer—and
that it would undoubtedly kill me—even
as other storm clouds gathered on the
horizon. The war we were fighting became
more dangerous than ever.

We Madrigals realized that the world
could never be safe unless Cahills came

together, once and for all. It became more
important than ever that the branches
reunite, so they could present a unified
front against the dangers that rise
around us.

"So—everyone's going to be involved in dealing with this other family?" Dan asked. "*All* Cahills?"

"We have always had a few friends in other branches," Mr. McIntyre said. "But now we're going to need many more."

"But some of the people in the gauntlet—Alistair, Sinead, Ian, and Natalie—they don't even trust *themselves* around the serum," Amy argued.

"No one should," Mr. McIntyre said darkly.

Dan went back to reading the letter because he was, once again, too aware of the papers in his pocket.

If you are reading this letter, then you
have accomplished a goal that no other
Madrigal has been able to accomplish in
five hundred years. I am so proud of you.

And, if you are reading this letter, then
you are in possession of a burden that no
eleven- and fourteen-year-old should have
to carry.

Dan blinked. It was like Grace *knew*!

Madrigals have always had a partial version of Gideon's original serum formula. In five hundred years, Madrigals have never been able to discover all the other branches' Clues. We always believed it was more important to work on reunifying the family and keeping the serum from falling into the wrong hands. We didn't want Gideon's serum.

Recent events have forced us to change our priorities.

When I began thinking about setting off a giant Clue hunt, I quickly realized that I once again had to choose between unbearable alternatives. I love my brother, Fiske, dearly, but he would be the first to say he could not have reunited the Cahills. I have a great deal of respect for William McIntyre and my other fellow Madrigals, but for one reason or another it was clear that they, on their own, would fail as well.

The only people I could possibly imagine achieving the Madrigal goals were the two of you—the two people I wanted to protect the most. I knew that, if asked, either one of you would have volunteered to save the world—even you, Amy, though you think that you are such a coward.

I am a coward myself.

Again and again in these past few days and weeks, I have wanted to tell you everything, to warn you of the dangers ahead. But I know I cannot do that without frightening you too much; without frightening <u>myself</u> too much. I grow weak. It is not just the cancer. It is fear of what I am about to do, what I <u>must</u> do for the good of the world.

I hope you are in a place now where you can forgive me for all the ways I have wronged you.

"Ah, come on, Grace," Dan muttered. "We wouldn't have been able to forgive you if you *hadn't* included us in the clue hunt!"

But it was easy to think that, now that it was over.

I instructed Mr. McIntyre to assist you as best he could, in his own judgment. And I told him to tell you, after my funeral, to trust no one. This was to be good advice for the beginning of the Clue hunt, when so much would be unknown to you. But I hope you realize that I do not want you to go through life with that philosophy. Many people have failed you — I myself have failed you, though I love you more than my own life. I can tell you that you will have your hearts broken more by the people you love than by the people you hate. But you must still dare to love. The rewards are worth far more than the risks.

Dan looked up and saw that Amy had tears streaming down her face.

"This *was* about love — '*Love's Labour's Won,*'" Amy murmured. "Grace thought we would win by coming to care about other people. And having them care about us. And, really, that is kind of what happened!"

"That's so sappy," Dan said.

Amy sniffled. Dan decided to poke her in the ribs just because — well, maybe that would help.

Amy poked him back, and he knew she'd be okay. And so would he.

I wish I could tell you what you face now, but I don't know how the dangers have grown since my death. I trust you will make the right decisions. And I trust that you will know whom you can trust to help you.

I know that you will have learned awful truths during this Clue hunt – you have undoubtedly discovered the facts about your parents' deaths that I could never bear to tell you myself. You have been victims of great evil. But you, no less than I, are not just victims. I trust that this Clue hunt has also shown you your great reserves of strength, courage, and goodness.

I love you. Your parents would be so proud of you.

With all my love,
Grace

Amy and Dan looked up from Grace's letter at the same time.

"You are going to need us to do more," Amy said. For someone with tears streaming down her face, she sounded incredibly calm. "With the serum, or—"

"No," Mr. McIntyre said. "Not yet. You do have time to recover."

Our adventures aren't over, Dan thought. *But—they are for now.*

It was odd how he could feel so relieved and so let down, all at once.

For a moment, everyone just stood there.

Then Nellie said, "So. Ready to go home?"

"Home?" Amy repeated, as if she'd never heard of the place. "But—we don't have a home anymore. Remember?"

"You've got four million dollars," Mr. McIntyre reminded them. "You could make your home anywhere you want, anywhere in the world."

A dreamy look came over Amy's face.

"We could live in Paris," she marveled.

"Or China, where I could work on my kung fu skills," Dan said.

"Venice, with all the canals," Amy said.

"Australia, where we could surf with Shep again," Dan said.

Nellie shrugged.

"I'm game," she said. "I just hope the Sorbonne or the University of Sydney takes transfer students. Because—you are not getting rid of me as your . . ."

"Don't say 'babysitter'!" Dan said. "Please!"

"Actually, I was going to say 'big sister,'" Nellie said with a grin.

That sounded perfect.

"Really," Amy said, "where I want to go is . . ."

Dan looked at his sister. Their mind-meld was working quite well right now.

"Massachusetts," Dan finished for her.

Amy nodded.

"We could have Grace's mansion rebuilt for you," Mr. McIntyre said speculatively. "We didn't tell you this before, but she did leave you that property—you're her primary heirs. And, fortunately, the house was insured."

"Thanks, but—it wouldn't be the same without Grace," Amy said. "Really, our old apartment is fine for now. We wouldn't want Nellie to lose any credits if she had to transfer away from BU."

"Just when I finally know what I want to major in!" Nellie said.

"You do?" Dan asked. "What?"

"Languages?" Mr. McIntyre suggested.

"No, although I want to learn as many as I can," Nellie said. "I thought about becoming a translator, but, you know, with that, you only get to say what other people are already saying. I was thinking more along the lines of going into diplomacy."

"What?" Dan said, gaping at her. "You're the least diplomatic person I know!"

"I got the two of you through the clue hunt without killing each other, didn't I?" Nellie asked. "I am so ready for the UN!"

Dan could almost picture it. She'd have everyone at the UN getting pierced noses before you knew it.

"I just need more student loans," Nellie said. "Because, I don't know, I've kind of got the travel bug now. . . . I might want to fly to Paris or Jamaica every now and then."

"No, you won't," Mr. McIntyre said.

"I can so fly anyplace I want!" Nellie objected.

"That's not what I was saying no to," Mr. McIntyre said. "It was the student loan part." He reached into the box where he'd kept Grace's letters and pulled out another envelope. He handed it to her. "Let's just say you're now as rich as Amy and Dan. It's only fair, for siblings. And this is what Grace wanted."

Nellie peeked into the envelope, which must have contained a bank account number. It was too thin to actually be loaded with millions of dollars.

"Really? REALLY? Sweeeet!" Nellie said, beaming. "Then—first month's rent is on me! Wow—it is so fun to be able to say stuff like that!"

"Oh, but if we go back to Boston . . ." Amy began. "Won't Aunt Beatrice have us stopped by Social Services?"

Mr. McIntyre went back to the box where he'd kept Grace's letter and Nellie's check. This time he pulled out a stack of paperwork.

"These documents transfer your guardianship

jointly to one Fiske Cahill and one Nellie Gomez," he said. "It's unconventional, but I know a judge who will approve it."

"You mean, Uncle Fiske will be, like, our adopted dad?" Dan asked incredulously.

Fiske blushed and looked at the ground.

"I don't have any experience being a father," he said.

"Lots of ice cream, that's the key," Dan said.

"Late bedtimes," Nellie said.

"Love," Amy said, smiling gently at him.

"So, back to Boston," Nellie said. "I might even be able to pick up some late-start fall classes."

A stricken look came over Amy's face.

"Ahhh!" she shrieked. "What's the date today?"

"September, uh," Mr. McIntyre looked at his watch, which was the kind with an entire month's calendar on its face. "September twenty-seventh."

"We were supposed to go back to school three weeks ago!" Amy cried. "I was so scared about starting high school! You know what they say about people putting freshmen in lockers and knocking books out of their hands and . . ."

She seemed to realize exactly what she was saying.

"Amy, you survived the clue hunt," Nellie said. "High school will be nothing!"

Dan rolled his eyes. He wasn't going to admit

that he'd been a little worried about starting seventh grade, too.

A new school year, he thought. *The old apartment. My old friends. Saladin will be happy to stay in one place. I can finally do the brass-rubbing kits I got in Stratford. We can hang the swords from Italy on the wall. I can buy all my baseball cards back.*

Going back to ordinary life sounded wonderful—for a while. But he knew all of that would just be like a recess before something bigger and even more important than the 39 Clues began.

I'm eleven years old, he thought. *I deserve to enjoy recess while I can.*

"All right, then," he told Nellie and Amy, "let's go home."